A LIFE WORTH DYING FOR

DYING FOR

RANDOM SURVIVAL BOOK 7

Ray Wenck
Glory Days Press
Columbus, Ohio

Glory Days Press
Columbus, Ohio

Publisher's Note: This is a work of fiction. Names, characters, places, and incidents are a product of the author's imagination. Locales and public names are sometimes used for atmospheric purposes. Any resemblance to actual people, living or dead, or to businesses, companies, events, institutions, or locales is entirely coincidental.

Book Layout © 2016 BookDesignTemplates.com
Cover Design by Mibl Art
A Life Worth Dying For/ Ray Wenck. – 1st edition
ISBN 978-1-7360350-9-2

Dedication

This story is dedicated to all those faithful readers who have followed this storyline since the beginning. It was for you I kept the story going. Thank you.

Author's Notes

With this, the seventh book in the series, I have decided to take a break. I'm not sure where the storyline goes from here, if anywhere. It has been a fun ride and whether it continues at some point depends on my own desires as well as how much grief you readers give me.

I have started an offshoot series entitled Random Survival: The Road, which views the pandemic from a different angle. Though I currently have no plans to meld the two worlds, that is always a possibility down the road.

Currently, four books are written and ready to go. You can find the first two on Kindle Vella. Once they have run their course, I will quickly release all four. If you enjoyed this series, the next one will interest you because it uncovers answers to the cause of the pandemic, and yes, brings up many more questions.

I want to thank all you readers who have followed my career and supported my work. You have inspired me to keep writing.

I'd like to thank Steve Wilhelm for another superb job editing.

You can view a complete list of titles at raywenck.com

Also, check out Ray's Ravenous Readers on Facebook. It's a private group for you. It features some free reads that have not been published, cover reveals, contests, and a chance to interact with me and other readers.

As always, read all you want, I'll write more.

Ray

PS If you purchased this book and want a free read, sign up for my newsletter, message me that you bought this book, and I'll send you two free prequels to this story as a way of saying thank you for the support.

A LIFE WORTH DYING FOR

Chapter One

Lincoln scanned the gathering assemblage with cold dread. They had much to discuss, some of which threatened to be explosive and open to heated and possibly physical debate. It wasn't for the first time he asked himself why he had been dumb enough to accept the leadership role. It was one thing to run for council, but to accept the chairman position was outright stupid.

The former NFL running back wiped his forehead. Was the sweat from the heat in the crowded space, or was he that nervous? He thought back to those wonderful days of busting through three-hundred-pound defensive linemen and outrunning speedy defensive backs with glory ahead of him. Had it not been interrupted, the new season would be six weeks in by now. Projections had him breaking the all-time rushing yard record by week eight. Damn! The glory, fame, and fortune were gone in a puff of what, disease-borne air? Replaced by what? The glory, fame, and fortune of heading a post-apocalyptic community? No. Hell, no. It just wasn't right.

He realized he was whining because it was better to do that than think about the battle yet to be waged. He released a deep breath and chastised himself for the momentary whine. He was one of the fortunate few who survived the deadly pandemic. Football fame aside, he was extremely grateful for that small miracle.

His head snapped to the side as his eyes locked on the one figure he hoped, no, prayed, did not show for the community meeting. Becca entered, surveyed the room, then caught and locked eyes with his. He gave a quick nod which she returned. The next few seconds were uncomfortable until she broke the eye contact and moved to the back of the room.

Lincoln sighed loudly. *Best to get this over with.* He looked left and right at the council, all seated behind two large eight-foot folding tables. "Ready?" He asked. Head nods indicated they were, and he picked up the gavel someone had found to use for the meeting and banged it twice. The sound was decidedly not as effective as if striking a wooden surface. The tables jumped, spilling two cups of water. He grimaced and mouthed sorry, then set the gavel down and whistled. The high-pitched sound was piercing but had the desired effect.

"I'd like to bring our inaugural community forum to order. First off, I'd like to thank Milo and his industrious crew for getting this building ready for use with such a tight deadline. No, it's not quite finished, and you all know its purpose is for the projected expansion of our community. However, until such a time as it is needed, it will serve as a community area for meetings, activities, and events. I have to say, despite it being the largest construction we've undertaken to date, it's surprisingly small once everyone is inside."

Milo glared at him.

Lincoln laughed and held up a halting hand. "Easy, big man. I'm not asking for an expansion."

"That's good," Milo barked.

"Yet," Lincoln added.

The crowd laughed.

"Anyway, we all know what we faced. We battled and survived and have grown stronger, but that's all behind us."

"We hope," someone said from the crowd.

"Amen to that, my friend, but here's the thing. We did get through a brutal ordeal and have rebuilt because of community. We stood together. We may not always agree about how things are done, but when we are needed, we answer the call for the benefit of all. I'm proud of y'all."

Someone started clapping, and applause rolled across the room.

"You know our council. You should since you voted them in. We will have a report from each person, which will be a routine occurrence for each meeting. Our meetings will be held monthly, the date and time to be determined. It may vary to allow those on guard duty or living off-campus to attend.

"Let's hear from our first council member, Elijah. You want to start?"

As the older man stood, Lincoln sat but kept his gaze down. His darkening mood was beginning to set. The hardest part was knowing when the time came, he was going to be trapped between his friend and the community.

Elijah said, "I am in charge of our vegetable and fruit gardens. In case you have not had the opportunity yet, go over and check out the new greenhouse Milo and his people built. It is not large enough yet to benefit everyone, but it's the first of four we plan by spring. Once ready, we will have the ability to produce fresh vegetables year-round. Come spring, we plan on plowing the field on the open corner, which is approximately two acres, and planting a variety of foods. We will also replant the cornfield though it won't be as large considering the land used for this building and our defenses."

That was said with a negative tone. He had argued a better use for the land was crops but had been soundly outvoted.

"For planting and harvesting, we will need all available hands. Remember this is for your benefit, so please, help. None of us has been through winter yet under these circumstances, so we are unsure about meat, but some of the ladies in our building have put together healthy and protein-filled recipes. If you'd like them, see Marlene over there. They sat up last night writing them out, so please take advantage of their hard work. Also, on a side note, we have begun nondenominational church services Sunday mornings at ten for any who would like to attend." He sat.

Lincoln stood. "Thank you, Elijah. That is wonderful news. And folks, he's right. You should go see the greenhouse. It's incredible work and will benefit us all eventually. Now, I think we'll hear from Caleb."

As the young man stood, a loud cheer erupted from his peers. He blushed visibly, which caused some laughter. Caleb had turned nineteen during the battle but had aged far beyond his years due to the extreme dangers faced and the current lifestyle. His long dark hair was brushed back in a failed attempt at neatness for the presentation.

"Hi, I, um, I'm Caleb. I'm in charge of hunting and harvesting. Though I expect the hunting and fishing to slow immensely over these next few weeks, we have brought in enough meat and fish to last at least a month if we don't bring in anything else. The meats and fish are being smoked for preservation. We'd like not to touch any of it until the winter when it will be needed but well, whatever. We'll just keep bringing in more.

"Harvesting is going well, but we've pretty much stripped the area of anything worth eating. Depending on what stores say, we may have to travel farther to make up for whatever we lack. I have a crew splitting wood for fires daily. What we don't use for cooking is being stored under tarps in both camps for heating the buildings in the winter. I estimate this will be an ongoing task to keep supplies filled for the winter months. Ah, I guess that's all." He started to sit.

"Great job, Caleb," one of the girls shouted. That brought another flash of red to his cheeks, which, in turn, created more laughter.

Lincoln stood to announce the next speaker, knowing he was purposely avoiding the one with the potential to inflame the crowd. "As long as we're on the topic, let's have stores give us a rundown."

Lynn stood and smiled at applause. "I'm pleased to report we have been extremely busy getting ready for the winter. Our stores are good. Not great, but we do have ample provisions, which I'll remind you does not include meats or produce, to see us well into January or February. All the corn that has been brought in has been ground into meal. We have a large surplus of canned and boxed goods. As we use those up, it is unlikely we will find much more. We'll be looking for substitutes, but whatever we come up with will be made from scratch.

"We are busy canning fruits and vegetables for the cold months, and if anyone has any time to help or Mason Jars, we can use both. Thank you. Oh, also, I have tried the recipes Marlene has, and you will like them, so make sure to pick one up."

"Milo, give us some words," Lincoln said, barely making it to a standing position.

The large bald-headed man stood abruptly, almost upending the table. "Well, as you can see, we've been busy. Our primary focus was rebuilding the dormitory across the road after its near destruction during the battle. We made it stronger and more defensible but having to rebuild allowed us the opportunity to make it larger and add a fireplace on both walls rather than just one. With this one nearly finished, we will be concentrating on what I think is the last project for this year—the wall surrounding the entire compound. We have a start, but it will take a lot more cinder blocks to complete. If the weather holds off, I hope to have it done by the end of November. We are searching for more solar panels for the hospital so it will have its own power source, which will increase the amount available for the other buildings. Eventually, if we find enough, all the buildings will have their own power.

"We have a list of projects that we may or may not get to depending on the weather, but if you have any you'd like us to consider, submit it to Desmond over there. I won't guarantee it will be approved, but you won't know until you ask." He started to sit and rose again. "Ah, thank you."

Lincoln knew he was running out of council people. He looked to each end. Caryn with good stuff or Maggie with bad. Best to finish with good. Wait, he forgot about himself. He could delay the bad for a few minutes more. He stood. "Next up is the one responsible for the community's defense and safety. He made a show of looking down the table in both directions before saying, "Oh, that's me." He got a few laughs.

"We have erected gates at the four intersections. It will be a pain now getting in and out because you have to be checked, and the gate has to open, but it is in the best interest of everyone here. After the attack, it is clear we can no longer allow free access to our land. Once the wall is completed, we will be enclosed. It will not prevent a determined adversary, but it will slow them down and make any who think us easy pickings think twice about attacking.

Each gate is guarded and has a schedule. We have fortified several of the buildings. Once the renovations on the house are complete, one of the new projects I'll be discussing with Milo is to build a watch tower attached to the house that enables us to see anyone coming from miles away."

Milo leaned over the table and glared at Lincoln.

"Don't worry, Milo. It's just on the list. It gets built when it gets built.

The big man nodded and sat back.

"Ah, what else, oh yeah, gas. We were blessed when Bobby brought in the tanker. However, it is down by two-thirds now. Without replenishing the supply with an unknown, I will be implementing gas rations. The bulk of the use should be saved for our hunting parties and the military vehicles. I want to keep some in reserve in case of an emergency. The ration will be determined on a case by case request."

A few people booed. "I know it's not popular, but until we can find another source, it's the way it has to be."

With that done, he had no other choice but to announce the next speaker. "Maggie, talk to us about medical."

Chapter Two

The person to best speak about the medical stores and conditions was the primary doctor, but she refused to run for council, citing too much to do already. Maggie came from a medical background and understood the current situation. She lived with Jarrod a few miles down the road and wasn't on the main campus often, so she had to check in with Doc to keep updated on the supply status.

The older woman stood. She had a lot of respect around the community and was always ready to step in and help whoever needed it. Her years belied her mental acuity and physical strength.

"All things considered, our medical facility and personnel are top-notch. Their hard work, superior skill, and determination kept many alive during our recent conflict. However, there is a price for all they have done, and that is the ever-lowering stores of vital medical supplies, medications, IV solutions and blood. We can all do something about blood. Please, everyone, consider donating a few pints. If something happens to you or one of your family members, God forbid, having that blood on hand may make the difference between life or death. What's the old saying? The life you save may be your own."

She placed her hands on the table as if steadying herself. Lincoln understood why. They had a very frank discussion with Doc and this moment was the one he dreaded.

"As stated, our supplies are low. Without a new influx from who knows where, we will deplete our valuable resources in short order. We still have three wounded in care in the facility, but all three are expected to recover and be out soon. But," she swallowed hard, "the long-term patients present a problem. We have two of them, and you know who they are. As it stands, neither has woken from their injuries. Myron's head injury is perhaps more worrying. Without the proper machinery, we can't determine if there's even any brain function. The machines we do have may be keeping him alive, but we don't know for sure, short of taking him off life support.

"Mark, on the other hand, has been on life support for two weeks. He may well recover, but our supplies will be depleted by the time we find out. If we have another situation where long-term care is necessary, we will not be able to provide it. That's just the sad truth of the matter. For discussion are our choices. Let it run until there are no more. Take one off life support to allow the other to go longer or take both off to save the remaining supplies for future use."

A man in the second row said, "What happens if we let them go until they run out? Does either have a chance to survive?"

"Unknown. It's a gamble either way."

A woman said, "Is there any way of telling if there's even a slim hope? A machine or something?"

"Yes and no. In Myron's case, we would need an EEG, CT, or MRI. Any will give us some idea. In Mark's case, his body took massive trauma and may just need time to recover by shutting down. However, if support runs out before that occurs, he may not make it anyway."

Lincoln sneaked a glance at Lynn. Her face was stoic, but he knew inside she was in pain. She was terrified of a council vote, fearing people might think her playing favorites. Even though they were no longer together, Mark and Lynn had been in love. No, still were, but perhaps too much distance had grown between them.

Lincoln was in somewhat the same situation. Mark was his best friend. How could he possibly vote against him? Yet he had a responsibility to protect the community, which meant making sure they had the medications available to everyone when needed.

"So, just so I understand this," a man said, standing up. "You're asking us to vote on whether two men will live or die. Like we're a jury."

Maggie sucked in a deep breath. "In essence, yes. The council could vote, but this is important, and we didn't want anyone to think we were playing favorites or taking advantage of our positions. This is a community decision."

A loud murmur rose and spread through the group. It was not an easy thing to ask. Mark had been a founding member of their community and a stalwart in its growth and protection. Though some would argue much of the troubles they'd encountered over the past few months would not have occurred if not for him.

Doc stood and faced the crowd. Lincoln spotted her and got to his feet. He shouted then whistled to bring order back. "Let's keep it quiet and peaceful. Doc would like to speak."

"I am in no way condoning taking either man off life support without an indication that a reasonable chance of life still exists. To do so in my opinion, is to commit murder, and I will not be a part of that.

"If we can find the necessary machines to give me that information, I can give a more informed opinion. Beyond that, I am not a brain surgeon. If I need to go into Myron's head, he may not survive anyway. Mark, on the other hand, may recover, but I can't say when or if. The trauma inflicted may prove too great for his body to overcome. It was a lot of work to fix the damage, but even if he recovers, he may never be the same. "I'm sorry," she hung her head. When she lifted it again, tears rolled down her cheeks. "I've done the best I could for both of them. For all of you. There are just some things beyond my abilities." She sat and covered her face.

"So, it's still back to a yes or no vote," the same man said.

A voice shouted from the back. It was the voice Lincoln feared. "You better think twice about that vote," Becca said, moving toward the back middle. "Anyone tries to unplug my dad will have to go through me." She held up the long knife to emphasize her statement.

Several people in the back stood and moved away. Voices in the crowd grew and became both fearful and angry. As Lincoln feared, things did not look good. A riot might break out and with it more injuries to further deplete their stores.

Lincoln snatched up the gavel and pounded it ferociously on the table like he was beating someone to death. The table bounced and bent under his powerful swings. "I. Will. Not. Tolerate. Violent outbursts in our meeting." He stopped banging and pointed the gavel at the crowd. "You will all sit down and come to order, or I swear there will be hell to pay." What that might be, he had no idea and was gratified to see them sit though few were quiet.

Becca still stood in defiant challenge.

Another voice lifted above the crowd, this one offering a solution and momentary peace. "So, if we can find more supplies and the machines you need, we can stave off this ludicrous and inhumane vote?" Bobby strode next to his sister and placed a gentle hand on her arm. He made no effort to pressure it down. He knew that was a mistake he might receive an injury from.

Doc stood and the crowd quieted. "Yes, Bobby. But I have no idea where we might find what we need. By now, everything's either been picked over or destroyed."

"Leave that to me. How much time do I have?"

"Life support will end in a little less than a month. After that, I have no idea. Maybe days, maybe hours."

"If I go hunting for what's needed," he said to Lincoln. "Do I have the council's word that no one will unplug either of them until I get back?"

Lincoln started to say yes but realized he was but one member. He looked down the table. Lynn and Caryn were looking at him with concern etched on their faces. He thought both would support him. Elijah was looking down at the table. Maybe not him. Milo was a maybe. Lincoln could not read his eyes. Maggie was a good person but took her responsibility to the community seriously. Though she liked and respected Mark, he thought she'd vote against the plan for the benefit of all.

Caleb looked frightened. Lincoln didn't blame him. He was too. He nodded to the young man, but he looked past Lincoln down the table to his mother. Yes, he'd vote the way his mother did. That meant at least four his way, which carried the motion.

The man who brought up the vote was still standing. "I disagree with allowing him a month to find the equipment to save his daddy." He said *daddy* in a mocking tone. Clearly, he was not a friend to Mark. Lincoln recalled the man. Sam Edwards had lost his seventeen-year-old son in the recent conflict. He blamed Mark for the loss. "If he doesn't return with the necessary equipment, we're out of supplies that someone else may need. Considering he's primarily responsible for the death and injuries that have cost us most of our supplies, he shouldn't be allowed to survive while so many have died."

This statement brought the crowd to its feet. Shouts and threats were issued along two sides. Mark supporters and Mark detractors. Lincoln spotted movement in the back. Bodies were shoved aside and chairs went flying. He recognized the determined and deadly glare of Becca mowing through the crowd to get at the man. Lincoln pulled the lightweight plastic table back and stepped through. He was about to jump down to intercept Becca when she was lifted off her feet and hauled backward a long stride and a lunge short of her goal. The fool wasn't even aware of his near death.

Jarrod, the large farmer and friend of both Mark and Lincoln, had her wrapped in a bearhug with her arms pinned. Bobby came up and bent Becca's fingers back to get the knife away. She kicked, snarled, and clawed to get free and cursed at Bobby when he pried the blade free. "Go near my father, and I'll kill you." Jarrod hauled her out of the building.

Edwards pushed away from a man who confronted him. "You see what I'm talking about. It's Mark and his warmonger kids who have caused the problems in our community."

Voices exploded again, each side trying to outscream the other. Scuffles broke out, but as yet, no punches had been thrown. Edwards shouted over the others. "With him gone, most of our problems are solved." Now fists flew.

Lincoln could not allow the melee to continue or escalate. He took the gun from behind his back, cocked the hammer, and aimed upward. He fired. The crowd ceased moving. Many dropped to the floor. "This will stop immediately. Look at you. You are supposed to be a community. Your strength and reason for your continued survival are knowing someone will have your back. How will that be possible if we are so divided? Now, no matter what side of this debate you align on, discussion is the only resolution.

Edwards started to speak, but Lincoln was beyond listening to him. "I have heard enough from you, Mr. Edwards. Sit your ass down and let us resume the meeting." He lowered the gun to his side and pointed at Edwards. "And Mr. Edwards, if I hear you have been spreading your poison to divide this community, I will take action to bring you before a tribunal to decide whether you are the type of person we want as a neighbor. Do you understand me, sir?"

Edward's face reddened. He glared at Lincoln. "Just cause you're a friend of Mark doesn't mean you have a right to decide for everyone."

"And just because you blame Mark for the loss of your son doesn't give you a right to exploit your personal agenda."

Chapter Three

Lincoln holstered the gun and stepped back. "Now, we will continue with this meeting respectfully and peacefully. The discussion before us is whether to allow time for the location of equipment and supplies before making a decision as to whether to unplug our two comatose patients. As we contemplate this obviously tense topic, think to yourself, if it was one of your family members lying in the hospital, what would you want for them? Despite their current situation, both of those patients are people. Let's keep our humanity and remember those patients are also members of this community and have fought and worked alongside all of you."

He pulled his chair back and sat, then popped up. "Milo, I apologize for the hole I put in your new ceiling. I will be happy to go up in the morning to patch it."

Milo frowned as Lincoln sat. "Now, who has something constructive to add?"

Hands shot up. "Before I choose someone, if you're just going to rant and rile everyone else up again, don't bother raising your hand." Most went down. Lincoln scanned the room and spotted the hand of Heidi Berry. "Heidi."

Heidi stood. "Most of you know me. I can't say I fall on either side but do see and understand both sides. I don't want to see either of those poor men die, but I have a suggestion. Instead of taking the entire month, which uses up our supplies, why not set a one or two-week deadline instead? That gives time to find what is needed but also leaves a few weeks' worth of supplies should the mission fail. It's a bit of a compromise." She hesitated as if she had more to say, then sat.

Lincoln nodded, then glanced up and down the tables at his fellow council members. Most stared out or down as they examined their own thoughts. Lynn met his gaze. Was there a plea in those watery eyes? He frowned.

"Is there anyone else who'd like to weigh in on this subject?"

They handled a few more opinions and suggestions as well as questions, then Lincoln said, "Let's put it to a vote. We have two. The first is whether to allow time for Bobby to locate more medical supplies. Council members?" He glanced to his right, then left. "The vote was unanimous. "The vote is carried seven zero."

He paused and swallowed. "The next vote is for the duration. Do we allow the full month or two weeks?" This time he started to his left. Caleb voted for a month, Maggie and Milo chose two weeks. He skipped himself for the moment. Elijah voted two weeks. Lynn and Caryn opted for a month. That left the decision to him as the final vote. He stewed over his decision, knowing his friend's life held in the balance.

"It's true, Mark is my friend." He heard Edwards moan then mumble something to the person sitting next to him. "He has been a good friend to all in this community. You have placed me in this position to do right by the community as a whole, regardless of my personal feelings. For the benefit of the community, I have to vote for two weeks." He picked up the gavel and pounded. The motion is decided." He flicked the gavel down, disgusted with himself, and sat back as the voices rose. He sighed then remembered Caryn still had to give her report. His hope was her presentation might shift the focus and lighten the mood.

"Hold. Hold everyone. We still have one more council member to hear from. Caryn has some exciting news to share with you all. Please, give her your attention."

The willowy woman stood. "Yes, I am in charge of special events and activities and have some fun things planned. First, with Halloween a week away, I thought it might be nice to have a celebration. We'll make it a joint Halloween and Fall Festival celebration. We don't have a lot of children, but there's enough that we can still have a costume contest and do trick or treating here to allow them to enjoy the occasion."

An excited buzz raced through the crowd. "I also want to do a Halloween party right here that same night." That announcement was met with applause and cheers. "Adults can dress up too if they want. We'll have a dance. We have some electricity reserved and should be able to play some music. A few of the teens have offered to do face painting. I have some ideas for fun activities and contests. I'll have details tomorrow and will post them on the community bulletin board on the wall over there." She pointed. "Volunteers are always appreciated. With everything that has happened to us all over the past six months, we deserve a chance to kick back and have some fun. Please, everyone join us. Thank you."

With that, Lincoln called the meeting adjourned, and the group began to disperse.

"I'm going to hold you to that patchwork," Milo said.

Lincoln smiled. "Of course, you will. Don't worry. Bright and early tomorrow morning." He motioned everyone close. "I hadn't realized there was such a divide in our ranks. We have to keep an eye on that so it doesn't widen and destroy us. That means we have to work hard to keep everyone together. Caryn, I think your celebration is a good start. I also think the daily work groups are important as well. It's hard to be against someone who stands next to you, working hard for unity. Just thought I'd mention it."

He stepped away from the tables and hunted for Bobby. He didn't especially want to face him and definitely not his sister, but it had to be done if only to explain his reasoning. He spoke to a few people who stopped him along the way. He was polite but craned his neck to see over everyone. When he didn't find them, he thought he knew where they'd be.

He opened the door of the barn where the hospital was set up. To the right was the recovery room. A series of curtains separated eight beds. The two farthest back held the two comatose patients, Mark and Myron.

When he pulled the front curtain aside, he found Jarrod, Bobby, and Becca. They had shifted the side curtain so both patients were visible. Becca turned her head away and folded her arms. "How could you? I thought you were Dad's friend."

Lincoln sighed. In a soft voice he said, "I am his friend, Becca."

"Didn't look like it." She wiped her eyes and whirled to face him. Her anger grew with each word. "It looked to me like you gave in to that asshole and his followers."

"No. I didn't vote because of *him*. My vote took into consideration everyone in our community. It was one of the hardest decisions I have ever been forced to make, but from my position as council chairman, it was the right one. I know that's not what you want to hear, but it's the way it has to be." He faced Bobby. "I will give you anything you need. A vehicle, food, weapons, whatever you think can help. I will protect your father and Myron. You won't have to worry about what is happening here. That way, Becca can go too."

"How do we know we can trust you?"

"Becca, come on."

"You won't have to," Jarrod said. "Trust me. I won't let anything happen to your dad. That's a guaranteed promise."

Lincoln sighed. Even Jarrod thought him a traitor. "Just let me know what you need." He backed away and left.

"You think we can trust him?" Becca asked.

"Come on, Sis, you know you can. He's in a tough position, but he won't let anything happen until we get back."

"He's a busy man. What's to stop someone else from coming in here and shutting everything off?"

"Me," Jarrod said. "I'll camp out here if need be."

Becca gave him a hug. "You're a good man, Jarrod. It is good Dad has at least one friend left."

"He has a lot more than one."

They all turned to see who had entered. Lynn stood there, eyes watering.

"Yeah," Becca said with attitude. "Who might they be?"

Bobby said, "Sis, stop. Now." His tone was forceful, and his eyes showed steel. Becca eyed him for a moment, then turned away.

"May I?" Lynn pointed toward the bed.

"Of course, Lynn," Bobby said. "You are always welcome."

"Ha," Becca said without turning.

"Despite what you might think, Becca, I do love your dad. Just because we can't live together doesn't mean I don't still care." She moved toward the bed and gazed down at Mark's unmoving body. The ventilator hissed and clapped, keeping his chest rising and falling. She brushed the hair from his forehead and whispered something in his ear. After wiping her eyes, she stood erect. "You will have nothing to fear. He will be well guarded. Good luck. I will pray for you." With that, she exited.

"We need to pack," Bobby said.

"You go. I want a few minutes alone with Dad. I'll meet you out front."

"Doc met him at the door. Here's a list of what we need. The fluids will be the hardest to find, even if they're still good. They are also the most important. The other thing is I'm concerned about this ventilator. It's old and is beginning to make sounds that make me think it's on its last legs. If we lose it, we may lose him. On the other hand, if you can find me one of those three machines listed there, I can determine if Myron has any brain function. That changes things."

Bobby glanced at the list. It was lengthy.

"The items near the bottom are more wish list. The priority is those items at the top."

He nodded, folded the paper, and stuck it in his back pocket. "We'll do what we can. For both of them."

"This might help." She gave him another list. "This is every hospital, medical facility, and urgent care center within fifty miles that I can think of. I'm sure there's a lot more."

"Thank you."

She embraced him then stepped back. "Go with God, Bobby."

Ray Wenck

"I'll go with whoever can help me find this stuff." He smiled and left the building.

Chapter Four

After packing a duffel for an extended stay, Bobby went
to the armory now housed in the garage. A wall had been
erected and a locked door kept everyone from taking what
they wanted as they once had done. As he stood in front
of it, wondering if he should pick the lock, the door
opened and Lincoln entered carrying the keys. "I thought
you might be here." He stepped in front of Bobby and inserted the key. "You weren't thinking about breaking in,
were you? Never mind. Don't answer that." He pushed
the door open and stepped aside. "Please, just take what
you need."

Bobby took an old Army green canvas bag off a hook
near the door and went down the rows of assorted ammu-
nition, grabbing boxes. He took two sets of night vision
goggles, flashlights, batteries, two extra handguns, and
two ARs with three magazines for each.

Lincoln looked pained as he exited.

"Don't worry. I'll return what I don't use."

"In other words, nothing." He smiled, trying to lighten
the mood. He locked the door. "I gassed up the Transit
and parked at the side of the house. That should give you
ample room to collect and sleep, so you don't have to be
outside and on the ground. I put two bedrolls inside too."

Bobby turned and extended his hand. As Lincoln took it,
Bobby said, "Thanks, Lincoln. Do the right thing here."

The two men held each other's gaze, then Lincoln nodded, and they moved outside. Bobby stowed the gear.

A small group of people milled around the van. One was Edwards. "Hey Council chairman, was everything they took approved? How about the gas and the van? I thought you said there was a shortage. Why is he allowed to take one of our vehicles and our dwindling supply of gas?"

Bobby walked past him, opened the rear doors of the van, and tossed in his gear.

"Seems like Mark's kids are getting preferential treatment, again." He blocked the door from being closed. "Let me see what supplies of ours you're taking."

Bobby hip-checked him out of the way and slammed the doors.

"Hey," Edwards said. "You all saw that. He assaulted me. What are you going to do about it, Council chairman? He should be locked up."

Bobby wheeled and cocked his arm, ready to throw a punch. Lincoln caught the arm before it fired. He patted Bobby's chest. "No."

Bobby was about to speak when Lincoln shook his head.

Edwards laughed. "Yeah, that's right. Lock his punk ass up."

Lincoln smiled at Bobby, then unleashed an overhand right that was planted squarely in the middle of Edward's face. His eyes rolled back and his body dropped. The others in the small crowd who had been laughing and jeering along with Edwards went deathly silent.

Lincoln squared up to them and began rolling up his sleeves. Before he finished with one arm, he asked, "Who else has a problem with how I do things?"

The crowd dispersed in a hurry. "Guess your friends don't like you enough to haul your loud mouth out of here, Edwards." He rolled his sleeve down.

Jin came around the van carrying a black garbage bag. He looked at each of them. "Mark, friend. I help."

Bobby smiled. "Awesome. Thanks."

"Yes. Awesome." He looked down at Edwards. "Still breathe. Hit again." He opened the door, tossed the bag in, and climbed inside.

Becca trotted over. "Trouble?"

"Not a speck," Lincoln said.

She looked down at Edwards. "You're almost forgiven," she said. "This our ride?"

Bobby said, "Yep." She stowed her gear. "I'm ready when you are."

"Guess it's time to go," said Bobby. He went around the van and climbed into the driver's seat. Becca moved to the passenger side door, but before she opened it, Lynn called, "Becca. Wait." She ran down the stairs carrying a wicker basket. "You'll need food for the road." She handed her the basket. It was filled with snacks, baked goods, fruit, and dried goods, along with two thermoses of water.

Becca was shocked. She tried to speak, if only to say thanks, but Lynn cut her off with a raised hand. "Be safe. Good hunting." She turned and hurried back up the stairs to the house.

Becca opened the passenger door to find Jin sitting there. The Korean man smiled. "Snooze. Lose." He grabbed the door and shut it, leaving Becca stunned and speechless.

Bobby laughed and fist-bumped Jin.

Becca climbed in through the side door. "I think I liked you better when you had a limited vocabulary."

"Jin speak much good English. Hot damn!"

She closed the door. "You've been hanging out entirely too much with Lincoln."

"Lincoln, man, good buds."

"Yeah. Great. Let's roll."

Bobby began backing down the gravel driveway. A voice shouted. "Wait! Don't go yet."

Bobby hit the brakes and scanned for the owner of the voice. Around the rear of the house came Darlene running hard. She carried a backpack in one hand and her long-bow stick spear in the other. She ran around the front of the van and stopped at Bobby's window. "Room for one more?" She beamed at him.

From the back, he heard Becca sing, *"And they call it, puppy love."*

Bobby shot her a warning glance and said to Darlene, "Always room for you." Her smile broadened. "But wait. Is your dad all right with this?" Her father was Elijah, and he kept her under a tight rein.

Her smile vanished. "Bobby, do you want extra help or not?" When her tone came out like that, she reminded him a lot of his sister. Having them both together might be scarier than whatever they encountered along the way. "Of course, we do." He emphasized *we*.

With the smile back in place, Darlene ran around the van to the side door. Becca had them open for her. "Room for one more?" This time she asked Becca herself.

"For you, sister. Always." The two had been bitter rivals when they first met, however, they came to an under-standing and now accepted each other as if they truly were sisters.

With his crew now aboard, Bobby finished backing down the driveway. He made the turn and drove to the corner. "Which way?" he asked.

Before anyone voiced their opinion, a voice shouted, "Darlene. No. Get out of that vehicle. Now, young lady."

Jin said, "Uh-oh. Busted."

Bobby looked. Elijah was running across the grounds heading for them. Becca and Darlene moved between the seats and peered out the window. Bobby felt something land in his lap. He jumped in his seat as he saw the tip of Darlene's spear. "Bobby. I like you, but if you don't drive, I'll cut your wiener off."

Jin tightened his knees together and covered up with his hands. "Oh, man. Snip. Snip."

Bobby jammed down on the pedal and the van lurched forward, sending the two women sprawling. He made a sharp right and sped away before Elijah reached them. He feared his reception when they returned, but that was a concern for a different day.

Chapter Five

The sun was all but set when they made the turn into the small city of Wauseon. Though they had been in the area before, they had never visited Wauseon, which seemed strange since it was less than an hour away from the farmhouse.

"According to the notes Doc gave you," Becca said, reading off the list, "there's Fulton County Health Center and a Wellness center."

"Which streets?" Darlene asked, spreading out a map. She held a small flashlight between her teeth. Becca read off the street names. "They appear to be near each other."

Becca said, "There's also a list of Doctor's offices that Doc tore out of a phone book, whatever that is."

"Let's do the hospital first," Bobby said. "Then maybe we can plot out a route to search the other facilities."

"I'll do that while you drive," Becca said.

After getting directions from Darlene, Bobby pulled into the lot of the hospital. It was not large, but the five-story building had certainly been invaded at some point. He noted six cars in the lot. That didn't mean anyone was inside, but it was something to be aware of. "There's a chance someone might be inside. Stay alert."

Bobby stopped under the overhang above the front door. The glass doors had been crashed through, leaving a large, jagged hole. Down the sloping circular drive was an extension to the hospital. The large letters on the wall said it was the Medical Office Building. The hospital was larger than he first thought. He studied the mirrors. "Since the doors are busted in, we know there are people in the area. We need to be alert."

"We don't know when they were broken," Becca countered. "It might have been way back at the beginning of the pandemic."

"True, but it's best to err on the side of caution."

Becca moved to the side door. "Okay, *dad*."

"Someone needs to stay with the van."

She yanked the door open and stepped out. "Thanks for volunteering, dear brother."

Darlene laughed as she exited. Jin hopped out. "Better you than me."

Bobby watched as they moved to the door. After an examination, they stepped cautiously through. While they were inside, Bobby checked the gear Lincoln packed for them. "Yes," he said to himself as he pulled out the long, clear plastic tubing they used to siphon gas. He grabbed the red, plastic five-gallon gas can. If any of the cars had gas left in their tanks, the five gallons would fill fast.

He started with the first car he came to and scored. Once the fuel was flowing, it took less than a minute to fill the tank. He took it back to the van and topped off the tank, then went back and filled the can again. After depositing it in the back, he replaced the tube and went back to the driver's seat. "Hope you score just as good, sis."

Becca stopped in the lobby and showed them the list. She wasn't sure Jin knew what they were searching for. "You and Jin take that wing. I'll go this way. We're looking for portable units, but if we can't find those, we may have to take the big boys. Not sure how, but we'll figure it out. If you see something and aren't sure if it has value, take it anyway. We can figure it out later.

Darlene moved right. Jin shrugged. "Jin go?"

Becca pointed. "With Darlene."

He gave her a thumbs up and hurried away.

Alone, Becca took out her handgun and advanced down the hall. Most of these rooms were for admission interviews. She searched behind the admissions desk discovering her first find. A half-full box of band-aids. She realized then she needed a bag to put her booty in.

Becca followed the hall as it wound through the building. Each room had been searched though from the lack of damage and debris strewn about the rooms, it appeared to have been more cursory than physical. She hoped that boded well for their success.

After finishing the first floor, she had a small plastic tray with a handle, the size of the small carry baskets in supermarkets, used for carrying products, supplies, or equipment though nothing specific came to mind. What it contained now was the band-aids, a glass container of swabs, a tube of some sort of cream with a long unpronounceable name, and a box of the elastic bands used to wrap around a patient's arm when drawing blood. Not a great haul, but other than the cream, the other items had a use.

She found the stairs to the second floor but wanted to finish the first floor. At the end of her hall, she found the cafeteria. At one of the cash registers was a large spinnable dispenser for plasticware. Becca found a metal cart on wheels and laid the dispenser on its side on the lowest shelf.

In the kitchen storeroom, she discovered a case of lime-flavored gelatin boxes. Every other food item had been taken. "Someone must not like Jell-O." She slid the box onto the second shelf.

She stopped the cart next to the stairs. No way was she going to muscle it to the second floor. She left it there and climbed. It was eerie how quiet the building was. With nothing but dark outside the windows, it reminded her of every horror movie she'd ever watched that took place in a hospital. The memories made her jumpy.

The rooms here were for patients. There wasn't much to find other than IV stands and monitors, but she thought more of those couldn't hurt. She rolled them down the hall to the stairs and left them. By the time she finished on the floor, she had quite a collection. It was unrealistic to take them all, but a few might help, especially if one of the units Doc had back at the farm ever failed.

Behind the nurse's station she found masks and gloves. Those always came in handy. Then she found a container of cotton balls and a box of tongue depressors. With nothing else to find, Becca went down the hall and carried most of her find to the first floor.

The third floor offered nothing new. The search was taking a long time. She wondered how the others were doing.

Chapter Six

Bobby grew impatient then antsy. It was too dark to see much in his mirrors. It was better to be mobile, so he got out of the van. He moved to the rear door and opened it pulling out one of the NVGs. He powered them up and slid them on. It took a while to get used to the strange greenish glow.

He stepped up on the bumper then hauled himself to the roof. There he had a good view in every direction. He scanned in a slow pattern left to right, then back, keeping his back to the hospital. After an hour, his eyes got tired and his focus began to wane. He slipped the NVGs off and powered them down to save on the batteries.

The night was calm and quiet. Not much sound at all. Over the next hour, he switched between the goggles and his naked eyes, going thirty minutes without and ten with. The search inside was taking longer than anticipated. He was into the third hour and was taking off the NVGs when he caught a distorted red blip. He quickly slid them back on and adjusted, but no matter where he looked or what he tried, the red splotch did not reappear. However, whether real or not, it made him more vigilant.

Thirty minutes later, he heard a racket coming from the building. He glanced back to see his sister wheeling a cart toward the door. Becca could not get the automatic doors to open. Not that they worked on their own without power, but she was unable to pry them apart. She was forced to carry the items from the cart to the van. While she slaved, he stayed where he was.

"A little help might be nice."

"Thanks for volunteering," he said, tossing her words back at her.

She scowled and loaded the van one trip at a time. When she was done, she rolled the cart to the side. "I'm going in to see what's taking them so long."

Bobby didn't respond other than to wave a hand.

Several minutes passed before he got a confirming blip on his display. It had been quick and small. An animal of some kind? Two more quick blips drew his attention into a deeper focus. Something was definitely out there but was it human? More importantly, was it a threat?

The shot convinced him it was. The bullet hit the angled roofline above the front seats, inches below his rifle and punched through to the interior. Shocked, he let out a cry of alarm and rolled off the side, dropping to a squat on the building side. Whoever took the shot was good. They had spotted him and placed a shot within inches of his head. Did they have NVGs as well? If so, then the shooter wasn't that good.

Bobby came up to the rear corner and squatted. He had a full array of blips now. He counted six and no longer had doubts as to whether they were human or not. He picked out a target, breathed out and squeezed. The first blip disappeared. The others stopped and backtracked.

While they regrouped, Bobby hunted for the sniper. A bullet exploded the taillight near his head. He ducked on reflex, but though close, it wasn't close enough. Now he had an idea where to look.

The shooter was elevated somewhat. He was also covered well. Only a small section of red showed in the display. He sighted and sent the round on the way. The blip vanished. He swept the rifle down and toward the others. They were all in full retreat.

Becca burst from the door, gun up and ready to engage.

"Relax, Sis. We're all good. Well, I am anyway. Not sure about you."

Five minutes later, Jin and Darlene rolled a cart laden with some sort of machine to the door. They could not get the cart through the opening. While Bobby covered them, they muscled each piece into the van. Once done, Darlene said, "We have more." Jin and Darlene ran back inside.

Becca gave him a look. "Go," Bobby said. "I've got this." She nodded and followed the others.

Ten minutes after, they returned, each carrying a clear plastic tub of unknown supplies. Jin also brought a heavy metal box. They slid their haul into the van. The heavy item was a toolbox. Jin winked at him as he slid it in.

After one last scan, Bobby drove them off the grounds and away from where he saw the intruders flee.

"I hear gunshot?" Jin queried.

"Yeah. I handled it."

"Good man."

"Wow!" Darlene said. "You should have seen this guy work. We found the maintenance room and Jin discovered a tool kit. When we reached the x-ray room, he went back and grabbed the kit and began disassembling the thing right off the wall. We found a bunch of, I don't know what you call them, x-ray thingies and grabbed them. Not sure how many but a bunch. We couldn't take the big unit, but this is one you stand up to take the x-rays."

"Doc has a portable unit, but I'm sure this one is better," Bobby said.

"After all Jin's efforts," Darlene said, "I hope so."

Becca said, "Where's the next place?"

Darlene fumbled the map across her lap and looked at the list. "Uh, where are we now?"

Bobby tried to find the streets. "Looks like Route 108."

"That's good. Looks like we have eight different medical facilities on or off this street, except I think they're all back the other way.

They hit four of the medical buildings before trouble came for them. Each building had been cleaned out, leaving little of value. Still, they managed to find a few items like rolls of the white paper used to cover examination tables and a box of syringes.

Becca came up with the idea of rolling out one of the examination tables, but without a ramp getting it into the van was a problem. It was while they were discussing options for doing so that they were attacked.

The suddenness of the gunshots drove them in different directions. Darlene and Jin raced into the building while Becca and Bobby took refuge behind the van.

"Can you see them?" Becca said.

By way of answer, Bobby crawled into the van and retrieved his discarded NVG. He slid them on and powered them up before coming out. On the way, he grabbed the weapons bag and left it on the edge of the van floor for Becca.

The gunshots were not overwhelming but more a steady and spaced attempt to keep them pinned down. Bobby scanned down the side of the van. He found one target moving along a building across the street from the doctor's office. He fired and the figure went down.

A shot pinged off the rear door of the van.

"They're behind us, Bobo," Becca said. She unleashed a barrage from an AR and all shooting ceased from behind.

He glanced back at her. She stood aiming the weapon with her NVG on. "Did you get them?"

"Don't think so. I think the firepower scared them away."

"You're standing in the open. Even scared, they may still shoot. A lucky shot will take you down."

"What are you saying, dear brother, that you care?"

"Not if you're dumb enough to stand in the open. Just proves my theory that you were adopted."

She snorted a laugh and climbed inside the van.

A sudden burst of gunfire came from down the street in front of the van. Though he had no way to know for sure, Bobby felt confident Jin was at work. Less than a minute later, the shooting stopped. Everything was quiet for several minutes, and then a voice called. "Don't shoot, Jin. I come."

"Come ahead, Jin."

Ray Wenck

Jin walked down the street with his head down as he reloaded the magazine of his handgun. As he reached them, he slapped the mag back in, chambered a round, and slid the gun behind his back.

"Most dead. Few run. All boys. How you say?" He couldn't find the right word, so he signaled with his hand holding it a few feet off the ground. "Boy." He raised the hand to about shoulder height. "Them."

Becca said, "Teens? They were teenagers?"

"Yes."

"How many?" asked Bobby.

"Kill four. Four more run."

"Man," Bobby said with compassion. "That's the type of people we need to reach out to. If only they had tried to communicate instead of attack."

There was nothing else to say. After moving everything in the cargo van to one side or toward the front, they managed to lift the front end of a rolling exam table onto the floor. Then with Darlene pulling and guiding from inside, the other three hoisted the back end and slid it in. Becca locked the wheels to keep it stationary.

They closed the doors but now had little room for the others to squeeze in. Jin insisted the two women ride in the passenger seat up front while he wiggled in through the clutter.

They finished the rest of the facilities but found little.

"We have to decide what to do," Bobby said. "Even if we find what we need, we no longer have the room to carry it."

"Can I make a suggestion?" Darlene asked.

"Of course," said Becca.

"Since we're still close enough to do so, why not drop the stuff off back home then start out again?"

"That's a great idea," Bobby said.

"Of course. I thought of it."

Chapter Seven

The sun was rising by the time they pulled up the driveway. Lynn, Caryn, and a few of the others assigned to cooking duties were already busy preparing the morning fires for cooking. Bobby drove to the barn and backed up to the door. As they exited, a small crowd began moving toward them.

Lynn hurried to the front and greeted them as they exited. "Did you find what you needed? Her tone was anxious, and her eyes hopeful.

Becca shook her head. "No, but we found other things that will be useful. We couldn't carry any more, so came back to unload."

Though Lynn fought to keep the smile on her face, the hope faded from her eyes. They organized a few helpers and unloaded in short time. As they moved to get back into the van Lynn said, "I'm sure Doc will be thrilled with her new equipment, but you've been up all night. Why not get some sleep before going out again?"

Bobby looked at the others. When none of them spoke, he did for them. "We're on a time crunch, Lynn. We'll sleep on the road."

"What about breakfast. Jarrod brought us a bunch of eggs."

Though it sounded good, Bobby declined. He started the engine. Before he could move, Elijah burst through the crowd and said, "Dar. Dar, please."

Darlene was angry. She ripped the side door open and faced her father. "Dad. Stop. I'm going. It's my choice."

Elijah looked at his daughter and forced a thin smile to his weathered face. Tears filled his eyes. "I know, sweet child. I know. I just didn't want you to go without saying goodbye. Is that too much for an old man to ask?"

Darlene melted as he opened his arms. She jumped out of the van and embraced her father. The emotional scene was both nice and awkward to watch. They kissed and said, "Goodbye," and exchanged "I love yous." Darlene got back in the van. As she closed the door, Elijah said, "Oh, I almost forgot." He offered her a tan canvas bag. "Something for you and the others for the road. Your favorite. Candied yams and ginger."

She took the bag. "Thank you, Dad. I love you."

"And I you. Be safe."

She closed the door and Bobby began to move. As they passed the house, Caryn called to them. She and Ruth ran up to the window and passed over a thermos of coffee, four plastic cups, and four egg and tomato sandwiches on the corn tortillas they were now making.

"Thank you, Caryn."

"Good luck," she said.

Jin sniffed at the sandwich then took a healthy bite. As he chewed, he said, "Good people."

Yeah, Bobby thought. The best.

They drove off feeling somewhat saddened yet anxious for their mission to be successful.

Not all who witnessed the return had been welcoming or happy. Sam Edwards and his good friend, Joe Merchant watched with disdain. "You think they'll find what they need to keep that asshole alive?"

Edwards spat a stream of tobacco. "Maybe. I'm surprised they found what they did."

"Yeah. Especially after just one day."

"I'll tell you what, Joe. I'm not about to stand by and let them save the man who killed my son. If I have to, I'll take matters into my own hands."

Merchant motioned with his chin toward Lincoln, who had just arrived at the community picnic tables. "Maybe we need to do a few other things too."

"What are we talking here? A shift in power?"

"Sure. Why not? You happy with the way things are going?"

"Hell no."

"So maybe we alter the power structure here by taking out a key member of the council."

Edwards looked into his friend's eyes for signs of sincerity. "You're serious?"

"As a heart attack."

"That's a bold step."

"Just has to be planned out right. If he dies of some accident, who's to know? Maybe he just outright disappears. If no one finds his body, there's no proof what happened to him."

"I have to admit, I like the sound of that, but what about the others on the council?"

"Elijah's an old man. Maggie's a hard one, as is Milo. We can control Lynn by threatening her daughter. Lynn can control her son's vote and Caryn's too. There'll be a special election to replace Lincoln. That could be you," Merchant said with zeal.

Edwards' eyes widened with sudden understanding and excitement. "Yeah. Let's do this. We take out Mark and Lincoln, put some of our people in the right positions, and this place is ours."

"I think we should join our people for breakfast today. I have a sudden hunger."

Merchant laughed. "I'll bet you do."

Lynn stopped at the rear door of the house as she noticed the two men across the yard by the garage. She did not like the way they watched the van leave, nor did she care for the sneers on their faces as they discussed whatever nefarious schemes were on their minds.

She did not trust the men, in fact, hadn't since they first arrived. There was always something off about them, something waiting in their depths like a tiger preparing to strike. They had arrived and joined the community a few months back, shortly after Elijah and his people. Two women, four men, a teenage boy, Edwards's son and a ten-year-old girl. They did not live on the farmhouse grounds, but instead took two of the three houses two blocks down.

No matter what the situation, Edwards was the type of person who always had a complaint. Unfortunately, his sort was always able to find a willing ear to listen to his poison. Lynn knew deep in her soul that these men were plotting something. Most likely something against Mark. It'd be just like that coward to attack a man who was unable to defend himself. Well, if Mark couldn't do it himself, she'd see to it he was protected. She needed to speak to Lincoln about keeping an eye on the two men and their companions.

She walked through the door with the two bowls of potatoes she had sliced for the meal just as Edwards and Merchant started for the table. She saw one nod to another man standing near the tables drinking coffee. The man smiled and nodded back. A thought came to her as she set the bowls down near the fire pit. It might be good to know who else was in Edwards' corner. They'd all bear watching.

Though she busied herself with the morning meal, her mind worked on the problem. By the time she was ready to serve the food, she had the makings of a solution.

Deep in his mind, Mark tried once more to reach his wife and son. They remained just beyond his touch. They made no effort toward him, nor did they speak. They just stood there smiling and waiting for him. They were so close. Frustrated with his failure, he pushed harder and felt whatever binds holding him back weaken. Yes. *It won't be long now, my love. I'll be with you soon. I've missed you so much.*

A deep voice penetrated his consciousness. With a start, he pulled back from his wife and son. His first thought was that God was speaking to him, but this voice was vaguely familiar, and to his knowledge, he had never heard God's voice before.

"Listen, you ornery son of a bitch. Don't you give in to death's call and, for God's sake, stay away from any lights." *Who was that? Why did he feel he knew?*

"There's trouble brewing here, and like always, your kids are smack dab in the middle of it."

He knew now. It was Jarrod. *Why was Jarrod here?* He glanced toward the fading image of his wife and son. *Wait. Don't go. I'm coming.*

"Don't you do something stupid like die just when your kids are working hard to save your ass."

Kids?

"You got some people who'd like nothing better than to see you die. If that don't happen soon, I'm thinking they may try to help you along that path. Don't you worry none. I'm here and ain't gonna let no one come near. It'd sure help matters, though, if you just up and woke on your own. Think you can do that for your old friend?"

Kids in trouble. Something changed within the construct his mind created. Something was different, something dire. With one more glance at the fading image of Sarah and Ben, Mark focused on the concerning words of his friend and how he might be able to help his children.

Chapter Eight

"Where to? Bobby asked.

"Keep heading west," Becca said. "It's been good luck so far."

"West it is."

Darlene rearranged the map. "Do we want to hit some of the smaller towns on the way or go for bigger ones?"

"What does the list show," asked Becca.

Darlene examined it. "Looks like they're all in bigger towns or small cities."

"Maybe smaller towns have been overlooked," Becca said. "Most will at least have a doctor's office. Do we gamble with our limited time?"

Good question, Bobby thought. One he had no answer for. It was going to take an extreme amount of luck to find the items on Doc's list. Even if they did, it still only delayed the inevitable. Eventually, the new supply would run out as well. It was going to be a never-ending search to keep their father alive for a little longer. If he didn't wake, what did it all matter? It will all have been for naught.

"Let's stick to the places on the list first," said Bobby. "If we strike out, we can hit the smaller places on the way back."

"You heard the man," Becca said.

A soft snoring rose from the back. Bobby angled the interior mirror enough to see Jin sprawled on the floor, asleep. He hadn't felt tired until that moment. This was still only day one. Well, actually, day two. It was going to take a lot of stamina and willpower to make it two weeks.

"First on the list in the direction we're going is the Archbold Medical Center."

"Okay. I know where Archbold is."

They found the building, which housed several medical practices, including a physician's group. The building had a modern look to it, with a slanted roof over the drive up. Bobby stopped on the street to observe the structure. The parking lot was clear of vehicles which made him think someone had moved them. Cars blocked the driveways preventing anyone from getting onto the grounds via vehicle. The only conclusion was that someone was staying inside.

He drove past the building then around to the back side. All entries were blocked, however, there were two ambulances backed up to the building as well as eight assorted vehicles, all parked close to the rear doors.

"Someone is most definitely staying here," Bobby said.

Jin woke, rubbed his eyes, and crawled between the seats scooting under Darlene, who was standing.

"What do?"

Becca said, "If they're staying there, it must be because they have access to supplies. Maybe we can trade something for what we need."

"It's possible," said Bobby.

Jin said, "I sneak in. Steal."

"Maybe," said Bobby. "Let's try it the peaceful way first."

Becca said, "Does that mean we can hurt them but not kill them?"

Darlene fist-bumped her.

Bobby looked from the women to Jin, who merely shrugged. "Man, is this the wrong group to send on a peace mission. I can't send any of you, or a war will start."

"So, you go," Darlene said.

"I was going to cover whoever went."

"Go," Jin said. "I cover."

"You won't shoot unless necessary, right?"

"No shoot. Go."

He looked at the women. "One of you has to go with me."

They looked at each other. Then, as if mentally deciding their course of action, Darlene said, "Best two out of three?"

Becca nodded, and they started a rock, paper, scissors game.

Bobby said to Jin, "You know how to handle this rifle?"

Jin cocked his head in a *seriously?* look and said, "Bitch, please."

Bobby wondered if he should correct the usage but decided not to. Jin was definitely hanging out with Lincoln too much.

Bobby stepped from the van. He had parked on the street a half-block away in view of the front door. Darlene stepped out with him. "Guess I won," she said with a smile.

"Or lost," Becca said. "Guess it depends on how you look at it."

"Thanks, sis."

"I think it's a win," Darlene said, sliding her arm around Bobby's. She did some rapid blinks and smiled, which cracked Becca up. "Okay, you two. It's not a date. You be home by the time the streetlights come on."

Darlene released his arm and gave Becca a wicked smile. "Sister, the streetlights no longer come on."

"Well then, sister, I'll see you in the morning."

They laughed conspiratorially and fist-bumped.

"Hey! Get serious here. We don't know anything about these people. They may shoot us before we reach the door."

Darlene slid a hand over her face from head to jaw, erasing the smile and replacing it with a stern expression. "Game face on, sir."

Bobby sighed. "Leave the rifle."

"What? No way."

"Yes, way. We don't want them to think us a threat, and if they do attack or take us prisoner, we don't want them to get our weapons. Handguns only."

"Man," Darlene said, handing the rifle to Becca. "Guess it was a loss."

"Amen to that, sister."

While Jin and Becca took up covering positions, Darlene and Bobby walked toward the facility.

"I lost on purpose, you know."

"How do you lose a game of rock, paper, scissors on purpose?"

"Cause your sister telegraphs her move."

Why would you want to lose on purpose?" He regretted the question as soon as it left his mouth.

"To be with you, silly."

When they first met, the two had kindled a friendship that everyone believed would blossom into a relationship. With all the hostile activity of the past few months, that never had a chance to develop. During that time, however, Bobby had developed a bond with Maretha, which he very much wanted to explore further. However, with the severe wounds she incurred during the defense of her home and the need to get back to his own, Bobby had no idea if she was even alive.

He glanced at Darlene. She was pretty with reddish hair that had been recently trimmed to shoulder length. She had a line of freckles across her nose and green-gray eyes. Her smile was thin, he guessed to cover the one tooth that was misaligned. She was a bit slimmer and shorter than Becca, but just as solid.

Darlene was a fierce fighter. Almost as good as Becca, who had bested her the first time they met and faced off. She was the third best female fighter he knew, well second, if he counted Maretha and Becca as tied. Not that being female or male mattered. Good was good no matter what your gender. Though he'd never say it to Becca, he thought Maretha had a slight edge over her. He hoped he never found out. He also prayed Maretha was still alive for him to ponder the outcome.

They stepped over the parking curb and onto the parking lot. With his eyes focused on the glass doors, he was sure he spotted movement inside the building. "Stay to the left of the door to allow Jin a shot in case we get in trouble. Let me do the talking."

"But of course, master. I'm just a simple female. I would never dream of speaking unless spoken to."

Bobby looked at her, unsure if she was joking though thinking probably not. "I just meant—"

"Relax. I was kidding. But just in case you want to know, I'm damn smart."

He didn't doubt that for a second.

They reached the edge of the overhanging roof when a voice commanded, "That's far enough."

They stopped.

"We're not here to attack or threaten," Bobby said.

"Got that right," a second male voice said from the opposite side of the door. He realized they were standing in the large bushes to either side of the entry. A young man of about Bobby's age stepped from the left side holding a handgun though not pointed directly at them.

Next to him, he could feel Darlene stiffen at the sight of the gun.

"Why are you here?"

"We're from a community a few hours from here. We're in need of medical supplies and thought you might have some. We'd be willing to trade for what we need."

The second man came out of the bushes to the right. He had a rifle and it was aimed at them. He was shorter and pudgier than the first man, but from the look on his face, Bobby knew he was hardcore and to take him seriously.

"Sure, we'll trade," the pudgier man said. "How about for her?"

Darlene bristled. Bobby tried to catch her arm. She stepped forward two steps and smiled, then swayed her hips. "You want to trade for little ole me?" She laughed.

"Oh, hell yeah, baby."

"Well, honey, first of all, you couldn't handle this. Secondly, ew! And thirdly, no. Just no."

As she talked and sashayed, she edged closer to the man. He was mesmerized by her body at first, and the barrel of the rifle lowered until he heard her words. Riled, he said, "You bitch."

He brought the rifle up again, but Darlene was fast. She ducked under the barrel, lifted it with one hand, and had the tip of her knife under his jaw before he knew what happened.

His partner, shocked by the sudden action, was slow to aim his handgun. "I wouldn't," Bobby said. He had his gun aimed at the man. He froze. "Just slide the gun into your holster and raise your hands." The man did as directed and slowly lifted his hands.

"Didn't anyone ever teach you it was impolite to call a woman B-I-T-C-H?" She spelled it. "Let the rifle fall to the ground."

He hesitated, and in a more forceful tone, she said, "Do it." The gun landed at his feet. She slid her foot under the barrel without looking down and flipped the rifle five feet away.

"We don't want trouble here," Bobby said. "We really only came to negotiate. Darlene, release him, please."

"That'd be a good idea, bitch," a woman said from the door. She had a rifle aimed at Darlene.

"There's that word again," Darlene said. She casually slid behind the man to block the woman's shot. The man sputtered, and a thin trickle of blood ran down his neck. He didn't appear so tough now. Bobby saw his hand fumbling for the knife at his belt.

"Dar."

"I've got it." To her shield, she said, "If that knife clears its sheath, I'll drive this through your jaw and into your brain. You understand me, Baby?"

"Hey! Hey!" the woman shouted. "Don't you hurt him."

Darlene glanced at the woman. "Is this man yours?"

"Please, I'm asking you. Woman to woman. Please don't kill him."

Darlene frowned. "Put your hands behind your back."

"What?"

"Just do it. I'm going to spare your life because your woman asked nicely." She leaned closer. "She seems like a nice person. Too nice for you. Put those hands behind your back, or I'll tell her you wanted to trade for me."

He swallowed hard and locked his hands behind his back. Darlene withdrew his knife and handgun and tossed them in the bushes behind the rifle. "Now, lady, I'm granting your request, but this doesn't work if you still have a gun aimed at me."

"Okay, I'm lowering it."

"Not good enough. Reach outside the door and toss it into the bushes."

"Don't do it, Sally. She'll kill me anyway."

"Sally, I'm a woman of my word. If I wanted this man dead, he would be already, and our sniper would've put a bullet through your head a long time ago. Now, please, so we can move this along, do as I ask."

The other man said, "It's all right, Sally. Do it."

"As long as we're doing this, "Bobby said. "Toss your gun back there, too."

The man went tight-lipped.

"Ah, with just two fingers, please."

The man complied. Once all guns were out of reach, Darlene pressed her body against the man's, reached down and squeezed his scrotum and said, "I was right. You couldn't have handled me." She smiled and shoved him toward the door. "There's your man, Sally. As I promised."

The man muttered, "Bitch."

"Now Sally, if he calls me that one more time, all bets are off, and I'll be wearing his tiny dick for a necklace and his little nuts for earrings."

Sally reached for her man and yanked him inside while giving Darlene a disgusted look.

Chapter Nine

"Now what," the man asked. "You gonna shoot your way in and take what you want?"

"No. We came to talk and maybe negotiate a trade. We did not come to make war. However, we are very capable of doing so. There's already been too much death in the world. We need to learn to live together and help each other. If you don't have what we need or won't trade, we'll go, but this might be to your advantage as well."

"How so?"

"First, we might have something you need. Second, forming alliances with a strong community makes you stronger. Third, if we form a trade partnership, it makes it easier on both sides when they're looking for something."

"What if we don't have what you want?"

"No big deal. We'll move on and try elsewhere. Tell me, is there anything you and your people are looking for?"

The man sucked in his lip. Bobby wasn't sure if he was thinking or deciding how much to tell.

"Food. We can always use food."

Bobby nodded. "I'm not going to tell you we have an abundance. We have a large community to feed and may need most of what we have to get through the winter, but if there is extra, it may be something we can trade. Why don't we do this first. Take my list. Check to see if you have any of it you can spare. If so, we'll go back and talk to our council."

"You have a council?"

Bobby paused, then smiled. "Yeah. When your community has grown as large as ours, you need some form of a governing body in place. Anyway, I'll check with them and see if a trade can be made."

The man nodded. "Okay. Let me see the list."

Bobby handed it to him but didn't let go at once." The man looked surprised. "Sorry," Bobby said, "it's my only copy."

"I promise to bring it back." Bobby released it and the man went inside. Bobby turned to Darlene. "Will you go tell them what's happening?"

"Sure." She trotted back to the van.

A minute later, the door burst open and three men and the woman who was at the door rushed toward him with guns aimed. The woman ran to the bushes to retrieve their weapons while the men ran straight at Bobby. "Keep your hands away from your gun," the lead man said. "If you make a move toward it, you're dead."

Bobby backed away. "This is a big mistake."

"You're the one who made it by coming here." He advanced while the other two men watched for anyone coming to Bobby's aid.

Bobby backed away and whipped his arm free of the man's grasp. "Is this a hostage situation? You think you can ransom me for what you want?"

"Stop moving, or I'll shoot."

"You won't shoot me. Not if you want to trade me."

"You don't have to be walking for me to trade you." The man altered the aim of his rifle toward Bobby's leg. One of the other men stepped forward, the rifle up and ready to fire. "Hey, Two women are coming."

"Fire a warning shot."

A shot was fired but not by him. A red mist blew out the back of his head, and he dropped.

The woman screamed. The second gunman said, "Oh God, they killed Doug."

The man reaching for Bobby said, "Well, shoot them." Before he got the chance, he went down like the first man.

The woman ran into the building.

While the man flinched at the second gunshot, Bobby made his move. He stepped toward the man fast, with the rifle aimed at his leg. He swatted the barrel down. It discharged, the round ricocheting off the blacktop. Then Bobby drove a fist into the man's face. He staggered backward, but Bobby stayed with him. This time he grabbed the barrel to keep it from moving on target and hit the man again. As he flailed to keep from falling, Bobby yanked the rifle from his hands, tossed it aside, and pummeled the man. Two solid blows sent him down, then sitting on his chest, he plowed one fist after another into his face until he felt a hand pull at his shoulder. He whirled, shoved the person back, and lifted his hand to throw another punch. This time someone grabbed his arm and clutched it tight to their body. A calm voice whispered in his ear, "He's done, Bobo. He's beyond feeling pain. Let him be."

His breath ragged, his throat harsh, he said, "I don't understand. What is wrong with people? Why does it always have to end in a fight?"

Becca helped him up. "Which answer you want? They're stupid, or they're afraid?"

Darlene came up and took his other arm. She held her handgun and had the fallen rifle slung over a shoulder. "Come on, Bobby. We don't need them as much as they need us." She walked backward, facing the door to ensure no further assault was coming.

"He has my list."

"We'll make a copy," Darlene said.

"But they might have had some of the stuff we need to save Dad."

"Think about it, brother," Becca said. "If they had the items on the list, they wouldn't have made a play for you. They must be desperate for food and knew we'd leave if they didn't have what we wanted."

It made sense, but it still angered him. Why not just tell them they didn't have what was on the list? They could have forged an agreement and made trades down the road. Now, two men were dead, and the third incapacitated. All for what? Greed? Power? No, more like fear and desperation.

They reached the van. "Nice shooting," Bobby said to Jin.

He smiled. "Guess figure gun out."

Bobby laughed. "Yeah, I guess you did."

"Now what?" Becca asked. "You want to storm the castle?"

"No, I think we move on to the next stop."

If the encounter had been disappointing, the remainder of their stay in Archbold was more so. Bobby's mood grew darker with each failure to find anything of use.

"Where to next? Becca asked.

Bobby sat sullenly in the driver's seat, staring at the road. He made no effort to respond and was only partially listening. His thoughts remained on the people in the medical facility. His anger simmered. He wanted to go back and confront them, to make them understand they were all in this together and the best way to survive was to help each other. Then he wanted to pound each one of them for being stupid and getting their people killed needlessly.

He was aware of rustling paper behind him.

"Here," Becca said. "Let's take Route Two to Stryker. Otherwise, we'll be driving a while to get to the next town. Stryker is small. Maybe no one hit it yet."

Darlene said, "But there's not even a doctor's office on the list. Isn't it a waste of time?"

"Maybe, but we're going that direction anyway, so why not check it out? Call it a hunch."

A hand touched his shoulder. "Did you hear that, Bobby?" Becca asked.

Bobby snapped from his angry thoughts. "Yeah." He made the turn onto Route Two. The Village of Stryker had fewer than two thousand people in residence before the pandemic. It was a ghost town now except for one thing. Every building they passed, whether house or business, had been broken into and ransacked. In several places, they found bodies. From the amount of decay and destruction by animals, they'd been there since the beginning.

"You think it's a wandering band that came through here?" Darlene asked.

"Maybe," said Becca. "It might be just a few people. My dad cleaned out an entire subdivision by himself in the beginning."

"You know what else is in the area?" Bobby said. "The Corrections Center of Northwest Ohio. I think there's a Juvee detention center here too."

Huh!" Becca said. "Let's go check it out. They have to have a medical facility on the site, right?"

"Where is it? It's not on the map."

"All I know is it's south of the village," Bobby said.

He followed Route Two as it curved south. Bobby noted both the fire and police departments had been cleaned out, including fire trucks and squad cars. He assumed whatever weapons had been locked up inside were in possession of the intruders as well.

When they reached the intersection with thirty-four, the facility grounds were easy to see. They were to the left across open farmland. Bobby made the turn as Becca and Darlene stood between the seats to eye the scene. Bobby drove closer, but with all eyes on the Corrections Center, they weren't watching the road ahead. Bobby was shocked when Jin bolted forward and shouted, "Stop."

Bobby braked on reflex. "What? he said, heart racing.

Jin pointed through the windshield. Down the way, blocking the intersection with the road the facility sat on, were two police cruisers.

"Guess we found who ransacked the town," Darlene said. "You think it was the inmates?"

Becca said, "I wonder how many they have in there."

Jin shook his head. "No good."

Bobby agreed, but with the memory of the last confrontation still vivid in his mind, he took his foot off the brake and let the van move forward.

"Bobby, what are you doing?" Becca asked in a curious tone with a hint of concern.

"I want to see."

"No, Bobby," Becca said with more force to her voice, "you don't. You think you can make what happened back there right, but you can't, and this can be worse. If the people staying there are former residents, they will have no hesitation attacking or gunning us down. Think. You

want a repeat of what just happened with us possibly on
the losing side?"

The van kept moving at low speed.

"We don't have time for this." Becca's voice increased
in volume and anxiety

The van rolled on.

"Think about Dad."

Bobby braked.

"What chance does he have if we fail?"

Jin reached out and touched Bobby's arm. He shook his
head, showing no emotion in his dark eyes.

Bobby exhaled, then reversed and turned around. As he
drove away, the tension within the van evaporated until
Bobby said, with a decided sinister sneer. "We didn't
have to go to them. They're coming to us."

Chapter Ten

Behind them, the flashing lights of a police car grew ever larger as the powerful engine quickly cut the distance between them.

Bobby hit the gas, but the van was slow to accelerate and no match for the cruiser. He swayed across both lanes to prevent it from pulling alongside.

"Looks like two inside," Becca said. "The other car is still at the intersection."

"We can shoot them through the rear door, can't we?" asked Darlene.

"We can, but I'm not sure we have anything that will penetrate," said Becca. "We might be able to scare them off though."

She picked up Bobby's rifle and made ready to lift the rear door hatch.

"Maybe we should see what they want first," Bobby said. "At least we can get information from them."

"You don't want information. You just want a confrontation," Becca said.

"Why would I want that?"

"To have a more satisfying conclusion than the previous encounter."

Darlene said, "Or to take out your growing anger and frustration. You're always talking about people getting along. Now's your chance to make that work. Either pull over and talk to them or we open fire and go to war. It's your choice."

Bobby glanced at Jin. The Korean man was stoic as usual, but his eyebrows lifted in question.

Without answering, Bobby angled toward the side of the road. "Becca, stay beneath the rear window. Once they move past, you keep your eyes out back for other approaching cars. Darlene, press behind my seat and try to stay out of sight. Stay ready. If trouble comes, I'll need you to take the man in my window. He'll see me move and have the advantage. Jin," he stopped. He didn't have to tell him anything. Jin already had a gun out, his hand between his seat and the door. The seat had been scooted back for protection and obscurity should he need to shoot. Bobby and his seat were that protection.

The cruiser did not pull up behind them as trained professionals might do. Instead, it passed them, did a one-eighty at high speed, squealing tires in a superior display, and faced them twenty feet ahead. Bobby glanced in the mirror and caught Becca's eyes. She nodded, already having the same idea. She left the rifle and slid out the rear door.

The two men in the police car made no move for several minutes. Bobby was unsure if that was meant to intimidate them or simply because they had no idea what to do next. A voice came across the bullhorn mounted to the roof. "You in the van. Exit now."

Dude has watched too many TV detective shows, Bobby thought.

When they didn't exit, the voice became more insistent. "Come out of there now, or we will shoot."

The two men were having an animated discussion that ended with the angry passenger getting out behind his open door and firing a shot through the windshield between Bobby and Jin.

The voice said, "That's your only warning shot. Come out now, or the next goes through you."

Jin slid to the floor with only the top of his head and eyes showing. Bobby opened the door. Jin nodded. "Got back."

Bobby nodded, knowing Jin would indeed have him covered. He opened the door and stepped down onto the step keeping his body turned sideways and as much behind the door as possible. The gun hung behind his leg.

"Come down out of there," the shooter said. He was an average size man with thin hair. He was not wearing a police uniform.

"I don't think so. I don't know you. We didn't mean to intrude on your territory. Let us go, and we'll move on."

The man spoke to his partner before saying, "Not until we see what's in the van."

"Why?"

He made a shrugging gesture. "Let's just say it's the toll for crossing our borders."

"I don't think so."

That surprised the man and made him angry. "I don't think you have much choice in the matter, bud. We've got the guns."

"So, if I let you search the van, you'll let us go."

"Sure," he said in an unconvincing voice.

Bobby leaned into the van. "Don't kill him, but as soon as he opens the door, we're taking this guy down. Then he leaned out a bit and added, "Wherever you are, I hope you heard that, Becca."

He slid the gun under the seat, knowing they'd ask him to move. "Okay, I guess if that's what we have to do, come ahead."

The driver opened the door but did not get out. The passenger stepped away from his door, keeping the handgun aimed at Bobby. "Move away from the door."

Bobby obliged, keeping his hands up. He took two steps, then two more when the man motioned him back. He glanced inside at Jin then back at Bobby. "Don't you move now." He gestured at Jin with his gun to get out. Jin was sitting in the seat, staring dumbly at him. "Hey, you, get out." Jin did not move. "I said get out." When Jin still hadn't budged, the man turned to Bobby. "Is he stupid or what?"

Bobby shrugged. "He's Korean. He doesn't understand English."

"Tell him to get out of there."

"I don't speak Korean."

"How do you communicate?"

"Mostly hand gestures," Bobby answered.

"Well, hand gesture his ass out of there."

"I don't think he'll go. He's afraid."

"How can you tell?"

"By the way he's shaking."

The man looked back at Jin. Jin played his role perfectly. He lifted a shaky hand to his forehead and wiped away imaginary perspiration.

Bobby walked forward. "Here. Let me try to get him out."

The fake cop flinched and swiveled the gun to Bobby's face. He backed a step but let him go by.

Bobby stepped to the door. He leaned inside. "Hey, you." He pointed at Jin with his left hand as he leaned over the seat. His body blocked the fake cop's view of the hand that reached under the seat, gripped the gun, and slid it into the front of his belt. Bobby motioned with one

hand. "Get out." He pointed at Jin. "You." Bobby panto-
mimed opening the door. "Out." He looked over his
shoulder at the cop. "Nope. Sorry. He won't go."

The fake cop used his gun to direct Bobby away from
the door. Bobby shot a glance at the cop car and noticed
the driver was now out, using the door as cover, and aiming his gun at Bobby.

The cop leaned into the van to look at the cargo area.
"Well, what have we got here?"

Bobby feared he discovered Darlene. The man looked
back. "What's in the duffels and bins?"

"Our personal stuff," he said, hiding his relief. "You
know, clothes and such."

"I'll bet you're hiding a lot more than that in there.
Come on," he motioned with his gun to lead him to the
rear of the van. "Open the door."

Bobby stepped forward, lifted the door open, and
stepped back. The fake cop kept his eye on Bobby as he
moved toward the door. He stopped when he felt the barrel press into his cheek. Bobby moved fast, pulling his
gun and snatching the surprised man's weapon from his
hand.

"You seriously messed with the wrong people," Bobby
said, moving up and pinning the man's legs to the bumper. "And I'm in a great mood for dishing out retribution."

"Bobby," Darlene warned. He shot her an angry glance
as if his mother had just told him to stop beating on his
younger brother. "Call to you, partner."

"Why, what are you going to do to us?"

"Nothing. We just want to be left alone and don't want
to get shot. Now call to him."

"What should I say?"

"Tell him he has to see this."

"Mitch, come here." His tone sounded frightened. "You gotta see this."

"What is it?"

Bobby whispered. "Food and weapons and a bottle of whiskey."

The fake cop repeated, "Food and-and weapons and a bottle of whiskey." His voice cracked, and he tried unsuccessfully to muffle a sob. "Please don't kill us."

"Andy, everything all right?" the driver said. "Andy?"

"If you bastards hurt him, I swear I'll bring the others down here and we'll roast you all." Mitch left the safety of his door and moved toward the side of the van. As he neared the passenger side door, Becca reached out from under the van and grabbed his legs like a defensive back diving to make an open-field tackle.

As soon as he started to fall, Jin opened the door straight into his head. The man had no way of avoiding contact. He struck hard, groaned, then hit the ground where, after Becca delivered a kick to his head, he was unable to move, let alone groan.

They stripped the men of their weapons and boots and left them on the side of the road. One bound with handcuffs, the second man carried on his belt like he was a real cop, and one unconscious. Becca and Darlene got into the squad car and sped off with lights flashing and siren blaring. Bobby did his best to keep up with them.

Chapter Eleven

They continued down thirty-four until they reached Bryan. Bryan Hospital was on Doc's list. It was located on the same road, across from a medical park. They slowed as they approached. Bryan was a city and much larger than the last two areas they searched. However, just a drive-by showed them stopping was a waste of time. The buildings looked not only looted, but physical damage had been done to them as well. Windows were broken out. Furniture lay in broken heaps on the grounds. One brick wall was blackened as if someone tried to burn the structure down. Whoever had been there had major anger issues and was not someone they wanted to meet. They kept driving.

They found two buildings that didn't show outward signs of damage and stopped to search them, but neither bore fruit. Bryan had been picked clean by someone, perhaps those from the prison.

They were outside the vehicles talking over the roofs.

"Should we check more?" Darlene asked. "Or is it a waste of time?"

"Waste," Jin said.

"Yeah, let's move on," said Becca.

Becca and Darlene led the way now with lights and siren off. Outside of the city they pulled over to discuss the next option.

Darlene yawned as she said, "We've got Blakeslee, Edon, and Edgerton, then the Indiana line. I don't know about you guys, but I'm hungry and tired. I can do either in any order."

Bobby said, "We should keep going."

"I know you're on a deadline, but we've only just begun the search. If we burn out now, we won't be any good later."

Annoyed, Bobby looked away.

Becca said, "Let's get to the next town and stop for a while. We can sleep in shifts."

"Works for me," Darlene said. "My turn to drive." She got back in the car.

"Bobby, I want to find what we need as badly as you do, but we can't kill ourselves doing it. This is only day one."

"Two," he corrected.

She had to think about that then agreed. "Okay, two, but we still need rest."

He thinned his lips but nodded.

They entered the small village of Blakeslee and drove the main street. It took less than five minutes at slow speed to cover the entire area. To their surprise, the houses and buildings looked untouched. They found a large house and pulled into the driveway. Bobby parked the van as far back off the street as possible. Darlene stopped in front of the second spot of a three-car garage with three separate overhead doors.

"What do you think?" Becca asked.

Jin shrugged and went to the side door.

Bobby said, "One place is as good as another."

"There's just no pleasing you, baby brother. Remember that about him, Dar."

Bobby said, "Huh! What?"

Becca and Darlene walked past him toward the house. "Oh, I will. Don't worry. I'll train him."

"Wait! What's going on here?"

The two women laughed and high-fived. Jin pushed the door open and stepped aside to allow the ladies to enter first. Becca said in an English accent, "Be a good lad and see to the bags, Bobby dear. That's a good boy." More laughter from inside the house had Bobby seeing red.

Jin moved past and cuffed Bobby on the arm. "Bobby dear. Bags."

Jin and Bobby brought the food, weapons and personal go-bags into the house and dropped them on the floor in the living room. Though the house had been closed up for months, other than a slight stale odor, there was no foul stench a body might leave.

They each took a bedroom and dropped their gear. When they adjourned in the living room, Becca said, "I vote food."

"Oh," Darlene yawned again and stretched her arms wide. "As good as that sounds, I think I'm catching some Zees. I'll catch you all later."

"Bobby said, "Just a nap. We're not going to spend the entire day here."

"Relax, Bobby. Let's eat, then check out the town. If nothing has been touched, we might be able to find things the community needs. Besides, it's getting late. There's only an hour of daylight left."

"Hey, Sis, screw the community. Half of them want to pull the plug on Dad."

She turned to her brother, a look of sadness in her eyes. "Bobby, that doesn't mean we can't do the right thing. Besides, if we bring back supplies, it will buy some goodwill with many of them."

He sighed and turned away. "Come on," Becca said. "Let's eat, then go exploring."

After a simple meal, they took the van leaving both Darlene and Jin to sleep. They headed north on thirty-four until they were out of town then hit a house. The first place was a treasure trove of food staples from beans and rice to flour and sugar. There was so much they had to find and empty some plastic tubs to haul it. They came away with four tubs full of food items, one of basic medical supplies, band-aids and ointments, and assorted automotive essentials such as oil and transmission fluid.

They also found three five-gallon containers of gas, two full, and one was half full. The haul had been so good they decided to move down the road to the next house. They passed open farmland on both sides of thirty-four. The next place was smaller but had a decent yield, including another five-gallon gas can.

As they drove back, Becca said, "Now see, that was worth doing, wasn't it?"

"Yeah," Bobby grumbled, "but it leaves less room for the medical equipment and supplies we're supposed to be looking for."

They came to an intersection and stopped. Becca counted seven houses to the right. Bobby tallied five on his side. "If we go either direction, it's going to be night by the time we're finished," Bobby said.

Becca said, "Bobby, it's already night. Let's go back and hit it tomorrow."

With grudging reluctance, Bobby acquiesced. He pulled up next to the garage, then went to the door. It was unlocked. He entered and slid the closest garage door up. Becca drove inside and parked. They entered the house and Becca swamped her brother in an embrace. "I'm going to stay like this all night until you hug me back. Annoyed, he did. "Nope. Not until you mean it."

"Becca."

"Stop whining and do it."

He squeezed her tight and lifted her off the floor, getting a squeak of surprise from her. He held her there for a moment until he was sure she was uncomfortable and struggling with air flow. Then he set her down, gave her a big wet kiss on the cheek, and walked away, leaving her out of breath. "Good night, Sis. Expect to be woken up at sunrise."

Chapter Twelve

Early the next morning, Bobby woke and was surprised to see Becca already up. She was nibbling on a cookie. "About time, sleepyhead."

"What happened to you? Couldn't you sleep?"

"Not really. I got a few hours in but couldn't stay asleep, so gave up around four and came out here."

"Dad?"

She shrugged. "Maybe. It hit me last night that if we fail, Dad might die. I'm not sure I can live with a failure."

"Then let's not fail." Bobby sat to put on his boots. "What about the others?"

"Well, Jin snuck out about an hour ago. I have no idea where he went. I don't think he knew I was awake. He's really sneaky."

"Yeah. It's eerie. Did he take the car?

"I don't think so. I didn't hear it drive away. Oh wait, I think Darlene had the keys last, so he couldn't have taken it."

"What about Darlene?"

"Still sleeping. I think we should go out ourselves and come back for them later."

"Works for me."

They drove away, stopping at the same intersection.

Becca said. "Okay. That's a lot of houses. Even with the two of us working, it may take all day."

"Gotta be done." Bobby parked in the driveway of the first house. They cleared it fast, finding a few good items, mostly food. It took about forty minutes. At the van, Bobby said, "Not as good as last night, but you're right. If we have eleven houses left just in this section, and it takes forty minutes each, it's going to kill most of the day. We need to fall into a routine."

"I'll tell you what. Since there are more houses in this direction, drop me off at the next house and go back and get them. Drop Darlene and the police car off here, and you and Jin go the other way. We'll meet back at the house and have a huge dinner. We should be able to finish in half the time and after we eat, maybe do some more."

Bobby sighed. "Yeah, the only thing is, Sis, there's nothing here that helps Dad."

"I know, but there's too much to pass up. Let's just see where we are when we're done. We can discuss what's next while we eat."

Bobby liked the idea of having a real meal but hated wasting the time. Still, Becca was right. The items they collected so far would help the community get through the winter months with less strain. He agreed and dropped Becca off at the second house with another one right next door.

He drove back to the house they had taken over. He hoped that was enough sleep for Darlene. He had a feeling an hour was good for Jin, but Darlene might be a problem. Was Jin back from where ever he went?

As he entered the house, Jin stepped out from the hallway with a gun ready. "It you. Good," he said.

The suddenness of his appearance had Bobby's heart racing. Jin sat in the kitchen and pulled on his shoes. "What do?"

"Where'd you go?"

Jin smiled but offered no explanation.

"We go?"

Bobby nodded and explained though he wasn't sure Jin understood. When he was finished, Jin sat and stared at the wall for a moment, then stood abruptly. "Good plan. You wake girl."

"Me? Why me?"

"She crazy. I not want die." He put a hand on Bobby's shoulder. "It be okay. She like you." His laugh as he left insinuated Bobby otherwise.

Like a death row inmate taking that last long walk, Bobby moved down the hall. He knocked on the bedroom door but got no answer. He tried again louder. Still no response. He opened the door but remained in the doorway. "Ah." He cleared his throat, nervous about being in her room while she slept. "Darlene." He kept his voice low and soft for some reason. "You awake?" He could hear soft snoring coming from under the blankets. "Darlene." Though it made him extremely uneasy, he stepped into the room. "Darlene." He increased his volume. He couldn't believe she was such a deep sleeper. She was out and heard nothing. He crept closer. "Darlene. We're leaving. You need to get up."

With a tentative touch, he extended his arm and touched her shoulder, giving her a gentle shake. "Darlene. Ah!"

In a blur, Darlene spun on the bed, grabbed his arm and whirled the other direction, pulling him off his feet and on top of her. "Do you often come into a lady's bedroom while she's asleep? That's rather perverted."

"I, ah, we—"

"I think you owe me something for this intrusion into my privacy."

"But I, uh, we—"

"You said that already. Let's see. What shall the payment be? Oh, I've got it." She grabbed the side of his head between her strong hands and pulled it down where she planted a long, moist, and tongue-filled kiss on him."

When she broke away, he was sputtering and breathless.

"Well, that will do—for now," she said, "but the next time you sneak into my room, you need to practice kissing first. It needs some work. Well, what are you waiting for? Get off me. You said we have things to do. I can't spend all day in bed with you." With a hard push, she shoved him against the wall and slipped out of bed. She picked up her boots and walked through the door. "No time for napping, Bobby. We've got work to do."

Stunned, Bobby lay staring at the ceiling, wondering what just happened, but not hating it.

Chapter Thirteen

They worked deep into the night, filling both the car and the van just in those first twelve houses. They still had a lot more to cover. The small town was yielding a lot of useful items though nothing on the list from Doc. However, it was encouraging to know there were still some areas untouched by looters. It gave hope that what they needed to find to keep their father alive might still be out there someplace.

Becca parked the cruiser in the garage. Bobby pressed the van against the garage and house walls, blocking all but the driver's side door and sliding door from being opened.

They were too tired to think about eating. After setting a watch for every two hours with Darlene taking first duty, they all went to bed. Bobby had third watch and Jin woke him five hours later. He checked his watch. "You woke me late."

"I sleep before. You need. I give more."

"Thanks. I did need."

Jin went down the hall and into a room. Bobby yawned and stretched, then made a circuit of the house's interior before going to the garage. It was colder in the garage. The weather had been so nice that he forgot they were well into fall. He decided to make a trip around the outside of the building but wanted his jacket first. He was about to go to his room to retrieve it when he heard a noise outside the garage door.

He froze to listen. A light metallic scraping drew his attention to a spot on the garage door. He moved closer. Something had rubbed against the door but was it animal or human? He thought about waking the others, but to do so, he had to leave the garage and possibly lose where the intruder was. Also, he didn't want to embarrass himself if it did turn out to be nothing more than a cat prowling the area.

As he leaned closer to the garage door, he thought he heard a grunt as if someone was trying to lift something, or—Bobby ran for the door into the house. He hurried through the kitchen to the back door, exiting and racing around the house. He slowed at the corner and peered around, looking at the van. A dark shape was leaning between the tiny gap between the garage door and the van as if trying to squeeze through.

The man's back was to him, so Bobby inched forward with his handgun out. He reached the man and said, "Come out of there with your hands up, or I'll shoot you."

The man screamed and struggled. "Oh, please don't shoot. My life isn't very important, at least not anymore, but it's all I have."

"Just come out of there, and I won't shoot."

"I, uh, I can't. I'm stuck."

Bobby wondered if it was some ploy by the man to reverse the situation.

"Son, can you help an old man?"

"What were you trying to do?"

"I just wanted to see what you took."

"Took? You mean from the vacant houses?"

"Well, they may be vacant now, but the owners might return at any moment. It'd be a shame if they found all their belongings gone when they arrived."

Bobby scanned the man. He was older, with thinning white hair and a long face with loose light brown skin like he had been much heavier at one time and lost the weight quickly. "Who are you? The town watchman?"

"Well, of sorts. I'm Father Bernardo. I'm the priest at St. Joseph's Catholic Church down the street. I kind of watch over my flock until such a time as they all return."

Bobby was stunned. A Catholic priest? Was he for real? He approached with caution and found where the man's black jacket was hung up on the grill. He pulled him free and stepped back in case it had been a ruse. The man looked relieved. He pressed a hand to his chest and leaned against the front of the van.

"Oh, thank you so much, dear boy. I didn't know how I was going to get free. Then you startled me with your sudden appearance and about gave me a heart attack when you threatened to shoot me. I need to rest a spell if you don't mind."

"Not at all. Take your time, Father. What were you trying to do anyway?"

"I couldn't get in the driver's door, so thought I might squeeze through that gap there and get in on the passenger side. Guess that was rather silly on my part."

"Were you going to take the things inside back to the houses?"

"No. No. That would be proper, of course, but only if you returned everything yourself."

"Father, you do realize that there's a pandemic going on, don't you?"

"I did hear something about that, but there's no longer any news. In fact, the TV and radio ceased working months ago."

"That's because most everyone in the country is dead. Haven't you noticed?"

"Well, I did have a lot of funerals. That was odd to have so many so close together. And there was no one to dig the graves. Fortunately, one other person was in town and helped me. I think we dug more than forty graves in about a week." He glanced up and crossed his arms. "I wonder where Fred went. I should go check on him."

"Haven't you left here at all to see what's going on elsewhere? Father, this is an apocalyptic event."

"Go on now, son, don't exaggerate. God would not allow that to happen unless it was the end of times, and I think he would've sent some word first."

Bobby couldn't believe what he was hearing. The priest either truly didn't know about the pandemic or was in total denial. Or perhaps he was just senile. "Father, you should get in a car and drive around. You'll see what happened here is not unique."

"I don't have a car."

"There are plenty around for you to borrow."

"Oh, I couldn't do that without the owner's permission. Besides, I don't drive. Haven't in more than ten years."

"How do you get around?"

"Walk, or depending on the distance or weather, ride my bike."

Bobby was in disbelief at the man's total ignorance of what was going on in the world around him. "Father, the people in those houses will never be coming back. We took food that would only spoil in time. We come from a rather large community that needs this food to survive the winter."

"But what if they do return? They'll have nothing to survive on themselves."

"I'll tell you what, Father. I'll leave you directions to our community. If they do come back, give them the directions and send them to me. I'll be happy to return what we have or replace what we used." He paused as a new thought came to him. "What about you, Father. Do you have enough food?"

"Oh, yes. I have a fully stocked pantry. My parishioners see to my needs. They spoil me. I have more than I need. I need very little to survive."

"Father, it's a new and dangerous world out there now. What once was is no longer. Everything has changed.

You have to accept that many of your parishioners will not be coming back. I'm sorry. Most everyone has gone into an everyone for themselves mode and are willing to kill for food, water, or medical supplies. You were fortunate that we are not like that, but others will be. You have to be careful who you approach."

"Son, I didn't get into this line of work to back away from problems. I will always be there, ready to help those in need or troubled in whatever way I can. It's who I am and what I do."

Bobby studied the man and decided he believed this was a good man. With a touch of sadness, he also accepted that a good man did not survive long in these hard times. "Father, it's getting cold. Would you like to come inside?"

"No, thank you, son. I'll be on my way. It's late." He started to walk away, then stopped. "Thanks for getting me free." He moved again and stopped. "Would you do an old man a favor?"

"If I can."

"Would you and your friends come to mass tomorrow morning? I haven't had anyone to share mass with in, oh, I don't know how long. It would be a great blessing for me, and hopefully you as well, and will go a long way for penance for all you stole." He looked at him, and Bobby saw the gleam of desperate tears. The priest had to be wondering about his role in this new world. Maybe he felt lonely without a flock to lead. Perhaps he felt he no longer mattered. But with so few humans alive, everyone mattered, and perhaps a priest was what was needed to remind the survivors of their humanity.

"I'll talk to the others, Father. Maybe."

He nodded. "Please do. It would mean a lot to me." He turned and strode into the darkness as if he'd been swallowed. His voice came from a distance, "Eight a.m. sharp." Bobby waited an extra minute to be sure the priest was gone, then checked the doors on the van to be sure they were still locked. He made a circuit around the house and entered through the backdoor. With the priest on his mind, he stood at the kitchen window, staring out at nothing.

How strange the encounter was, he thought. It made him realize there were other concerns in the world besides his own. He cleared his mind. Though that may be true, none were as crucial as the one that faced him now. His father's life depended on him, and it was a life worth dying for. He vowed to God and his father, "I will not fail you, Dad."

"Everything alright, Bobo?"

Bobby was so lost in his thoughts he had not heard his sister approach. To his surprise, he discovered his cheeks were wet. He pretended to sneeze. He turned away as he did to cover the act of wiping his face and clearing his eyes. "Yeah, fine. Maybe allergies."

Becca came up next to him and slung an arm around his shoulders. "You don't have allergies, brother." She kissed his forehead. "Go. Get some sleep."

He gave her a hug. "We can't fail, Sis."

She drew him close. "We won't, baby brother. We won't. Now. Go." She released him, and he walked down the hall.

"Don't let me oversleep. I need to be up by seven."

She snorted a laugh. "Why? Got a hot date?"

"You might say that."

"What?"

"I'm going to church."

"She snorted louder. "Oh, God, that's a good one."

He stopped. "I'm serious, Sis. And you know what's even funnier? You're going with me."

Bobby entered the bedroom, relishing the astonished and confused look he left on his sister's face.

Chapter Fourteen

"Well, look at you," Darlene said. "You tried to clean up. You got a hot date?"

That's what I asked him," Becca said.

"And what was his reply?" Darlene asked with a raised eyebrow.

"Get this. He's going to church."

Darlene's mouth dropped open.

"Why is that so hard to believe?" Bobby asked. "Maybe I need to lighten my soul."

Becca scoffed. "More like search for the sacramental wine."

Darlene laughed. Then she saw the look on Bobby's face. "Wait. You're serious?"

"I am. You ready, Becca?"

Darlene looked at Becca and her jaw dropped further.

"I think I'll sit this one out," Becca said.

Bobby moved closer. "Not even for Dad."

Becca averted her gaze but it was clear his words sparked anger. "That's not fair, Bobby. Besides, after everything we've been through, the world's been through, I'm not sure I even believe in God anymore."

"I met a priest last night who is desperate to maintain his belief. I think he's struggling with his faith and perhaps wondering whether all those years of service to an entity he believed in was a waste. I may not believe, but I'm not going to take a chance that my prayers might help Dad. If my attending mass can help a man reassure himself that he still has a purpose, all the better."

"I believe." Dalene's voice was meek, her eyes downcast. If they hadn't heard the words come from her lips, they might not have recognized the voice. She looked up through her filled eyes. "I want to go."

"Good," Bobby said. He faced his sister.

She looked from Darlene to Bobby and frowned. "Man, don't guilt me." Exasperated, she threw her hands into the air and said, "Fine, I'll go if only to get you off my back."

Bobby looked at Jin, who had been following the exchange. "I stay. Protect supplies."

They walked down the street toward St. Joseph's church. It was a block away. As they walked, Darlene fidgeted with her clothes in an effort to look presentable. Seeing Darlene smooth down her wrinkled shirt, Becca became self-conscious about her appearance, which Bobby thought funny. At one time, his sorority lifestyle sister would not have dreamed of going outside her dorm without being dressed and made up to the nines. He wondered when the last time was she cared about her clothes and appearance.

Bobby noticed the bulge at Becca's back. "You brought a gun? To church?"

"Don't give me that. I don't go anywhere without a weapon."

He looked at Darlene. She answered the unspoken question. "Of course. Just because I believe in God and want to worship doesn't mean I'm going unprotected."

The church was not large, though it was probably adequate for the needs of the small community. It looked like a Catholic church with its tall center steeple, the red brick, and the decorative arches around the doors and windows. It reminded Bobby of the small church he used to attend when he was young.

They climbed the stone steps to the glass double doors. Bobby stepped ahead and opened the door for Darlene and Becca.

"Well, how chivalrous," Darlene said. "Does this only happen when entering a church?"

Bobby ignored the sarcasm and smiled.

Becca said, "He's making sure God doesn't strike us down first before he enters."

Darlene gave him a withering glare but stepped inside first.

As they entered the vestibule, Father Bernardo came through the door, head down and unaware of their entry. Upon seeing them, he froze, then broke into the largest, toothy smile Bobby had ever seen. The older man's eyes filled with tears, and he gushed. "Oh," he choked, "you came. Thank the Lord, you came."

If nothing else came from this side excursion, the sight of the pleasure they brought to the priest was well worth the time. "Hi, Father. "This is my sister, Becca, and my friend, Darlene. Ladies, this is Father Bernardo."

"I am so pleased to make your acquaintance." He stepped forward and took their hands in both of his, and gave a warm shake. "Ah, please, have a seat. Mass will begin as soon as this old man can compose himself."

Darlene looked down to avoid embarrassing the priest. Becca shifted her gaze to Bobby and a strange, soft glint entered her eyes. They seemed to smile at Bobby, which made him uncomfortable. He cleared his throat. "Ah, shall we, ladies?" He extended his arm toward the doors.

As they entered the church, Darlene walked past, but both Bobby and Becca, with a childhood of training, stopped for a second to dip their fingers in the holy water and crossed herself. Bobby and Becca followed suit.

"Wow!" Becca said. "That came right back."

"Yeah. Like we've been doing it our entire lives."

Becca put her arm through Bobby's as they walked. "You like the old guy, don't you?"

"Hey, have some respect. He's a priest. But yeah, I do."

They sat in the front pew, Bobby between the women. He noticed Darlene had a strange peaceful expression and seemed to have sunk within herself. He wondered what memories stirred in her mind. He studied her for a moment while she was lost in thought and didn't notice. Though tough and battle-hardened, she was also soft and quite attractive. Her reddish-brown hair had been chopped short by someone with little skill. Her pale skin showed the signs of someone who had lived in the wilderness for an extended time, not to mention fighting in several violent and bloody battles. Had he ever really noticed her external beauty before? Did her appearance matter? She was the same person regardless, and he thought her to be just as beautiful on the inside where it all counted.

He wanted to explore his new perspective further, but Father Bernardo rang a tiny bell. "We no longer have anyone here to play the organ or the guitar, but if you would join me in Hymn four, twenty-three in your hymnal, we'll wing it." He began to sing and start down the aisle before they even got the books open to the proper page. Bobby and Becca stood as they fumbled for the page. Darlene sat still lost in her thoughts while flipping pages absently.

She snapped from her fugue as Bobby and Becca began to sing. She looked around as if waking from a nap, then stood and nudged Bobby. "What Page?" He told her, and she joined in the song.

It was the typical mass doing all the ritual parts. When Father Bernardo began the sermon he prepared, he gazed out across the church and the rows of empty pews and sighed. He looked down at the three of them and went off-script. "My new young friend there told me last night that this was a new and dangerous world. Though I haven't witnessed the danger, I have to accept that the world has indeed changed, and not for the better. I miss my flock, if you will. I miss the interaction and the opportunity to converse and to assist others in whatever way I am able. I cannot begin to tell you how much your presence means to me." He paused for a moment, some lost memory likely interrupting his thoughts. He wiped at his eyes and stood erect. "Sorry. Forgive an old fool." He continued where he left off in his sermon.

Afterward, he stood at the door as Bobby expected he did at all masses and shook their hands. "Thank you again for coming. It meant so much to me."

"You're welcome, Father," Bobby said, "and thank you for reminding us that there are still good and important parts of our former lives that still remain. This meant as much to us as it did to you."

"Would you do this old man one more favor? Have lunch with me. Oh, it won't be fancy, I can promise you that, but I do have solar power, installed by a parishioner a year ago that keeps my refrigerator running, and in the freezer I have a few burgers. Not sure what I've got to go with it, but it would be my honor to share the food with you."

They looked at each other. Bobby anticipated push back from Becca and possibly Darlene, who hadn't said a word since the service began but to his surprise, Becca said, "We'd love to, Father."

"Oh, wonderful. Why don't you meet me at the rectory behind the church in, say, two hours? No. I can't wait that long. Make it an hour."

"That's perfect, Father. We'll be there, and thank you for the generous offer."

They moved outside and Bobby turned. "Father, we have one other friend with us. Would it be all right to bring him?"

"Yes, of course. The more the merrier."

As they walked back toward the house, Darlene came alive again like she'd been asleep. She snaked an arm around Bobby's and leaned close. "I do feel special. First, you hold the door for me, then you call me a lady—twice.

Wow! If I didn't know any better, I'd think you were try-ing to seduce me."

The look on his face must have been precious because one look had her bursting out laughing. She didn't stop the entire walk back.

Chapter Fifteen

Ruth was making her morning rounds. It was an easy job most days, especially now that the war was over. She still had two wounded to look after, one man, one woman, each with a bullet wound to an extremity. However, she also looked in on the two comatose patients, Myron, who she secretly liked though he only had eyes for Becca, and Mark, her mother's one-time boyfriend.

She was a tall, spindly seventeen-year-old who hadn't filled out her womanly body yet. Her hair, eyes, and nose left no doubt as to whose daughter she was. Though Lynn was a few inches shorter, they were duplicates.

Forced into assisting her mother in medical emergencies early in the pandemic, Ruth had found she liked the medical field and studied all she could from books taken from the library. She volunteered to help in the hospital and soon became Doc's number one call when she needed non-surgical assistance.

After doing her daily rounds, she always said a prayer for both men as well as her mother. She knew her mother still cared for Mark, and sometimes she wished they'd get back together. Her father had been abusive to all of them. When he died, it had been Mark to guide her mother from the darkness. She had never seen her mother so happy, at least when there wasn't some earth-shattering event going on, which was often back then.

Finished with her ritual prayer, she touched each man's arm. "Good morning, men. Sleep well, have happy dreams, and come back to us soon." She always talked to them. She remembered watching a TV show from the before days as she called them, where the patient's love interest talked to her comatose boyfriend. He supposedly heard her voice, and it helped him wake. Ruth didn't know if that was true, but what could it hurt?

She turned to walk away but something caught in the back of her mind that made her stop and wonder what had just happened? Her face scrunched up, perplexed by the nagging feeling that whatever it had been was important.

Ruth whirled as if expecting an entity to jump out at her. The flickering eyes made her scream just as loud as if it had been a ghost. "Oh, my God!" The clipboard dropped from her hands as she fled the building. "Doc! Doc!" she shouted as she ran. "He's awake. He's awake."

Those sitting around the picnic tables chatting after breakfast stopped to see what the commotion was. Ruth did a joyful leap and shouted again. "He's awake."

The words now clear to the group caused them to stand. Doc set down her coffee mug and ran to meet Ruth. Lynn and Caryn were close behind, as was Lincoln.

"Who, Ruth? Who's awake?"

"See for yourself," Ruth said with glee and sprinted toward the hospital. They burst through the door, Doc on Ruth's heels. She yanked back the curtain to find the same two comatose patients, neither appearing any different from the last time she checked on them.

She looked from Mark to Myron then back to Mark. However, a flicker of movement caused her to swing back to Myron. There. His eyes were open. She rushed to his side and immediately began checking vitals. "Myron," she said in a soft but breathy voice from her run.

Others crowded into the space while Doc turned to Ruth. "Escort them out please."

Ruth nodded. "Please, everyone. You need to leave. You know Doc will inform you of whatever changes there are. Please. You have to go."

No one spoke, but as they turned to go, she caught her mother flick a glance at Mark. Disappointment showed clearly on her face.

Merchant snagged Edward's arm and pulled him through the pine trees that lined the side of the road next to the newly reconstructed farmhouse. "Did you hear?"

"What?"

"One of them coma guys woke."

"No! Which?"

"I think it was the nerdy kid, but I'm not sure. It doesn't matter, though. Even if Mark woke, he'd be too weak to do anything."

"Still, we gotta make a move before he wakes up. We ready?"

"Yeah."

"How many we got with us?"

"Seven. But two of them's that man and his son who live in the house between ours and the others."

Edwards considered the statement. "Yeah, I'm still not sure they're on board. Let's not tell them. We need to put the plan in motion tonight."

"You want to do them all?"

"Yeah. We take out Lincoln and that farmer, Jarrod, then kidnap the daughter. That eliminates any real opposition and gives us leverage to buckle Lynn. Once we control the daughter, we can count on three votes in our favor. At best, we get one more vote to win and get on the council. At worst, it's a tie and goes to a runoff vote of the community. By this time next week, we'll have control of the entire place."

Merchant said, "That sounds good to me. There're some people I owe some payback to." He eyed Caryn through the branches as she returned to the tables. "Then there's some other stuff I'd like to do just for fun."

"We need to tell everyone we're on for tonight."

They moved away in separate directions. It was hard to contain the excitement Edwards felt. Soon, revenge would be his. Then came the power. Yes. It was going to be an epic night.

As Lynn approached the tables, she caught movement through the branches on the other side of the pine trees. Two men turned and walked away from each other. It should have meant nothing to her, but in a glimpse between two trees she was sure one of the men was Edwards. She made a note to speak to Lincoln about her fears concerning the man.

She looked for him. He was nowhere in sight. Perhaps he went to tell Jenny, his friend who lived with him. She'd talk to him later. For now, the excited faces around the table had drawn others to them and were busy talking about Myron's miraculous recovery.

Jin decided the opportunity to have a real burger was worth the risk of leaving their newly acquired things unprotected and the bother of listening to an old religious man prattle. He came with them, and if the quickness of his pace was any indication, he was anxious for the hot meal. He slowed to speak with Bobby. "You tell priest I speak no English. Okay? Good." He walked ahead again.

They found Father Bernardo by following his singing voice around the back of the rectory, which was attached to the rear of the church. Still dressed in black and wearing his collar, the man belted out a song Bobby guessed to be from the fifties, while standing in front of an old gas grill.

The aroma of the cooking meat greeted them like long-lost friends. Bobby's mouth watered and his moan of delight escaped his lips before he could prevent it. Both Darlene and Becca heard and snorted laughter. Darlene hip-checked him. "If you moan like that just smelling the burgers, I can't wait to hear you when you taste it."

Father Bernardo heard the laughing and turned. His smile beamed. "Welcome. Welcome one and all. Grab a seat and a drink from the cooler. The food will be done in minutes." He went back to his work and his singing."

At the mention of drinks, Bobby, Darlene, and Becca all looked at each other, excitement and wonder playing across their features. They darted for the cooler only to find Jin already bending over it. He withdrew a bright red, recognizable can with remnants of ice dripping down the side. "Ah, things go better," he said and smiled with pleasure. It was one of the few times Bobby'd seen the man show actual sincere joy. The snick of the pop-top and the effervescence of the released bubbles had them drooling. They reached for the cooler at the same time and jockeyed for position to grab the next can.

Inside were six ice-cold cans of red, blue, and green. Bobby grabbed another red one. Becca seeing it was the last, slapped it out of his hand and scooped it up. She ran before Bobby could snatch it back. He almost called her a name but remembered where he was and refrained. Instead, he snarled at her and grabbed a blue can. Darlene had a green one. They drank with sheer enjoyment, trying to hold back from downing the entire contents.

As they sat around the table, Father Bernardo said, "Bobby, would you open the umbrella, please?"

"Sure thing, Father." He stood and wound the umbrella up. As he did, Darlene kept reaching over and tickling him playfully. He jumped out of reach and moved to the opposite side of the table as the women laughed conspiratorially. Something was going on with them but especially Darlene. She was being flirtatious, and although he couldn't deny enjoying the behavior, it was out of character.

Father Bernardo said, "I know it's outside the current acceptable practices, but I've always enjoyed my burgers cooked medium-rare. If anyone wants theirs done differently, now's the time." No one wanted to wait longer to eat, so no one spoke up. "Medium rare it is."

The table was set with real plates and silverware. There was a tub of real butter, a plate of sliced tomatoes, slices of cheese, a plate of buns, and a bowl of baked beans. They stared at the food with growing anticipation. Jin's leg bounced in an uncontrollable fashion. When Father Bernardo bent to turn off the gas and plate his masterpieces, Darlene let loose a moan of anticipation. Bobby laughed and elbowed her.

"Hey, don't make fun of a woman and her food."

He laughed again.

Father Bernardo set the plates down on the table. Five large hot burgers, their juices running down the sides, filled one plate while eight ears of grilled corn were on the other. As soon as the plates hit the table, Jin was reaching. Bobby kicked him under the table, and Jin sneered like a dog ready to fight for scraps. Bobby gave a quick head shake and Jin sucked in a breath and sat back. However, his leg went into overdrive.

"I am so pleased to have you all here to share this meal with me. Let us pray."

Jin barely made it through the short prayer. He reached for the burgers, but Father Bernardo was faster. He lifted the plate and Bobby feared Jin might go over the table for the food. Like a good host, Father Bernardo passed the plate to Becca, who was sitting to his right.

"Thank you, Father."

"You're so very welcome, child." He passed the corn to his left. Darlene accepted the plate, used the tongs to take one then passed it to Jin. Though Jin took a cob, he didn't take his eyes off the burgers. They ate corn with almost every meal back home, but burgers were a rare treat. So rare, in fact, they had never had them.

Father Bernardo said, "And who's our new friend?"

Bobby said, "Father, this is Jin. He is Korean and speaks little English."

Jin almost jabbed the corn plate into Bobby's chest like a quarterback giving a handoff as he eyed the burgers. Both plates reached Bobby at the same time. With a plate in each hand, he offered the burger plate to Jin, who snatched it greedily. Bobby took corn and sent the plate to Becca. When he turned back, Jin had one burger on his plate and was eyeing Bobby's. "No want?"

"Bobby grabbed the plate back. "Of course, I want." He plated the burger, then for fear of Jin snatching Darlene's, he skipped Jin.

"Thank you, kind sir," she said and winked.

Though he knew she was teasing him, heat still rushed to his cheeks.

He topped his burger with cheese, tomato, mustard, and ketchup, then took a deep breath before taking his first bite. Yes, he moaned and didn't care. In fact, no one else heard over their own appreciative sounds.

Chapter Sixteen

No one spoke for the next few minutes as the meal was consumed noisily in record time. Bobby looked around the table. After an initial assault on their burgers, Becca and Darlene had settled into a slower pace. Bobby took note of Jin's nearly gone burger and realized he was almost on the same pace. He set the burger down and started on his corn.

As expected, Father Bernardo was the first to speak. "So, tell me, young folk. What's the world like out there?" He swept his arm out to the side."

Bobby knew the others had no interest in speaking, so he answered. "It's not easy, Father. In those early months, food and water were still easy to find. Now, it's much harder to find food. Our community—"

"Community?" he interrupted.

"Yes, Father. We have close to two hundred people living together. We found many of them along the way. Some we saved from bad situations while others wandered to us searching for a safe place. Armed groups of marauders roam the area looking for anything they can steal. They are willing to kill to get it. That's one reason we all came together—for protection. The thieves might be bold enough to attack an individual or a family, but they leave us alone. We are well organized and very protective of each other."

"That sounds like a wonderful place. Maybe I can see it someday. Tell me, though, Bobby. How is what these marauders are doing any different from what you and your friends have done?"

That stopped everyone but Jin from taking their next bite. Becca set her burger down, wiped her mouth, and Bobby feared the tirade that was about to come.

"Becca—"

She held up a hand to stop him. "Father, with all due respect, you don't know what it's like out there. You think we're stealing from your parishioners. We see it as survival for two hundred people. The main difference between us and the lawless mobs that will eventually come here is that we would not touch their things if people were still living here. We are not thieves. We take what is available. Others who will come won't care if anyone lives here. If you have it and they want it, they'll take it even if they have to kill you. I'm not trying to be mean or scare you, but that goes for you, too. If we were like the lawless mobs roaming the area, we wouldn't be having this meal. We'd have already killed you and stripped your pantry."

"Becca," Bobby said with a pleading tone.

"No, Bobby. He needs to know the reality of what life is like out there. I truly mean no disrespect, Father," though her tone and rising voice spoke otherwise, "but you wanted to know what life is like. It is the hell you have warned about your entire priesthood come to Earth. You need to get your head out of your ass and wake up to what's going on around you."

To his credit, Father Bernardo showed no reaction other than a quick flare of fire in his eyes. "If it is so dangerous out there, why do you risk it?"

"Not because we enjoy it but because we need to ensure the survival of our people. Our current search is of a more personal nature. Our father was shot by one of those marauders we were talking about. Our doctor managed to patch him up, but he is in a coma, and we are running out of the necessary supplies needed to keep him alive. We also have a friend who was injured during a battle in the same situation. With two people in comas, there aren't enough supplies to keep them both alive for more than a month. They are depleting the supplies we have, making it imperative we find more so others can benefit should another crisis occur."

Becca said, "They have given us two weeks to find what we need, or they have threatened to pull the plug and save the supplies for future patients. We have ten days left."

"I understand your motivation. It sounds as if you and the entire community have been put in a bad situation with lives balanced precariously in the middle. I feel for you. It can't be easy."

Perhaps it was the reminder of the stakes that were involved, or maybe it was the soft, comforting words spoken with sincerity, but Bobby was surprised to see a tear escape Becca's eye and roll down her cheek. She made no move to wipe it away.

"Your tone as you explained the realities of this new world was angry. Whether at me or your situation, doesn't matter. Words spoken in anger wound no different than a bullet, only they bleed on the inside. I gave no offense. In fact, only invited you to what I think was a splendid meal, yet you attack me with your words like I do not matter. Is that any different from those you say slay without remorse to steal your food? For all intents and purposes, you have assaulted me in my own home and have taken my food. All I asked was companionship and information. If this is the way of the new world, you are welcome to it."

Becca burst into tears and lowered her head. Father Bernardo placed a gentle hand on her head. "It's all right, dear child. I hold you no ill-will. All is forgiven as it appears you are penitent."

Becca nodded, and through sobs, said, "I'm so sorry, Father. Please forgive my rudeness."

"There, there, child. It is already forgiven and forgotten."

She lifted her tear-streaked face. "Thank you, Father."

"Now, if the histrionics are finished, is oxygen on the list of items you need to keep your father alive?"

Bobby was stunned. He wiped his mouth and set the last few bites of his burger down. "Yes, Father, it is."

"One of my parishioners has been on oxygen for years. He can't go anywhere without it. He has the in-home unit for constant air as well as a lightweight, portable unit that he wears in a bag slung over a shoulder when he goes out, which for him is mostly when he comes to church. I know for a fact he will not be returning as he has moved on to a better, less complicated world." His eyes took on a distant look. "I make daily rounds, you see, in hopes someone has returned. I think I already suspected what you told me was the reality of the situation. Perhaps I just didn't want to accept it as truth." He gave a sad smile. "Guess I'm not sure if I should be glad or sad that you have come here and dissolved my charade that all the trouble is temporary and the world will be made right in time. Anyway, that's off the topic, and I apologize.

"While making my rounds, I found several residents had passed, including Mr. Hoffman. His wife never returned from wherever she went, and with the electricity out, the poor man perished. I suppose he suffocated. I only wish I had thought to search houses sooner. I said a funeral mass for him and buried him in the small cemetery down the road. He was the first of six I buried that same day. I hope they and their families will forgive me for the simplicity of the service. It was truly the best I could do under the circumstances." He sighed. "I'm not sure what I'll do if no one returns. What's a priest without a parish to serve?"

He stood. "If you'll excuse me, if you're finished, I'm going to clear the table." He picked up his plate and carried it inside the rectory.

Bobby sat back, both ashamed and excited. As usual, Becca had gone overboard and insulted their host, but was it possible this supply of oxygen would work for their father. Doc had asked for a ventilator and oxygen canisters. Wasn't this the same thing?

Jin tapped him on the shoulder and pointed at the last bites of Bobby's burger. "You eat?"

His appetite gone, he slid the plate to Jin.

They pitched in to clear the table, then Becca and Bobby guided Father Bernardo to a chair in the kitchen and took over dishwashing duties. While they worked, Darlene sat with him and engaged him in conversation. "Father, I am not Catholic and, truthfully, haven't been to a church in a long time, but I have to say being there today was perhaps the single most peaceful time I've had since the pandemic began. Thank you for that."

"You're quite welcome, dear girl."

"But Father. Though I wouldn't have put it as harshly as Becca did, she is right. You may not be safe here alone."

"What would you have me do, carry a gun like you all do?"

"We only carry them because we know the risks of not doing so. I don't want anything bad to happen to you."

He smiled. "The pat response is to say I don't fear death. I know heaven awaits me. However, I'd be a liar if I did. I'm not a brave man, though I won't back down from evil. However, with the stories you have told me playing through my mind, I'd be a fool not to be concerned."

"You need a backup plan, Father. A way of escaping if someone does come. I hate to agree with Becca, but she is right. Eventually, someone other than us will come."

"I promise to give that serious thought."

With the dishes done, they stayed another hour talking trying to stay away from any morbid or threatening subjects. Then Bobby said, "Father, are you willing to show us where the oxygen is?"

He studied Bobby for a moment, then nodded. "Yes. If it helps your father live, of course I will." He drew them a map, and they all said goodbye, including Jin, who shook the priest's hand and said, "Good eats. Thank you."

They walked while Jin went back to retrieve the van. They found the house down the street and a block over. It was a small, brick ranch with a fenced yard and a detached two-car garage. As Father Bernardo had said, the rear door was unlocked. They entered and found six canisters of air on the landing of the rear door. "Wow!" Bobby said, "We might have caught a huge break."

"They might be empty if they're by the back door," Darlene said.

"Father Bernardo said the man suffocated," said Bobby. "That means all the canisters might be empty."

They walked through the kitchen into a living room where a hospital bed was pushed against the wall. Along the wall was an additional four canisters of air and a home oxygen concentrator machine. On a small table to the right of the bed was a smaller portable unit in a shoulder bag. Three canisters for the portable unit were inside the table, along with a roll of air tubing, cleaning supplies and accessories. Darlene found a plastic bag and she set about filling it with the supplies.

Jin pulled the van into the driveway. Bobby ran out to open the gate and allow Jin to move closer to the rear door. They hauled out the equipment as well as whatever food and medicine they found. Their haul also included two and a half cases of bottled water and two twelve packs of diet coke.

As they finished loading, Bobby said, "I'm not sure what we should do now. Go back and see if this helps or continue searching."

"How much time will we lose if we go back and find out we have to search more?"

Bobby frowned. "Probably four hours."

Darlene said, "That's not bad considering. We drop all the food and equipment off and go back out."

"I'd like to strip the town down further but feel bad about doing it in front of Father Bernardo," Bobby said.

"I no feel bad," Jin said. "Need food for family. You go. I stay."

Bobby nodded. "Okay, I'll drop the stuff off and come back here. I should see you in about four hours if there're no delays."

"I'd kind of like to go too, if you don't mind," Darlene said. "I want to assure my dad I'm okay."

"Fine by me if you two think you can handle it."

Becca buzzed her lips at him. "As if."

Bobby laughed. "One of you should come with us. I'll drop you off at the house, and you can get the cop car. We can also unload what's inside."

Jin motioned with the back of his hand. "Go."

Becca prodded Darlene to get in front with Bobby while she crawled through the side door over the collected items. They reached the house a minute later and unloaded the car. Bobby gave his sister a hug, then Becca and Darlene embraced with Becca whispering in her ear. Bobby didn't know what sinister plot was being hatched but wasn't sure he wanted to.

They left the little town of Blakeslee and headed for home.

Chapter Seventeen

Darlene traced the fastest route on the map with her finger. "We're on thirty-four, so I'd go left of Rural Route G. That will take us back to Stryker, where we loop south around the town and pick up Route Two. Two is what we want, right?"

"Yeah. That takes us all the way home."

"Wait. Okay. I see. Once we get to Archbold, we cut through the town and go north, and then it's a straight shot from there."

Bobby nodded as if she could hear him. His mind was on other things, such as the encounters they'd had in both those areas. That had been two days ago. Surely no one was looking for them if they ever had been. Regardless, this was the quickest way home and back. Though he wouldn't admit it to her, Bobby was concerned about leaving his sister with so little protection. Sure, Jin was a killing machine, but he tended to go off and do his own thing.

It was only four hours, five at most. She'd be okay that long. If only his mind believed his thoughts.

"You worried about something?"

"Yeah. A little."

"I hope it's not being alone in the van with me."

"Huh? What?" He blushed. "Oh, ah, no." Eager to change the subject, he said, "I'm worried about leaving Becca alone."

"She's not alone. Jin will keep her safe. I'd sure feel safe with him watching my back."

"Yeah, I guess. Still, she's my sister. I can't help but worry a little."

"Aw, how sweet. I'll have to tell her how much you care and missed her even though we've only been gone fifteen minutes. Is that separation anxiety?"

Bobby smiled but offered no comment.

"Oh, here's G. Turn here." She pointed left.

Bobby made the turn. They drove until they hit Stryker and Darlene guided him until they reached Route 2. Bobby was about to turn left when Darlene said, "Oh Shit!"

Bobby braked reflexively. When he looked at her, he didn't have to ask why the exclamation. Down the road to the right, a cop car was racing toward them with its lights flashing. Bobby had to think fast, but he knew outrunning the cruiser was not possible. Coming to a decision, he said, "Darlene, switch seats with me. Now." He shifted into park, then slid from his seat while Darlene climbed over him. As he dug out his rifle, he said, "Shift and get ready to jam the pedal down."

The cop car closed the distance fast. Bobby wanted to see what they did before deciding a course of action. He squeezed to the side door and cracked it open, placing his foot against it to keep it from rolling further.

"If they stop short of us and get out, slide low in the seat. When I fire, you take off. If they try to block us, don't even give them a chance to get out. Just ram them and drive them as far as you can. Shove them off the road if possible."

The cop car slowed as it neared, perhaps wondering why they hadn't tried to run. The cruiser slowed even more, approaching with caution. Bobby wanted them closer. The only hope they had was to either kill the phony cops or incapacitate the car. The car stopped thirty feet away. Through the gap, Bobby saw two men in the front seat. They appeared perplexed and unsure of what to do.

"Darlene, do a quick jump forward about ten feet, then brake. Let them see you. Look afraid."

"What are you going to do if they don't approach?"

"I guess chase them away."

"Brace yourself. Here goes." Darlene jammed on the gas and the van lurched forward. Even with the warning, Bobby was pitched sideways. The door gapped more. It quickly slid back and closed when Darlene slammed on the brakes. The tires gripped the road and Bobby fell against the front seat.

"They're moving again,' she said.

He righted himself and moved to the side door. If they block you, don't wait for me. Just go."

"They stopped five feet in front of me but only halfway across."

Damn! Bobby set the rifle down and drew his sidearm. He unlatched the sliding door but waited before opening it.

"He's pointing at me to get out. I shook my head. Now he's giving me a sterner glare."

The crackling of the onboard megaphone came to life. "Get out of the van now." He paused a moment before adding, "I will not ask you again."

If Bobby didn't know her better, he'd think Darlene was too terrified to move. Her eyes were as wide open as they could go. Her hands went up to her face, fingertips curled to her mouth. She shook her head then lowered it to the steering wheel.

Bobby pressed an eye to the space between the passenger seat and the door. The two men were arguing. Then the passenger opened the door. He made a few final comments to the driver then got out. He stood with one foot out the door and peered over the roof at Darlene. "Get out, bitch," he shouted.

"Get ready," Bobby said. "Don't even lift your head until you make contact. I don't want him to have even a fraction of a second to react."

The man aimed his gun over the roof. "I'm going to shoot." A second later he did, but the shot was aimed over the van.

Darlene reacted with appropriate behavior. She jumped and screamed. Real tears streamed down her face. Was she that good of an actor? Bobby watched, ready to spring. He didn't think they'd actually shoot her but was he willing to risk her life?

The man stepped away from the car, keeping his eyes on her and a two-handed grip on the gun.

"Slide down. Punch it. Now," Bobby said.

Darlene slid lower in her seat and at the same time she stomped on the accelerator. The van lurched forward, smacking the driver's door. The shooter's eyes widened as the van burst forward. He fired, but the shot was hurried and the round went high. He attempted to jump back into the car, but the door frame struck his leg and knocked him down. Bobby could hear his scream.

The car was moved fifteen feet before striking the opposite curb. It tilted upward, but the van didn't have the power to push it further.

Bobby yanked the sliding door back hard and far enough to lock in place, then hopped out. He aimed the gun with his left hand at the driver, then made a backhanded jab with his knife at the rear wheel. The blade hit and skidded without penetration. He tried again, but though the tip bore in, it didn't go far enough to cause damage.

Forced to holster the gun, he noticed the driver was trying to get the window down. The door was crumpled inward, preventing it from opening. However, if he got the window down, he could shoot at Bobby. Bobby gripped the knife with both hands and drove it down hard into the tire's sidewall. The blade bit and penetrated. Once inside, he dragged it down to elongate the gash and ensure the tire went flat. He drew the blade out with effort and was rewarded to hear hissing.

A sound drew his attention. The man on the outside had recovered and now leaned over the roof, bringing his gun online with Bobby. He ducked as the shot fired, but the round was nowhere close to him. "Hurry," Darlene said. "Get in."

He kept low as he hurried to the van's door catching a glimpse of her gun extended out the passenger window. She was already reversing before he closed the door.

"You think they'll come after us?" Darlene asked.

"Maybe, but not in that car. If they have others on the road, we'll have to keep an eye out."

Darlene raced through Stryker and made the turn onto Route Two. With Archbold ahead, Bobby shifted into the passenger seat. They remained quiet over the next fifteen minutes as Bobby scanned the windows and mirrors for signs of pursuit. Though he didn't spot any, he did discover something worse. A wisp of smoke curled up over the hood. He sat erect to watch. More smoke came in an increasing stream. "Oh, no."

"What?" Darlene asked, looking at her side mirror. "You see someone?"

"No. Something." He pointed at the windshield. "I think we have a radiator leak."

Instinctively, she let up on the gas.

"No, keep going. We need to find someplace to pull over so I can look at the damage."

Bobby leaned forward, placing his arms on the dashboard as he searched for the best place to hide while he worked. "There," he said, pointing at a street that ran into a small wooded residential area. "Gaslight Drive."

The fall colors were vivid oranges and yellows interspersed with the earthy browns and greens. Darlene turned left. The street was narrow, and houses stood on each side buried amidst the trees. "Move toward the rear of the development."

"You realize if there's no other way out, we could get trapped in here."

"Guess we'll just have to be quiet."

"Will they be able to see the steam rising?"

The steam had billowed into a cloud-like dispersal. "Doubtful. It will most likely dissipate at that height. Pull in there." He pointed at a house near the back of the development. There was no road leading out the back.

Darlene stopped outside the garage, and Bobby told her to shut the engine off and pop the hood. Bobby lifted the hood and stood back to allow the steam to thin. With a glance, he could see the problem. A portion of the grill had snapped off during the collision and punctured the radiator a third of the way up. He studied it for a minute, thinking of possible solutions.

Darlene exited and stood next to him, looking into the engine. "Well, boss man, how you gonna fix this one?"

"Not sure yet. I need to find something to seal it with and a sealant that will hold under the heat. We only have about an hour's drive to reach home, so the patch job doesn't have to hold long. We also need water. I don't want to use up our limited supply, so maybe we can find a house with a well or water in the line."

"I'll look for water," Darlene said. "You figure out the leak." She walked away. "Oh, and keep in mind, the sun's setting. Soon, you won't have light to work by."

That made Bobby's frown deepen.

Chapter Eighteen

Ruth left the hospital in high spirits. According to Doc, Myron's vitals looked much improved. Though his eyes were open, his mind hadn't yet gotten the message to wake up. Doc anticipated it might be soon. Unspoken was her concern for brain damage. The impact with the windshield had been severe. Still, she was hopeful. She had spent the day at his bedside, holding his hand and talking to him, trying to coax his mind to focus.

What was he seeing? Did he recognize where he was? Who she was? She sighed. All in time. She had done lots of praying today, more than normal, and decided to offer up one more before she went to bed.

As she walked toward the house where she shared a room with three other girls, she heard a noise behind her. It didn't alarm her, but she glanced over her shoulder in time to see a shadow descend upon her. Rough hands pressed against her mouth. She recognized a smell. The hand had a cloth with what she knew to be chloroform on it. She tried not to inhale, but as she was lifted off her feet and panic swelled within her chest, she couldn't help it. One man held her torso and kept the cloth over her mouth while another lifted her feet. She inhaled deeply to scream, but it seemed trapped inside her throat. Everything became foggy and distant though she was aware of being carried at a fast speed. She knew she was in trouble. Then darkness came, and she knew nothing else.

Edwards and Merchant were outside the second and furthest barn on Jarrod's farm. According to their nightly surveillance, they knew the big man always did a check of the animals in the barns before locking them in at night. He had the doors alarmed with strings of cans in case intruders tried to steal his sheep, chickens, pigs, or cows. Edwards thought he wouldn't mind getting one of the chickens for himself. Maybe if there was time and they didn't make too much noise taking Jarrod down.

They decided to beat the man to death, not wanting to risk waking everyone with a bullet. The noise might still be loud but not as loud as the gun, and if they got a good first strike in not for long. They each carried a baseball bat for that purpose.

"Here he comes," Edwards nudged Merchant. They had another man waiting on the other side of the barn in case somehow the farmer got away and ran toward the house. It was that man Thomas who lived next door to them with his son. Edwards wasn't sure they trusted him, but he came, so maybe he was all right.

Jarrod passed the first barn and angled toward the second. Thomas raced out of the shadows swung the bat at Jarrod's head. The two men closed, and a struggle ensued.

Edwards and Merchant were stunned by the sudden attack and were unprepared to move. In the dark they witnessed the attack then saw the big man go down. They were up and moving as Thomas stood over the man pounding his head into the ground. As they approached, someone shouted from the house. Thomas stopped his assault and ran toward Edwards and Merchant before they made it to the body. "Hurry," Thomas said, "before someone sees us."

"You sure he's dead?" Edwards said.

"Oh, he's more than dead. I pulverized his head."

They turned and ran into the bean field and were lost in the darkness. Merchant said, "Man, I didn't think you had it in you."

"I hated that guy. He was going down. Sorry I didn't let you get in any hits."

Merchant laughed. "That's all right, buddy. You did good."

Neither man noticed how quiet Edwards was. He was replaying the scene of the attack. It was too dark to see details, but something seemed off. He wished he had the time to be sure the man was dead.

Lincoln was out making the rounds of the four gates like he did every night. Being responsible for the defense and protection of the community was no small task and was not one he took lightly. He had developed a routine of checking every post, staying up late to ensure all defenses and personnel were working as they should. Because of his late hours he slept in late. He got used to the hours over the past few weeks and had come to like the night. It was quiet, and he didn't have to deal with people other than those guarding the gates.

He had checked three of the four gates. The final one was the southern gate, the one furthest from his house. He passed by the new construction in Elijah's section and neared the woods that lined both sides of the road. The southern gate was beyond the woods.

"Psst! Mr. Lincoln."

The voice came from the right near the woods. He stopped, his hand automatically moving to the sidearm he carried in a holster on his belt. "Identify yourself, or I will fire."

"Shh! Keep your voice down. It's me, David Bedrosian."

Lincoln recognized the name. David and his father had been instrumental in thwarting the final assault in the battle just a few weeks ago. He heard rustling of branches and leaves and drew his gun.

"Please don't shoot and be quiet. I'm here to warn you."

Despite his caution, Lincoln found himself moving closer. "Warn me about what?"

"There's men ahead in the woods. They're here to kill you. Don't go down there."

Lincoln froze and glanced down the dark road. "Who are they?"

"I don't know their names. They're friends of that Edwards guy."

The mention of Edwards brought everything to light and made sense. The man was not happy with the way things were being done and had a personal grudge against Mark. If he was out of the way, Edwards had a better chance of gaining power and with it control over what happened in the community, which included pulling the plug on Mark.

"How do you know this?"

"Because my dad and I are a part of it. We're just pretending to go along," he said hurriedly. "We just wanted to hear their plan then report them."

"How many are involved?"

"Five. Edwards and four others I don't know."

"Okay. I need you to do something."

"What?"

He sounded nervous. "Run to the western gate and tell two of the guards to enter the woods at the far end and work their way toward me. Tell them what you told me. Go. Hurry."

David broke into a run across the open ground. Lincoln turned to face the deeper darkness that ran like a tunnel between the trees. His feet began to move as if without his knowledge. His mind worked. Where would his assassins be? Not too close to the gate where guards might intercede. Not too close to Elijah's camp where help might arrive, though most likely too late. They'd be toward the middle of the two groups of trees.

The woods ran east and west until they reached the next block. To the east were wide open fields that offered no cover. However, the woods continued past the next road quite a distance which would keep the assassins covered.

They most likely had a vehicle stashed somewhere off-road. Yes, west made the most sense for an ambush.

He kept moving ever closer to his possible death yet was unable to stop his progress. Instead, his mind continued to work the scenario. The shooters would be separated ten to twenty feet. The closest shooter would allow him to move past before shooting, thus ensuring to catch him in a crossfire from front and back. Three or four quick shots each, then escape. The ensuing chaos would help cover their retreat.

He was at the edge of the trees. He estimated another twenty steps would place him within the kill zone. The thought that he was a potential assassination victim both terrified and electrified him. Though afraid, he was not going to back down from these guys. He had a brief reflection of what he was doing then thought about the stupidity of his actions. He'd been hanging around Mark and Becca far too long. Still, despite his rising fear and the understanding that his actions may lead to his death, his feet moved forward again.

He pushed all thoughts aside and focused his energy on picking up any unnatural sounds from the woods on the right. He picked up the radio that hung from his belt. He had the ability to check on all posts via radio but opted to do them in person instead saving the radio for emergencies.

"Southern gate, report."

"This is the southern gate, sir. How you doing tonight. Listen carefully. I need two of you to walk down the road keeping special attention on the woods to your left."

"Problem, sir?"

"Do it now." He replaced the radio on his belt. As he moved, he angled away from the woods on the right trying to blend his black skin deep within the shadows on the left. He raised the gun and focused on the trees picking out a spot.

From down the road he could hear running footfalls on the blacktop. In the distance the sound of crunching leaves underfoot came through clearly. Whoever was in the trees, if anyone was there, was now trapped.

A whispered voice called to someone else. He could not make out the words but now had a tighter target area. He shifted his aim. It was time to end this ambush with one of his own. "Step out of there now. We have you surrounded and will not hesitate to shoot."

In response, shots erupted almost directly where his gun was pointed. He returned fire as the assassin's shots went wide. Lincoln continued to fire, changing his aim inches to each side with every shot. Something crumpled to the ground.

Running steps crunched through the woods, moving away from him. The two guards arrived from the southern gate. 'You two check on whoever just fell." He pointed. "I'm going after the other one." Without looking to see if guards knew where to go, Lincoln broke through the first line of trees and followed the runner.

Ahead he heard, "Stop, or we'll shoot."

Two shots were followed by six or eight. They came so fast it was difficult to tell. He kept moving until he heard voices. The same one commanded him to stop. "It's me. Lincoln. I'm coming forward." He could just make out the young man. "Is everyone all right?"

The speaker said, "I'm fine. Jimmy was grazed by a bullet. He's in pain but okay."

"What about the assassin?"

"Assassin? Oh, he's down. We shot him. I don't know if he's dead. I've been busy helping Jimmy."

Lincoln made a mental note to correct the guard's decision making. He should've made sure of the threat first. "Where is he?"

"To your left."

Lincoln took out his flashlight and played the beam on the ground. He found the body folded over on the ground, with its head pressed awkwardly against a trunk. He shone the beam on the man's face first, then the hands. He spotted the handgun dangling loosely from a finger and took it, then focused on the face again. He recognized the man though his name did not come immediately to mind.

He dug his hand into the man's collar and dragged him back toward the road through the trees. "Jimmy, go see the on-duty nurse. You," he couldn't remember the other man's name either, "go back to your post and stay alert."

He broke through the trees to find twenty armed people on the road. Several swung weapons at him as he emerged. "Whoa! It's me. Don't shoot."

He slid the body next to the other one and released it.

"Seems I was the target of an assassination attempt. Man, I just love politics."

Chapter Nineteen

Edwards paced the front room. Merchant approached. "What's the problem?"

"Something was off about what Thomas did, but I can't put my finger on it. Did you actually see him hit the farmer?"

"Well, yeah. He hit him, but the first blow wasn't enough. He knocked the guy down then wailed on him. What am I missing? It's not like the guy got back up like some zombie."

"That's just it. I don't think he was hitting the guy at all. I think he was pounding the ground next to his head."

"There's one way to know for sure. Let's check his bat. If he pounded the man's head in like he says there should be blood and brain matter all over it."

Edwards snapped his finger. "Good idea."

They went into the kitchen, where Thomas was sitting staring at the table. "Hey Thomas, where's your bat?"

"Huh? Bat? I uh, I guess I dropped it when we were running."

Edwards and Merchant glanced at each other. "What about your hands?"

"My hands?" He studied them. "No, didn't drop them."

"Let me see them." Without waiting for them to be shown, Edwards grabbed and examined them. "No blood."

"No. Should there be? I'm not hurt."

Merchant said, "No, but if you pounded that farmer's head, like you said, there should be some splatter. I don't see any on your face or clothes. I think you lied to us and faked that attack."

"Why would I do that?" but the nervous look on his face was all the evidence they needed.

Merchant ripped him from the chair by his shirt and shook him. "What did you do, asshole? Did you warn him? Were you two in it together?"

"I-I don't know what you're talking about."

"We gotta get out of here," Edwards said. "If he talked, they might be coming for us."

"We should wait for the others. If they killed Lincoln, we might be okay. We'll have one down and still have the girl to use as leverage."

Edwards nodded. "Yeah. Sure, but we should at least move just in case."

"Okay." He pitched Thomas back in his seat. He fell and the chair tipped against the wall. "You watch him. I'll get Terry and the girl."

When Merchant left, Edwards said, "Man, I knew you weren't really with us. I'm going to take great pleasure in killing you." He pulled his gun.

"No. No. I can still be useful. Keep me as a hostage."

"What value do you have?"

"I can get to Mark. You want him dead, right? I can get to him. They trust me. I'll pull the plug. That's what you want, right?"

"Yeah, but how you gonna manage it? And I already don't trust you. How do I know once you leave here, you'll do what you say."

"Hey," Merchant said, poking his head into the kitchen. "We're leaving. Kill that slug and let's go."

Edwards aimed the gun but hesitated. He lowered it and said, "You're coming with us. If I can work this out, you get to live. If not, I can kill you anytime."

They walked to the car. Merchant was in the driver's seat. Terry and Ruth were in the back. "I thought you were gonna kill him."

"Not yet," Edwards said. "I've got an idea and need time to work it out." He pushed Thomas into the back and got in the passenger seat.

Milo said, "What's going on?"

Lincoln answered, "I guess these two men were sent by Edwards to kill me."

"What?" Milo said.

Gasps and murmurs spread through the small crowd.

"I think it's a coop. Edwards is trying to usurp power."

Just then, Lynn came running toward them. "Lincoln. Lincoln." Panic resonated from her voice. "Ruth is missing. She never came home after her rounds at the hospital."

"Did you check there?"

"Yes. They said she left hours ago. Please. I'm so worried. Something has happened to her."

Lincoln looked at Milo and they both said, "Edwards."

"Who knows where Edwards lives?" Lincoln said.

David Bedrosian stepped forward. "I do. Him and his friends live in the two houses on either side of us. My dad is with them. They were going to kill Jarrod and my dad was going to warn him. Please, you have to help him too."

Elijah said, "If Edwards is doing a power play, I can see why he'd take out Lincoln and Jarrod, but why take Ruth?"

Lynn answered. "To control me and Caleb."

"This man has been a pain for too long," Lincoln said. "Milo, round up a team. We're going after him."

They paraded down the road toward the farmhouse. As they went, Lincoln had time to think. He said to Milo, "Only take people we know we can trust not to go wild. We want people who can think and take orders. We don't want to risk Ruth's life in a gunfight."

When they reached the house, headlights were approaching from the north. Whoever it was had to be cleared by the gate there to enter. The truck braked hard, screeching its large tandem tires. Jarrod almost fell out of the truck. "Assassins. Assassins. They're coming for you."

Milo caught the big man as he stumbled from his truck. Maggie and Doc hopped out the other side.

Lincoln said, "What happened?"

Jarrod seemed too winded to speak.

Maggie said, "Some men jumped him, tried to beat his brains in with a bat. Guess one of them tried to help Jarrod."

Doc said, "He's bruised but okay. I think he's just adrenalized and slightly panicked."

"Doc, we've got one with a bullet graze in the hospital," Lincoln said.

She nodded. "Thought there might be injuries. That's why I came." She jogged toward the hospital.

"Easy, Jarrod," Milo said. "Tell us what happened."

"First," he sucked in air, out of breath. "First, I have to warn Lincoln."

"No, you don't, buddy," Lincoln said. "The killers have been dealt with. You just need to calm down so you don't have a heart attack."

At seeing Lincoln, Jarrod visibly relaxed. "I was worried."

"We're all good here. You take a few breaths and tell me what happened."

A few seconds later, Jarrod inhaled one deep breath and began his narrative. "I was walking to do my nightly rounds when a madman carrying a bat attacked me. He hit me on the shoulder. Though not hard, it was enough to knock me off balance. He closed on me and said men were there to kill me and that I should go down so he could pretend to do the job so they wouldn't. I recognized him. It was Thomas. I decided he was telling the truth since the hit he laid on me wasn't very hard, so I went down. He pounded the ground next to my head a few times.

"I heard him shout to someone, 'Hurry before someone sees us.' Someone else said, 'You sure he's dead?' and Thomas said, 'Oh, he's more than dead.' I waited for them to get far enough away so they didn't notice I wasn't as near death as expected, then drove here to warn you.

Milo asked, "Do you know who the other man was?"

"Nope. Didn't get a look, though I might recognize the voice If I hear it again."

"We think it's Edwards," said Lincoln.

"The fella who wanted to unplug Mark?"

"Yeah."

"Well, that bastard's due some payback."

"We're heading down to Edwards' house now."

"You best hurry then. When I came here, I looked down Thomas's street and saw headlights. They was leaving."

Lincoln turned to the crowd. "We need vehicles and teams."

Jarrod said, "Got one ready to go right here." He didn't wait for a response but climbed up into the cab. Lynn was the first to react and got in on the passenger side. Milo and Lincoln followed. Lynn moved to the back seat. Caleb tried to get in too, but Lincoln stopped him.

"She's my sister."

"Exactly," Lincoln said. "One emotional family member is more than enough. You stay. We'll get her back." He closed the door and Jarrod backed over the curb then shot forward. Lincoln glanced in the mirror and spotted two other sets of headlights.

The street where Thomas and Edwards had their houses was one block outside the northern gate. They made the turn fast and wide, running up over the curb and bouncing back down. Jarrod stopped fifty yards down from Edwards's house. There was no activity and no car in the driveway, however, there was one across the street from the house.

"Let's do this smart," Lincoln said. "Jarrod, you got your shotgun?"

"Yep. Like my underwear, I wear it wherever I go."

"You cover me. I'll go to the front door. Milo and Lynn take the back. Don't barge in until we have an idea what we're facing. If they're inside, I'll try to draw them to the front, then you can break in the back. Don't shoot unless you're sure of your shot or until we know where Ruth is."

The house was dark though that was not unusual. None of the three houses on this block had electricity. All three, however utilized lanterns and none were lit.

Lincoln crept low until he was beneath the large picture window in front of the small bungalow-style house. He called to mind the interior. A family room and kitchen to the right, with the bathroom and two small bedrooms down a hall to the left. A large dormer was upstairs. He lifted his head, keeping his ear to the window. He could pick up no sound, so he turned his eyes to the glass. He could see nothing even if there was something to see. He moved to the front door. A glass storm door covered it. He pulled it open slowly and had Jarrod hold it out of his way. Then, he took one step forward and slammed his foot into the door just beneath the knob. The door cracked and flew open, splintering the jam.

He raced in, gun up and ready. Jarrod followed. They heard the back door crash open and Milo entered. With flashlights on, they searched the house. In one of the bedrooms they found rope and a chair. Ruth had been there but was gone now.

Lynn moved to the chair as if able to absorb her daughter's essence from the rope and chair. She cried silently.

Outside, a multitude of cars screeched to abrupt stops. Voices shouted, and an army of potential rescuers streamed into the house.

"Everyone out," Milo ordered. "There's nothing to see here. Ruth is gone."

"What about my dad?" David asked.

Lincoln stepped into the family room. "If he was here, he's not now. We have to assume he went with Edwards."

"But you have to understand he isn't with them. As soon as we found out what Edwards was planning, my dad and I pretended to be a part of it until we learned what they were going to do. Then we warned you. You can't blame my dad. Please, don't hurt him." The frantic boy was desperate for anyone to believe him.

"I can vouch for Thomas," Jarrod said. "If he hadn't attacked me before the others and told me what was going on, I might have been killed. Let's make sure nothing happens to him until we can sort this all out."

"That's fine," Lincoln said. "I don't want a witch hunt, but we do need to find where they took Ruth."

"All I know," Jarrod said, "was when I passed by, they were heading east. That's a lot of ground to search."

"We need to organize search parties," Milo said. "Each team needs a radio. Let's go back to the farmhouse and get organized."

Chapter Twenty

"Milo," Lincoln said, pulling the big man aside. "Jarrod and I are going to start from here. I don't want to lose any more time than we already have. Get the search teams set up and on the road. I have a radio and will be in contact."

Milo nodded. "Okay. I've got it." He didn't seem pleased.

"Problem?"

"Well, it just seems to me that this is your job sending people out on a rescue mission."

Lincoln sighed. "Okay. Point taken. I'll go back and handle it. I'd appreciate it though, if you go with Jarrod."

Milo looked away. "No. I'm sorry. You go. I never should have said anything. I'm happy to help. We can talk about it after we find Ruth."

Lincoln nodded. "Thanks, Milo."

"Go. Hurry."

Jarrod and Lincoln jogged to his truck. As he was about to close the door, Lynn and Caleb appeared. "We're coming," Lynn said in an end of discussion tone. Lincoln knew better than to argue. He pulled the seat forward and allowed them to climb into the back seat.

They drove down the road, each of them shining their flashlights outside the windows hoping to find a sign of where Ruth might be and praying that it wasn't too late when they found her.

They drove straight down the road for fifteen minutes before Jarrod asked, "How far do you think they'd go?"

"Far enough to be out of a search grid but not so far that they couldn't get back to do whatever other damage they might have planned."

"So, in other words, no idea."

Lincoln didn't bother answering.

Jarrod said, "Well, from the time I seen them leaving til now, I'm guessing it's been twenty minutes. If they got a place to go we might be too late to find them now. If they're winging it like we always seem to be, then maybe we catch a break and see some taillights."

Lincoln didn't respond.

"Wait! Wait!" Caleb said. "Back up. I saw something down that last road."

Jarrod braked hard, throwing them all forward, then reversed, squealing the tires. He stopped in the middle of the intersection as all eyes swung down the road. "You sure?" Jarrod asked.

"It was a quick flash of red. You know, like when someone taps the brakes."

"Good enough for me," said Jarrod. He turned and accelerated.

They traveled miles and searched for hours but did not catch sight of lights or a moving vehicle again.

"We're not going to find them in the dark," Jarrod said.

"I'm afraid you're right," said Lincoln. He turned to look at Lynn. "We should go back and regroup in the morning." He hesitated, not knowing how to broach the next subject but decided it was best to just say it. "They won't hurt her, Lynn. They need her for leverage. By now, they know their friends have at the very least been captured. We'll find them. I promise."

Lynn didn't speak, but it was apparent to Lincoln she was fighting to maintain control of her emotions. She gave a reluctant nod, and Caleb embraced her.

Jarrod turned the truck around. On the way back, they passed other vehicles. Though they encouraged them to continue the search, many took their cues from Jarrod's retreating truck and followed them home. It was a somber group that gathered at the picnic tables. Someone had thought to make coffee. Several, including Lincoln, took a cup while most of the others wandered away to bed after Lincoln told them it would be an early morning to begin the search again.

To say Bobby was uncomfortable was a gross understatement. Not only was he forced to sleep on the couch instead of one of the three beds in the house, but Darlene had curled up next to him, well, half on top of him, preventing sleep or even rest. It wasn't that her presence bothered him. In fact, her warmth and nearness were quite pleasing. It was more that her nearness made him nervous to the point of perspiration.

When she crawled up next to him, he suggested a bed might be more comfortable. She snuggled in deeper, a hand around his waist, and just said, "Umm!" as if in agreement, yet she made no effort to relocate. His next attempt was to tell her he'd take first watch so she could get some sleep. Her comment was, "That's sweet."

"But I can't keep watch if you're—"

She wrapped around him tighter. "Sure you can."

He started to speak again, but she shushed him. "I can't sleep if you're talking."

Bobby gave up after that but had trouble settling down. He wanted to be up and moving—actually on watch. She must have felt his anxiety. "Do I make you nervous, Bobby?" She didn't wait for his reply. "Relax. I won't take advantage of you." She squirmed her cheek against his chest.

He marveled at how easy she fell asleep. He watched her for a long while. His hands, held over his head to prevent contact with her, not wanting her to think he was *trying something,* grew weary. He needed to bring them down, if only for a few minutes. Also, he wanted to move his legs. She snored softly, making him smile and feel comfortable about having her so close.

His thoughts turned to Maretha, the young, fierce, black woman warrior who he thought he'd developed a bond with, like kindred spirits. He was sure she felt the same, but in the midst of a battle was no place to discuss such things, as she'd been seriously wounded. Had she recovered? Was she even alive? He might never know the answer and doubted he'd ever see her again. If so, what was so wrong with developing a relationship with Darlene?

Unable to hold his arms up any longer, he began the slow process of lowering them. His muscles protested, and it took great effort not to just yank them down. He searched for resting spots and placed his left hand on top of the sofa back and the right one on the edge of the cushions under his leg.

Darlene must have felt the movement and altered her position. Bobby discovered he was holding his breath as one might do when praying a newborn stayed asleep. When she ceased moving, he let the breath out slowly. Though he didn't want to wake her, in truth he wanted to rest his hand on her arm and feel the pleasure of holding her. However, he wasn't sure he was ready for whatever his touch and her closeness might lead to. It was better to keep a distance and not get too involved.

He lost track of time. His eyes burned, wanting very much to close. His head bobbed. The constant snapping up of his head when he realized he was dozing was giving his head and neck an ache. If they were doing it right, it should be her turn to keep watch so he could sleep. Though he knew he should wake her, he was unable to do so.

Fifteen minutes later, her eyes opened. She glanced up at him and smiled. "Umm! I could stay here next to you forever."

He didn't know what to say.

"I hope this was all right."

"Ah, yeah. It was fine."

"It's my turn to keep watch." She pushed up, moved up his body and planted a kiss on his lips. "Thank you." She swung one leg over him and straddled his hips. "You should go into one of the bedrooms and get some sleep. You look exhausted. Your eyes are all red." Before she moved, she let her gaze travel down his torso stopping at where her body sat. She gave a wry smile and he was sure the grinding of her hips into his crotch as she stood was intentional.

He took his time standing to make sure his legs had enough blood flow to prevent his falling. Before he could move toward a bedroom, she wrapped her arms around his neck, pulled him down and kissed him deeply. When she broke the kiss, he was embarrassed to find she left him breathless. "Thank you for a magical evening." She released him.

"You're welcome." His voice was a bit high, which embarrassed him further.

She laughed. "Did you just hit puberty?"

He walked past, and she smacked his butt. Though he paused, he did not look back. He made his way into what he thought was the master bedroom. It took a while for him to relax enough to fall asleep.

Chapter Twenty-One

His dreams were tormented. When he woke what felt like minutes later, he was startled to see Darlene leaning over him. He realized she had been shaking him. "Oh, thank God. I thought you were unconscious."

"What? What's the problem?"

"They found us."

Now, fully awake, Bobby bolted upright but had to wait a moment for her to get out of the way of his legs. "Where?"

"They're blocking the end of the street, and I counted six, maybe more armed men coming down the street. By now, they're about three houses away."

He ran into the front room with his rifle in hand. They didn't have time for observation and flight. It was one or the other. At all costs, they had to protect the medical items in the van. If they got in the van, he was sure they could drive through the backyard and into the field next to the house. How far they got depended on what crop had been planted. He doubted they'd get far if it was corn.

They'd give chase. The van was not going to outrun many vehicles. Was it better to defend in the house or to make a run for it? The other concern was if the van over-heated with pursuit close behind. The walls of the van offered less protection than did the house. He made his decision.

"You cover the front. I'm going out back to work around them. I'll try to whittle down the odds. I'll close the door but leave it unlocked so I can reenter. I'll say your name when I do. If you don't hear your name, shoot cause it won't be me."

"Don't you think we'd both be better outside?"

"No. One of us has to remain protected. I won't be long." Not wanting a debate or argument, he turned and ran for the back door.

Outside, he went right. There was a grouping of trees at the end of the street that separated the houses from the field. Bobby now saw it was indeed a cornfield. The stalks and ears had browned and thinned, making it more difficult to move unseen through them. Staying in the house was a good decision.

Keeping the house between him and the attackers, he reached the trees. They were not thick enough to conceal him, so he ran deeper into the woods, then worked his way tree by tree until he had a line of sight down the street.

The six men separated, sending three to the back while three found shooting positions across the street from the house. He used the scope to take in the roadblock. Two vehicles formed the blockade, a police cruiser and a Tahoe. They sat broadside to the road and one man stood behind them with binoculars.

Now that Bobby knew the setup, he moved toward the rear of the house. Darlene could handle the three out front, but she had no one to watch her back and he had left the door unlocked.

By the time he found a position giving him a full view of the yard, the three men were already in place. One stood at the rear corner of the garage, one was at the front of the van, while the third slid along the back wall of the house toward the back door. Bobby decided his shooting sequence then acquired his first target, the man behind the garage. Though he was covered from the house, he was not from Bobby's position. He could take him and still have an open shot at the man who had no cover near the house. He contemplated taking the man by the van hoping for a momentary freeze at a shot from an unexpected place. However, it was not a sure shot, and he might miss his chance at the third man. In the end, he concluded it was better to have two down for sure rather than one and a possible second.

He waited for the shooting to start. It was only seconds later. The shooters out front fired. Bobby guessed it was to keep them occupied while their friends snuck in the back. He pulled the trigger and the man behind the garage spun around from the impact to his chest and fell. Quick but not hurried, he swept to the next target. The man near the back door heard the shot and froze while trying to locate the origin. That was the last moment of his life as Bobby's next round bore through his forehead.

The third man found Bobby and slid to the far side of the van. He fired over the slanted hood and had Bobby pinned down. He was a good shot. No matter where Bobby moved, the man would be able to track him, so he waited him out. Once he had a lull in the shooting, he'd line up his own shot. Even if he missed, he'd return the favor and keep him locked down. It all depended on how many rounds the man had in his magazine.

Bobby's only held five, so while the other man fired at him, he dropped the box magazine and slid two more rounds in. His opportunity came seconds later. It was obvious the other man had a magazine that held significantly more rounds than Bobby's. That being the case, it was doubtful he was reloading. He'd exchange magazines which only took seconds.

Bobby sighted on a spot above the hood where the man had been shooting. If he was smart, he'd change positions. Shooting accuracy was one thing. Being a skilled hunter of men was another. Bobby'd know a lot about his opponent from his next appearance.

As he waited, he noted the shooting out front had lessened. He kept any conclusions from forming, choosing to concentrate on his target instead. The man's face appeared and Bobby fired. Whether to draw a shot or some premonition of his demise, the man ducked before the shot struck. The bullet zipped past.

Disappointed and surprised, Bobby decided it was time to relocate before the man reappeared and reacquired him as a target. He dashed to his right toward the cornfield. As he neared the field, he realized it was a mistake. He had placed himself in a corner. He had a small section of smaller trees to use for cover. The shooter could track him easily in the corn unless he got a good distance away. That distance might take too much time to arrive. He wasn't daring enough to chance his speed against a bullet.

The only advantage to his new position was the man now had to move to have a line of sight at him. He did a quick peek. He saw no one and nothing happened. He set the rifle against the tree so the butt was visible from the back of the van, then sprinted toward the rear of the garage. It was a forty-yard dash across open ground, but the angle changed with every step he took. If the shooter spotted him, he'd have to move and adjust his aim while moving himself. It could be done but Bobby hoped the man hadn't seen him break.

When the shot came, he grabbed his body in reaction to the impending pain. It did not happen. He reached the back of the garage and pressed to the brick wall. His breaths came in huge gulps. He tried to keep them quiet but near panic and a racing heart made that all but impossible.

He glanced at the tree. The rifle was gone. That must have been where the shot was aimed. By now, the shooter knew Bobby was no longer there. He had to suspect where he was. Neither man was in a good shooting position. The advantage went to whichever man guessed right about the direction his opponent would move to. It was either going to happen fast or agonizingly slow.

A window was in the middle of the rear wall. Bobby moved to it with stealth, placing all effort into his hearing. He reached the window and slid his handgun into the holster. Pressing both hands on the lower sill, he pushed up and walked up the wall with the tips of his boots. Once he was able to rest a knee on the narrow sill, he shifted his hands to the sides and stood. The garage was not high, with a sloping gray shingled roof. The roof overhung the wall by a foot, and Bobby had to lean back to clear the end. It had no gutter. As his head cleared, he thought he heard movement out front of the garage. If the shooter was making his move now, he'd have an easy shot at Bobby.

He shifted his hands to the roof and pressed down. His feet scrabbled for purchase on the wall. He rose easily and slid a leg on the roof. Then he pulled himself up and sprawled flat to listen for his foe. As he did, his hand slid down his leg to withdraw the gun.

A faint scraping sound came from someplace nearby. He had trouble placing the sound until the barrel of a rifle appeared over the roofline. His counterpart had the same thought about getting to higher ground. Trying not to make noise but knowing he had to get his gun online before a head popped up, Bobby leaned to the side to allow room for his arm to swing unobstructed and without dragging across the course shingles.

The top of the head rose slowly. Did he know Bobby was there, or was he just trying to be cautious about making noise? The rifle barrel inched higher, then the head did the same. Bobby had the hairline for a target. Not enough to risk the shot. All he wanted was an inch of forehead.

He was subconsciously aware that no shots had been fired from anywhere for quite some time. Sweat rolled down his head dangerously close to his eyes. He did not have the luxury of time to wipe it, but if it reached his eyes, the burning might blur his vision. Time slowed. The only two people in the world were on the garage roof. Only one would come down alive.

A half inch of head crested the peak. Bobby's finger tightened on the trigger. He was only a fraction of pressure away from sending the round.

A voice shouted from the front, "Hey, Jessie." Running steps followed. "We got—whoa! Oh, man, Ed."

Bobby saw the flick of fingers rise and fall above the roofline. The shooter was trying to quiet the man below. Whoever it was couldn't take the hint. "Jessie, we got the shooter in the house. It's the woman. She cried out when Matt fired and now we can hear her moaning and crying inside. We're going in but wanted some help. Adam's down. I see Ed is too, but at least Adam's alive. Where's Wayne?"

The announcement sent first ice, then fire through Bobby's veins. Could it be true. Was Darlene shot— wounded? All he could think was to kill these men fast and get to her side. Bobby dug in his toes and lifted his knees, balancing on his left forearm. His foe spoke. "I've got the other behind the garage. See if you can flush him, then we'll go see to the woman."

Bobby placed his left palm flat on the roof, pushed up, then took two fast steps toward the peak to the left side of the rifle barrel. He shoved the gun over the peak and began firing as his opponent slid the rifle toward him. Bobby fired until the rifle slid from sight, then without rational thought or regard for his safety, stood, spotted the other man, and fired. The other man was stunned by the sudden appearance and action and took a moment to react to his friend getting blown away. He got off two shots before Bobby fired.

Though the man triggered first, he panicked and backed away from the garage, so the bullets were inaccurate.

Bobby gave them little thought as his second and third shot found their mark and dropped the man to his butt.

He looked shocked at seeing the circular blood patterns forming on his shirt. He kept patting at them like he was putting out a fire. Bobby took careful aim and pulled the trigger, but the slide was back. He was out of bullets.

He slid to the edge of the roof and leaped off, landing and rolling on the lawn. Disregarding the wounded man, he broke into the house at a run and with worry and fear controlling his mind. He ran through the doorway to the front room and was shot. The bullet struck his right side and spun him around. He gripped the door frame to keep him standing.

Behind him a gasp and an "Oh, God. No," reached him before the edges of blackness surrounded his vision. He heard Darlene run to him. "Bobby. I'm sorry. I thought you were one of them." Tears streamed down her face. "You said you'd call my name when you came in, Bobby."

He gave her what he hoped was a reassuring smile. "It's okay. I'm fine." Then the darkness became complete, and he had the feeling of falling.

Chapter Twenty-Two

Darlene tamped down her emotions and went into action. Bobby's life depended on her staying calm and focused. While she worked on stemming the flow of blood from Bobby's wound, she thought. How many attackers were still outside? What items did she need to bring with them?

She grabbed two gauze pads and a Kotex mini pad she found in the house and pressed them over the wound. A roll of duct tape found in a drawer was wrapped around Bobby's body to keep them in place. Then she grabbed him under his arms and dragged him to the rear door.

After setting him down, she stepped outside to make sure no ambush awaited them. A man was sitting in the driveway crying and trying to stop the blood flowing from his wounds. He looked up at her. "Help me."

"Yeah, as if. You should have just left us alone."

She dragged Bobby from the house and used all her strength to lift him into the van, laying him as flat as the room allowed. As she climbed into the driver's seat, she glanced back at the wounded man. "You should move."

She started the engine, looked in the mirror, and saw the man still sitting. Bobby was a hell of a lot more important than the man was. Without hesitation, she put the van in reverse and pressed the pedal down. She heard the scream before she felt the thump. *I warned you. Plenty of clearance. You should've moved.*

She hit the street, staying low in the seat in case snipers were in place. Down the street, she saw two men behind the vehicles in an animated discussion. They stopped talking and looked at the van as it started forward. Both men took out guns and leaned over the vehicles. *How dare they get in my way.*

Darlene floored the pedal. The van did not have the horsepower to lurch but gained speed steadily. She closed on the barricade fast. The two men began firing. She slid lower. Bullets punched through the windshield all around her. She knew she could not afford a collision at full speed with the vehicles, as the van might not survive another impact. Though they had blocked the street completely, they hadn't bothered with the grounds in front of the houses.

Trees filled the right side, leaving her only one option. As she was about to swerve left, a severe pain shot fire up her left arm. She cried out and released the wheel with her left hand. Though the pain blurred her vision and filled her brain, she retained one thought, escape. She turned the wheel with one hand, riding up onto the grass and bouncing toward the main road.

The two men continued to fire. Darlene could hear the rounds puncturing the van's walls. One thumped into the back of her seat. She whipped the wheel hard still with one hand, but the wheel suddenly spun away from her grasp. The van teetered first one way, then the other. She was forced to brake to keep from flipping. In the mirror, she saw the two men notice her predicament, and they advanced at a run. She was tired of being shot at. Darlene slammed the stick into park, buttoned down the window, picked up the gun she set on the passenger seat, and leaned as far out the window as she could without falling.

Leaning on her wounded arm caused excruciating pain, but though she moaned, she focused, lined up her shot and fired. Though her first shots were inaccurate, the first shooter walked into the rounds and was spun to the ground. His partner squatted, then knelt to return fire. When Darlene saw him eject his magazine and reach for another attached to his belt, she opened the door, stepped out, and fired nonstop as she advanced toward him.

The panicked man, seeing Darlene approaching, fumbled the magazine and dropped it. He reached for it as a bullet ricocheted off the blacktop inches from his hand. He turned and fled, abandoning the magazine. Darlene's last round caught him in the ass. He reached back at the wound as he ran, tripping and falling.

Darlene bent to pick up the dropped magazine and ejected hers. She walked toward the fallen man as she pushed the magazine in. It did not fit. Frustrated, angry, and in pain, she tucked her gun under her armpit, thumbed two rounds out of the old one and went back to retrieve her fallen magazine.

The man, now aware she was coming, scooted backward on the blacktop holding up a hand toward her in defense. "Please. No. Please don't. I'm sorry."

She advanced, ignoring his pleas. He got to his feet and hobbled away as she seated the magazine. After chambering a round, she stopped walking, took careful aim, and fired. The first shot was a miss. The second bullet took the man in the back, sending him sprawling face first. She desperately wanted to end his life, but Bobby needed her. She turned and ran back to the van.

Unfamiliar with the area, Darlene tried to recall the streets from the map. She was on Route Two and knew that took her all the way back, but she wasn't sure of the roads she had to turn on to get to the farmhouse. She turned down the first street that looked familiar and wound her way through the area, searching for home.

In the back, Bobby began moaning. It spurred her on hearing him endure such pain but also added to her anxiety over her failure at not getting him home faster. She began to cry more for Bobby's pain than her own. Steam began to rise above the hood. The engine had to hold out.

After several more turns showing her nothing she remembered, she spotted something ahead. Something was in the road. She advanced slowly, not wanting to get too close, concerned it was another enemy roadblock.

She braked at the next intersection wanting an out in case of trouble. She reached into the back seat, snagged her rifle and used the scope to examine what lay ahead. It was a gate across the road with three armed guards. It was home. She let out a hoot of joy and sped forward.

Darlene was aware of the guns aimed at her. Her first thought was to bust through the gate and hurry to the hospital, but she thought better of it. The guards might be able to help. She lowered her window and leaned out as she slowed.

One man held up a hand and stepped forward while the others covered him. "We need help. Bobby's been shot.

"Darlene?"

"Yeah. Bobby's been shot. Hurry, let me in."

"Can't do that. You know the rules. We have to verify the contents before we allow you in."

"Well, hurry, dammit. He's lost a lot of blood. He's in back." She opened the door to get out. The guard stepped back and put a hand on his sidearm. "Stay in the van."

She released a frustrated shout. "Okay. But if he dies while we're waiting, I'm coming back for you."

Steam billowed, now obscuring her vision. She scooted to the left. Just a little longer, she pleaded.

The guard waited until she returned to her seat and shut the door before moving to the rear. He opened the door and she heard him cry out in surprise. He ran around the van. "Open the gate and call in that we have a wounded man and need the hospital." He ran to the back and got in.

Darlene did not wait for him to close the doors. As soon as the gate was up high enough to clear the van, she floored the accelerator. This time the van did lurch forward. She glanced back to see the guard was no longer inside the van. That brought a sadistic smile to her face.

When she reached the farmhouse, a dozen people were waiting. She was barely stopped before people were offloading Bobby onto a stretcher. The engine coughed, hissed, and sputtered to stillness. She climbed out and was assaulted with a myriad of questions from several sources. It was all too confusing and increased her angst. All she wanted to do was make sure Bobby was all right, but no one would leave her alone. "Stop!" she screamed at the top of her lungs. Then, she felt faint from the effort and fell back against the van.

Someone said, "She's been shot too. Quick. Help me get her to the hospital."

Her head felt heavy and her mind foggy, like that time that guy shared his weed with her. It was her first time, and her father was furious. She never saw that guy again. That was her last thought before waking hours later, with her arm wrapped in bandages and her body attached to machinery.

Her mind cleared in increments as the memory worked to return. When she recalled she had shot Bobby, her eyes bulged. She tried to call for someone, but her mouth and throat would not cooperate. Croaked sounds elicited a response. A young woman she knew by sight but not by name entered.

"Ah, you're awake. That's good. Let me check your readings, take your temperature and blood pressure, and then I'll get Doc to come in and talk to you."

Darlene tried to speak, but a thermometer was stuck in her mouth. When it was pulled, the woman examined it and made a note on a chart. "Slightly elevated, but I guess that's to be expected." She wrapped the blood pressure cuff around her arm and began pumping air.

Darlene tried to speak again, but her throat was too coarse. She swallowed several times.

"That's all right. You just relax. Your voice will return. Oh, my. That's high," the woman said, reading the results. "Are you in pain?"

Darlene reached out, snatched the woman's arm, and pulled her close. In a whisper, she said, "How's Bobby?"

The woman did not respond to being yanked, but she did react to Bobby's name. The sight sent a wave of mental anguish through Darlene like she hadn't experienced since her mother had passed from the virus. She released the woman and turned her face away to allow the tears to flow unobserved.

Chapter Twenty-Three

"There," said Caleb. "Down the street on the left." It was yet another silver car. They had gotten the color of the car from David Bedrosian but not the make or year. It wasn't much to go on, but at least they knew it was a car. Without knowing more, they were forced to check out every silver car they saw. However, Lincoln was of the mind that wherever Edwards and his gang were hiding the car, it was not in sight.

They had six cars out doing area searches. The areas had been divided up, and each car did a block-by-block search grid. They left before dawn and had been out for a little more than two hours.

Lincoln stopped three houses down from where the silver Buick sat in the driveway of a small brick ranch. Caleb and Lynn got out. Lynn carried a scoped hunter's rifle while Caleb carried a pump-action shotgun. Lincoln had an M-4 taken from one of the soldiers in last month's war.

This was the seventh house they checked and had developed a routine. Caleb took the front with his mother covering him from across the street. Lincoln took the back. As soon as Lincoln entered after kicking in the rear door, it was apparent no one was there. No one living that is.

The foul smell caused his eyes to water. No one had been in this house since the start of the pandemic. He stepped back outside and walked toward the street. He waved them toward the car and without a word, they got in and drove on. "Dead bodies," was all he said—all he needed to say.

They patrolled for another forty minutes before Caleb sat forward and leaned into the front seat. "Lincoln, back up a bit."

Lincoln did so without question.

"Stop." Caleb extended his arm and pointed through the windshield. "There."

Down the block, five houses from the corner was a silver Cadillac parked in the backyard. What lent hope to the find was that the car was pulled off the driveway onto the grass behind the house.

Lincoln pulled forward, using the corner house to block their car from the target house. As Lynn moved to get out, Lincoln put a restraining hand on her arm. "Just a hunch, but let's do this one a little differently."

"How so?" Caleb asked.

You both stay here." He cut off protests with a raised hand. "No. Listen. I'm going out to observe only. I want verification before we make a move. If they are in there, we can't risk Ruth's life on an assault. We need to—well, let me check to see if they're in there first. We'll go from there."

He picked up the binoculars and got out before any arguments ensued. He was right about this. It had to be just him.

He climbed the fence around the backyard of the corner house then ran crouched to the one-car garage. He squatted and focused the glasses on the suspect house. The angle wasn't good. He couldn't see inside. He had to move to the next house. Each move brought him closer to discovery.

Edwards paced the small front room. "We have to assume they were all killed or at least captured. Either way, we're blown."

"Maybe, maybe not," Merchant said. "We have to find out if they were successful taking out Lincoln. Even if they only took down Lincoln, we still have a chance here. As long as we keep the girl, we have leverage over Lynn and her son."

"What I don't understand," a man began to say. He entered the room carrying a can of warm beer. His name was Herb and he owned the house. When the pandemic first swept the country, he didn't hunt for and store food and water like other survivors. Herb broke into every liquor and convenience store in the area and took the beer and booze. His basement was stocked to the ceiling. He would have joined the community but didn't want to share his beer. "Is how you thought it was gonna help you take control of the community. Even if you did manage to kill those two guys and they agreed to your terms, once they got the girl back, what was to stop them from killing you? You'd've had to keep the girl hidden for a long time until you were sure you had the numbers to keep control."

He popped the top of the can with a snick and a hiss. "Don't sound like much of a plan to me. I think you screwed up."

"Shut up, Herb," Merchant said. To Edwards, he said, "What do you want to do?"

Edwards peeked through the drawn curtains. "We giving up on the plan?"

"No. I got one last thing I want to do. I want to kill Mark."

Edwards stared at him open-mouthed. Herb stopped drinking his beer. "How do you plan on getting in there. They might be out here searching for us now."

"The wall they're building is not complete yet. There's a lot of space between the two gates on the eastern side. We can slip through easily. We come up behind the hospital and sneak in through the back door. We can be in and out in minutes."

Merchant said, "Someone will be in the hospital. They keep someone there all the time."

"Then they die too. We make it to the hospital. I go in, do the deed while you cover me. Then we're gone. We come back here, pack up and take off."

"And we take the girl. She's young, she'll last a long time." Merchant said, rubbing his hands together eagerly. "In fact, if she no longer has value, I think I'll take her for a test drive now."

Herb stood. "Not here, dude. I won't have that kind of abuse in my house."

Edwards said, "Yeah, hold off until we see what's going on at the community. She may still have some value. She might still be leverage in case we get caught."

"What about Thomas?" Merchant said.

"He has no value to us at all," Edwards replied. "We can finish him anytime."

Herb gulped the entire beer, belched, and crushed the can. "Sounds like a job for me."

Edwards said, "He's all yours. We're going to go find some food, then scout out the farm. Don't hurt the girl. Keep her safe, in case we need to trade her. Hurt the man as much as you want. Unless something changes, we won't be back until later tonight."

"Okay, but if you're not back by morning, I'm claiming the girl as mine."

Edwards and Merchant collected their gear and went out the back door. As they moved to the car Merchant said, "We may need to lose the car and find another. They may know what you're driving and be looking for a silver car."

"Man, I love this car."

"Cut the cord, dude. It's gotta go."

They got in and Edwards backed down the driveway.

Chapter Twenty-Four

Lincoln saw the men leave. They were in the right place. *Was Ruth inside? Thomas? Was she alive? Was anyone else in the house?* Lincoln decided not to tell Lynn. He didn't want an emotional reaction that would lead to her charging the house. He also didn't want to inform her until he checked the house to ensure Ruth was there and alive. If she wasn't, he wanted to prevent Lynn's last sight of her daughter in the position of what he feared he might find.

He moved around the corner but ducked back fast as the storm door slammed open and a large man with wild unkempt hair dragged another smaller man outside. He tossed him on the ground and pulled a handgun. "Go ahead," he said. "Make it more challenging and run."

Lincoln recognized the man as Thomas. He was about to be executed.

"I'll give you to the count of five. One."

Thomas scrambled to his feet and tried to run but tripped over his own hastily moving feet. Lincoln had to act. He dropped the binoculars, drew his gun, and ran toward the metal chain link fence typical to this neighborhood separating the next house. Even if he managed to scale the fence without being seen, he was still four houses away. The best he could hope for was to draw the assassin's attention to him, and he'd be standing in the open. The secret was to keep moving and shooting. To keep the man off balance.

He reached the fence and in one fluid motion, placed a hand on the crossbar and swung both legs over. He landed on the run. The four-time all-star NFL running back sprinted toward the next fence like it was the goal line and he was in the Super Bowl.

The shooter was still counting, which told Lincoln he had not yet been seen.

"Four."

Thomas had managed to get to his feet and was attempting to climb the fence at the back of the house. It was obvious to Lincoln Thomas was not going to make it.

Before the gunman reached five, he must have caught movement in his periphery and turned his head toward Lincoln. He was out of time. The next fence was coming up fast. He had to fire but was still too far away to be accurate, not to mention being on the run. Without thought, he triggered his first round as his body took flight. He hurdled the fence like the high school track star he had once been. However, the fence was significantly higher than a hurdle and he was many years from peak form. His trail leg caught the crossbar and he fell while still shooting.

The surprised gunman ducked and fired blindly as he scampered toward the house. With Lincoln tumbling on the ground, the shots were nowhere close to him. He shoulder rolled and came up on one knee, firing toward the man, but his shots were hurried and did not score a hit.

The man stood inside the doorway, covered from the chest down and fired back at Lincoln. Exposed as he was, he was a much better target than his opponent. He had to move or die.

A shot was fired behind him and echoed off the houses. A chunk of the doorframe splintered away, causing the man to duck back inside. Lincoln took advantage of the man's disappearance and scurried toward the rear of the nearest house to cut the other man's shooting angle. He edged toward the next fence, gun up and trained on the door. He hadn't bothered to look behind him. He knew either Lynn or Caleb had his back. He did glance right, however, to make sure Thomas was safe. The man had rabbited and was nowhere in sight.

With one hand keeping the gun aimed, he reached down with the other to grab the crossbar and leaped to put his foot on top. He paused for an instant in case the shooter made an appearance, then jumped down. He moved forward in steady, consistent steps, now one backyard away from the house he hoped held a living Ruth.

As if in answer, he could hear the man screaming inside the house. "Get up, bitch. Move, or I'll split your head open." Crying filtered through the brick wall, followed by a squeal. Though it pained him to hear Ruth cry, he was happy to know she was still alive. Now all that remained was to see what condition she was in.

He kept close to the rear wall of the neighboring house as he advanced. The rear door slammed open with such force the glass storm door shattered. The large man stood behind Ruth, using her as a shield. He had one hand entwined in her long hair, yanking her head back at an uncomfortable angle for the much shorter girl.

"Back away, or I splatter her brains all over the yard." His face looked maniacal. His eyes were wide open and slightly bulging. His wild hair looked like he'd stuck a finger in an electrical socket.

Once Ruth spotted Lincoln, she stopped squirming and crying. An eerie calm settled over her as if she knew he'd make things right. She closed her eyes and stood still. Her confidence only served to increase his angst. His mouth went dry as he shifted his gaze to focus on the wild, insane-looking eyes of Ruth's potential killer.

"Drop the gun and back away," he said to Lincoln, "or I swear she dies first, then I'll kill you."

From behind him, Caleb shouted, "Ruth! No, you madman, let my sister go. If you hurt her, I swear I'll kill you."

Now Lincoln knew who was behind him but he doubted the boy would be much use in his current emotional state. Where was Lynn?

The crazed man noticed Caleb for the first time. For some strange reason, his appearance made the man smile. "Ah, sister. Well, isn't that nice." He looked at Lincoln. "Now you know you have to drop the gun. You don't want me killing this sweet young thing in front of her brother now, do you?"

Lincoln caught movement past the gunman. In a calm voice, he said, "Ruth. Look at me." Her eyes opened. There was no hint of fear displayed within. "You trust me?" She blinked twice. *Yes.* He smiled inwardly. Ruth was as cool as they came. Her mind was working faster and smoother than his. "Stand perfectly still. Do not move, and don't worry."

"Hey! What's going on?" He crouched lower behind Ruth, so only his wild hair showed. "Stop talking to her. I'm warning you."

"Okay. Okay." Lincoln held up one hand and lowered the gun. "You win."

He looked at Lincoln from over Ruth's shoulder then shifted his gaze to Caleb. "What about him?"

"Caleb. Set the rifle down and move away."

"What? No."

Lincoln shouted. "Caleb. You want your sister safe? Do what I say, now."

He didn't look behind him, not wanting to take his eyes off the man. He read Caleb's acquiescence in the gunman's expression. The wicked smile spread across his face. "Toss the gun."

Lincoln did. That emboldened the man. He stood more erect and dragged Ruth away from the door. Though he knew it was coming, the gunshot still made Lincoln jump. To her credit, Ruth did not move even after the brain matter and blood coated her hair and face. She stood still until the body fell away. She turned to see her mother, her handgun still up where it had fired inches from the man's head.

"I knew you'd come," Ruth said. She stepped into Lynn's arms, and they hugged each other tightly. Seconds later, having scaled all the fences between them, Caleb appeared and joined the embrace.

Lincoln retrieved his gun and entered the house to make sure it was clear. He had no idea who this guy was, but he was an obvious friend of Edwards and Merchant. He moved room by room, clearing each. When he reached the basement, he was unable to refrain from an awe-struck gasp at the mountain of beer and cases of booze. In his mind, he heard a chorus of angels in perfect harmony.

Chapter Twenty-Five

They found Thomas four blocks away jogging. He flinched and turned to run the other way when he heard them approach. "Thomas. Wait. It's Lincoln."

It took several attempts before the man slowed enough to look at the large black man leaning out the car window. He was so happy to see him he wept. "How's my son?"

"He's safe," Lincoln said. "He warned me of the ambush. He's my hero. He's back at the farm."

They made room for Thomas in the back. His small frame squeezed into the back. They started to drive and Thomas slid forward in his seat grabbing Lincoln's. "Hey, I need to tell you, I think Edwards and Merchant are planning something at the farm."

Lynn turned her head to look at him, new concern displaying on her face. "Like what?"

"I'm not sure. I only heard about every third word. They said something about checking on their friends, then something about doing one last thing at the farm. I have no idea what?"

Horror registered on Lynn's face. Her hand shot across the console and grabbed Lincoln's arm. "Mark? They're going after Mark."

Lincoln didn't ask questions. He knew she was right. He pressed the pedal down and sped back toward the farmhouse. Lynn picked up the radio. "Lynn to base. Lynn to base. Come in, anyone."

Milo answered. "Lynn, it's Milo. I've got two teams checked in and waiting on the others, but so far, they found nothing."

"Milo, listen," she said, her tone intense. "We have Ruth and Thomas—"

"That's great, I'm—"

She cut him off. "Milo, listen," she snapped. "We think Edwards and Merchant are on their way there to kill Mark. Is someone with him?"

"Yes, Jarrod's there. How do you know?"

"I'll explain when I get there. Just increase the guards. Please."

"Doing it now. What's your ETA?"

She looked at Lincoln.

"Fifteen," he said."

"Fifteen minutes."

"Okay. See you then."

They pulled up the gravel driveway in twelve minutes, with Lincoln powering on the speed. They were met by a host of armed people. Many hugged Ruth and commented on how glad they were she and Thomas were safe. David threw himself into his father's arms. It was a joyous reunion, but while that was occurring, Lincoln, Lynn and Milo moved to the side.

"I recalled all the other search parties, sent word to the gates that Edwards and Merchant might be coming and to refuse them entrance, and added four more people to guard Mark. If they show themselves anywhere near here, we'll take them down."

Lincoln said, "I've been thinking about that. I think we should keep to our normal routine."

"What?" Milo said.

Lynn said, "Why?"

"If Edwards and Merchant see we are waiting for them, they'll leave. They may run, or they may wait for a time when we are not prepared for them and sneak in. I think we let them in and capture them here. That way, we have them."

"Then what?" asked Milo.

Lynn answered. "We put them on trial, so the community can see we are making an effort to handle problems with some form of code."

"Ah, that wasn't what I had in mind," Lincoln said, "but okay. We can do it that way. I see the merit."

"However, I want to make a few changes to your plan. First, everyone in the hospital needs to be moved to someplace safe in case shooting starts. Second, everyone except for a select few needs to be kept away from here to ensure no one gets caught in the middle and either shot or taken hostage."

Milo said, "Moving the patients might be a problem."

"Why?" said Lynn. "There's just two minor illnesses and Myron and Mark. Since Myron is somewhat awake, I don't see the problem. We can ask Doc."

"Those aren't the only ones there. While you were out, Bobby and Darlene returned. They've both been shot."

"What happened?" asked Lincoln.

"I don't know. I haven't had a chance to talk to them. They were in with Doc, and then I got involved with co-ordinating the search. All I know is Bobby was bad while Darlene was just grazed. They should be out of surgery by now. You'll have to check with Doc."

Lincoln sighed.

Lynn muttered, "It never ends."

"Well, at least no one can blame Mark this time," Lincoln said.

Lynn shot him an angry glance.

"We should still have some time before Edwards and Merchant try anything," said Milo. "I'm guessing it won't be until dark. I'll take care of things while you go check in with Doc."

"See that Ruth stays inside and out of sight," Lincoln said. "If they see her, they'll know it's over. As long as they think they have her as leverage, they'll make the attempt."

Lynn and Lincoln moved toward the hospital. "That comment about Mark was uncalled for," Lynn said.

"Was it?"

"You know damn well it was."

"Maybe you need to take another look at what we're dealing with here on an almost daily basis. Mark has done more to protect this community than most people give him credit for. This is not an easy world we live in. Never was, but more so now." He paused and turned on her. "And maybe it's time you reexamined your own feelings for him before it's too late. You've almost lost him several times. Cut him some slack. If he survives, don't let a moment go by wasted on reasons to stay apart. You love him. The entire community knows it. Let it happen. You'll both be much happier and facing whatever comes our way will be easier together."

"It's not that easy, Linc."

"Sure it is."

"No, it's really not."

"Lynn, do you care for Mark?"

She blew out an exasperated breath. "Yes, but—"

"No buts. You do or you don't. Make up your mind. How are you going to feel if he never wakes up and you never had the chance to tell him how you feel or make up with him. All I'm saying, from Lincoln's advice to lovers, is if he wakes, let your heart free from its restraints."

He stepped back with hands raised in surrender. "Okay. I'm done preaching."

They entered the hospital and found Doc at a desk near the back of the space, making notes in a chart. She was still wearing her dirty surgery worn scrubs displaying sprinkles of blood. She glanced up from her work, eyes bleary from lack of sleep. Her face brightened with hope. "Any word?"

Lynn nodded. "We found them both. Unharmed."

Doc stood and hugged Lynn. "I'm so happy." She pushed back and held Lynn by the shoulders. "Do you want me to do a complete exam?"

Lynn shook her head. "She says they roughed her up a bit and threatened to do things but never touched her."

Doc cocked her head in a question.

"Yes. I trust she's telling me the truth."

"Okay. Good. I'm glad she's home."

"What have you got here?" Lynn asked.

"Ah, that's right. You were away when they came in. Darlene had a through and through to her arm. I patched her and gave her some meds. She's sleeping now. Bobby's wound was a little more serious. He took it in the side. It too passed through, but he had significant damage to a kidney that required a lot of work. He's resting quietly now and, in fact has not been awake since he arrived. I'm keeping a close eye on him for infection or if I missed something."

"So, he can't be moved then," Lincoln said.

"Ah, no, why? What's going on?"

Lynn said, "We think Edwards and Merchant are coming to kill Mark."

"Seriously? Well, there's no way they can get in, so there's little to worry about."

"That's the thing. We'd rather have them get in and take control of them so we know where they are."

Doc looked from one to the other. "So, you what? Want to use Mark as bait? No. Not a chance. Not in my hospital."

"Okay," Lincoln said. "We respect that decision but we are going to let them in so we can capture them. We can do it before they get here. But we'd feel better if all patients can be moved away from Mark in case they somehow manage to elude us."

"God, you are just trying to make my life more difficult, aren't you? Why can't you just shoot them on sight?" She covered her face with splayed fingers. "I can't believe I just said that. I need a break from the daily grind. This place is worse than the emergency room I used to work in. Okay. I'll do the best I can. Are you leaving the guards at least?"

"Yes, but they'll be hidden."

"You're taking a big risk with a lot of lives. I hope you know what you're doing?"

"Yeah. Me too."

"Well, that's not encouraging."

Lynn said, "We will take every precaution. We will try to take them outside before they get near here. Moving the patients is just a backup plan in case something goes wrong."

Doc said, "Which around here is a guarantee." She looked at them and shrugged. "Okay. If you're determined to go this route, you need to help me move people."

Chapter Twenty-Six

Edwards crept through the undergrowth until he had a line of sight of the compound. He scanned the grounds and spotted Lynn and Lincoln leaving the hospital. He lifted a finger and aimed it at them. "Bang. Bang. You're both dead." He took several more minutes sweeping the grounds but did not see anything that made him rethink his plan. Mark was dying tonight. No matter what else happened, he was paying for his son's death.

He backed away then walked the two blocks where Merchant waited in their new pickup. He slid inside.

"Well?" Merchant asked.

"Obviously, our people failed. I saw Lincoln."

"You think they're dead?"

"Most likely. If they survived, they'd have been out looking for us."

"We still doing this?"

"Oh, hell yeah. Mark dies tonight. I think we also take out whoever else we can, too."

"Hold on, partner. I understand your need for revenge. I'm all in on that, but if we go shooting up the place, we're going to get killed. There're too many of them, and they've gotten quite good at killing attackers. I think we sneak in, take Mark out quietly like maybe slicing his throat, and sneak back out to fight another day."

Edwards sighed. He hated not finishing what he started.

"Hey, look at me." There was steel in Merchant's voice.

Edwards did.

"I'm not doing this unless I have your word."

Edwards nodded.

"No. Not good enough. I want to hear you say it."

"Okay. Okay. I agree. We do Mark quietly and get out. That's fine. None of the rest of them are worth dying for anyway."

"Okay. Let's go find something to eat, then get back here after dark."

Merchant drove the truck away from the farm and hoped his friend had enough self-control not to get both of them killed, well, at least not him.

"Jin! Shh!" Becca said, holding up a hand. She angled her head and leaned forward as if the added inches increased her ability to hear whatever it was that caught her attention. When the sound did not return, she wondered if she had heard anything at all. However, the hairs on her arm were still standing. She had heard something. She was sure of it, but with all the noise Jin was making, perhaps they heard them too.

She backed up two steps and leaned toward Jin. "Someone's outside." She did not say *I think* someone's outside. Her senses were screaming it was fact. He nodded and without a word, moved with the silence of a ghost to the rear door of the house they were searching. In the day and a half since her brother and Darlene had left, they had amassed a large inventory of food, beverages, medical supplies and equipment to take back to the community. It was an amount to be proud of, and that might feed them well into the winter.

Without the van, moving the items they found took a lot of time, but they had settled into a routine and once the police cruiser was full, they moved it to the house they had taken over and piled it in the garage. The fear was always that someone might come along while they were out searching and relieve them of their stockpile, but they had not seen one person, at least until today, and that person or persons still had not been seen.

Becca crouched and crept toward the front picture window of the small brick ranch. The houses they were searching now were on the southern outskirts of the small town. They were choosing to do the furthest houses first and work closer to their home. She crawled under the large window and inched up to the corner. A fraction at a time, she peeled the heavy drape back until she had a narrow view of the front of the house.

Open ground stretched in all directions. There was no cover and no place to hide. They had finished the larger ranch next door twenty minutes earlier and had debated whether to go back and unload or check this house. They decided to see what was here first before making an extra trip. So far, they hadn't discovered much of value, but the search had been cut short.

Becca got to her knees and changed her angle. She looked right. The road ended at a large field just past the house and continued as a two-lane dirt track. The field had at one time been farmland, but for whatever reason, whoever worked the land hadn't planted anything. That left the ground unobstructed for a long way. Patches of brown and green dotted the land, but no growth was high enough to conceal a person. The only possible place for a person to hide in front of the house was behind the cruiser, which they had parked in the driveway directly in front of the house.

She inched back and peered to the left of the house. At the fringes of her view, she spotted a bumper. That was all she could see from her position. From the height it belonged to a truck. *Was it the van? Had Bobby returned?* She did expect him sometime today. Although Bobby insisted he'd be back with four to five hours, it was late when they left, and she knew Darlene had some plans of her own.

She had to find an angle that allowed a fuller view down the road. She moved to the side of the house. The only window in the eastern wall was in the kitchen and the view was blocked by the neighboring house. Though it offered no line of sight down the street, she did catch a flash of movement near the rear of the house. Was it Jin? She glanced at the rear door. It was closed. If he went out, he had done it with such stealth she was unaware.

She focused on the spot she had seen the movement. The house next door was fifty feet away. She did not have an angle to see behind the house, but the only spot blocked from view was against the rear wall, and that's where she had seen the flash. She closed her eyes and recalled the image. She replayed it several times before opening her eyes. She was sure now. It had been a face. It did a quick peek at the house.

A noise from out front drew her attention away from the kitchen window. She moved toward the picture window. If she heard a sound out front and spotted a face in the back, there were at least two intruders. Becca decided there might be too much curtain movement at the front window so instead moved to the door. A small window filled the top quarter panel. She was forced to stand on tiptoes to see with a downward angle. To the driver's side of the car, a man's head was visible through the window. It was working with a pry bar to open the driver's door. She couldn't allow that.

Becca placed a hand on the knob but stopped before opening it. She had no cover to protect her from the second person. She ran toward the short hall where the bedrooms were located and chose the farthest one to give her the best angle.

Through the sheer curtain with a floral pattern, she could make out the form of a man squatting next to the car with the pry bar inserted into the door frame near the base of the window. He had created a gap and was inserting a long slender tool to unlock the door. He was close to getting inside.

She slid inside the curtain and slid the window up. It was a newer double-hung vinyl window, and after unlocking, it slid easily with little noise. A screen covered the window. She feared the noise it might make and the time to lift it without alerting the man. Instead, she took out her knife, made an incision, and cut out a square.

Outside, the man was unaware of her actions as he popped open the door. It made noise which made him freeze for a moment. She slid the barrel of her handgun through the gap in the screen, lined up the shot and fired as he leaned inside to work on the steering column. Her shot hit him in the butt. He howled and jumped, smacking his head on the column.

Clutching his butt with both hands, he crawled out of the car and ran. She could have killed him but was so pleased with her shot, and knowing the pain he'd be in for a long time, she decided to let him go.

That might have been a mistake, however, when seconds later, bullets rained on the window shattering the glass. Becca ducked back as glass splinters went flying. The shooter had no angle to hit her. His obvious intent was to keep her from shooting again.

Another shot was fired but did not come in her direction. She wondered where Jin was. Becca ran from the room and into the kitchen. She reached the rear door and edged it open. She was forced to open the storm door to get a peek at the neighboring house. On the ground behind the house was the body of another man. Jin was at work.

Becca ducked out of the house and ran to the far side away from the shooter, working her away around to the side and stopping at the front corner. She peered around to the front and spotted two men moving toward a large white delivery truck. One supported the other as they hobbled along. Jin darted out from the far side of the other house and closed on the two men.

"Jin. No," she called, but he was already in motion. She sprinted toward him as he sliced into the unwounded man. He went down, blood spurting from his severed throat. The second man fell and tried to crawl away, pleading. "No. Please. Don't."

Becca closed the distance fast as Jin advanced on the defenseless man. Why did she care? They tried to rob them. Yet, for some reason, she did. Perhaps it was that he was wounded already or that they were in retreat and no longer a threat. She had no answer, only that she didn't want Jin to kill him.

"Jin," she shouted. This time he stopped and looked at her. She pulled up next to him. "Let him go." She glanced at the other man. His body still twitched as the last drops of life pumped from his parted artery.

Chapter Twenty-Seven

Jin looked confused. "Mistake."

She nodded. "Maybe." She squatted a few feet from the whimpering man. "Please. I don't want to die."

"I'll make you a deal. Information for your life."

"With this bullet wound, I'm going to die anyway."

"Okay. Fair enough. That's true. You will die without medical assistance. We can give you that if you talk."

"You'll kill me anyway."

"Well, let's say that's true. Wouldn't you rather it be quick instead of the prolonged agony of an infection that ravages your body? One way offers hope, the other pain."

"Wh-what do you want to know?"

"I'll make it easy on you. I just want to know if anyone else is going to come that we have to worry about. Tell me the truth and I promise medical help and food. My word may not mean much to you, but it does to me. You will not be harmed."

"Will you let me go?"

Becca frowned and looked at Jin. He lifted one eyebrow as if wanting to know the answer himself. "I'll tell you what. We will be leaving here in another day or so. I will let you go when we leave. That way, you can't run off and bring back a larger party."

He didn't speak.

"I'm guessing you don't have many others where you're from, otherwise you wouldn't worry about dying from the wound. Someone would be able to help you. Where you're shot it shouldn't take much to dig out the bullet and wrap the wound. The problem will be infection and if you have the antibiotics to treat it. All I need to know is how many others are there and will they come looking for you. I don't even need to know where they are."

He refused to give them up.

That fact alone told her that others existed, otherwise he'd just lie and say he was alone. "Okay. I tried to do it the nice way. Say a prayer." She stood. "He's all yours, Jin."

Jin flicked open his knife with a flourish and took a step forward. By the slowness of his movements, Becca guessed he was intensifying on the man's fear. It worked.

The man scooted back, holding one hand up. "No. No. Please. Don't kill me. I'll tell you."

Jin took another step and made circles with the blade. His eyes shone a sinister glint.

The man turned his pleading gaze on Becca. "Please. I'll tell you. There're four others. They won't come looking. I swear. They're no threat."

Jin stopped and winked at Becca. Becca smiled. The man was good. "Why won't they come?"

"For one, they don't have a vehicle. We took the only one."

"And for two?"

"Ah, well, they're all women."

Becca bristled. "Excuse me!"

"No offense. Honest. It's just, well, one of them is pregnant. One is a little, ah, incompetent. One is the pregnant woman's four-year-old daughter and the other is a teenage girl."

Becca drew in a long breath and released it in a gush. "You have a child and a pregnant woman? Are they able to defend themselves?"

The pregnant woman can, but she's close to her due date. The one young woman has been spoiled her whole life and doesn't know how to do much. The teen has a gun, but I'm not sure she could shoot someone."

"And the two dead men?"

"One is the guy who knocked her up. The other is just someone we met along the way."

"Are you related to anyone?"

"Sort of."

"Meaning?"

The pregnant lady is my ex-wife."

Becca rolled her eyes. "Are they someplace safe?"

"Yeah. In a house. We were out scavenging for food and supplies."

"And thought you'd steal ours."

"Hey," he said in a stronger voice. "It's not like it hasn't been done to us."

"Can you drive?"

"Ah, I don't know. Maybe."

"If I let you go, you need to collect them and bring them here."

"Why would I do that?"

"Relax. If I wanted to hurt anyone, I'd start with you."

"I think you already did."

"And yet you're still breathing. Go get them. We have food and supplies that can help. I also know where there's a doctor for your pregnant wife."

"Ex."

"Whatever. It's up to you. If you don't come back, so be it. Have a good life and stay safe." Now, we've wasted enough time with you. Go."

"You're really letting me go?"

"Don't press your luck. If you're still here by the time we finish, you're dead."

To emphasize her words, Jin flicked the knife open again.

They loaded the car with the few things they found in the house and were climbing into the car when the truck appeared down the street. It braked two blocks away. He was probably catching an earful from the women in the truck about trusting them, Becca thought. They got into the car drove to the first street, then she rolled down the window and motioned them to follow.

Jin rounded the corner.

"I'm thinking we take them to Father Bernardo," Becca said.

"Yes. Good plan."

Jin drove past the house they were staying in and turned into the parking lot for St. Joseph's Church. He moved to the back of the lot and the two got out. The truck stopped at the driveway apron, unsure whether to proceed.

Becca motioned them forward, but they did not move. The rear door opened and Father Bernardo looked down at them from the top step. "Visitors. I'm so glad you stopped by. I was just thinking about you."

"Father," Becca said. "We have new members for your flock." She pointed.

Father Bernardo leaned on the wrought-iron railing and looked at the truck. "Who is it?"

"People in need, including a pregnant woman, a child, and a wounded man."

At the announcement of a wounded man, Bernardo looked at her inquisitively.

She shrugged.

The good Father trotted down the stairs and moved up next to Becca. He shielded his eyes with a hand against the overhead sun. "Why have they stopped?"

"I think they're afraid."

"Afraid? Of me or you?"

Becca laughed. "Maybe both."

"Well, we can't have that now, can we?" He walked toward the truck. Becca got instantly nervous. She didn't know these people. Though she didn't think they'd attack, if they did, she vowed to hunt them down and kill them all. She might not be overly religious, but she had great respect for the priest.

She hesitated to pull her gun, not wanting to spook those in the truck. Sensing her unease, Jin moved behind the car and once out of sight, did pull his. Becca felt her chest tighten with the anxiety of the unknown. She narrowed her gaze and tried to see into the truck. The man she wounded was in the driver's seat. That had to be uncomfortable for him.

Father Bernardo walked to the driver's door and looked up. A discussion ensued. Becca saw a woman move up next to the driver and lean over him to see the priest. They talked for several minutes before Father Bernardo stepped back and the truck moved up the drive into the lot.

Becca breathed a sigh of relief. The truck stopped at the far edge of the lot, and the driver's door opened. The man almost fell out. He grabbed the door for support. Becca made no move to help, not wanting to appear as a threat. Once he could stand unaided, he reached a hand up and helped a woman out. She didn't look pregnant, nor did she look like a teenager. Becca assumed she was the incompetent one. The teen came next. After her, a young girl hopped down the steps like she was on some great adventure. The pregnant woman did not appear.

The party moved toward them, all bunched together and clinging to each other. All except the four-year-old, who hopped and ran like she was in a playground. As they came closer, Becca examined each. The teenager was typical of her age and gender. She wore a dingy shirt of some band Becca had never heard of with horizontal tears in several places exposing skin, cut off blue jeans with fringe, a floppy red hat, and a jean jacket vest.

The incompetent one struck an instant sharp chord. The woman looked like the debutante Becca had been a mere six months ago. How Becca loathed who she had been. She was so much more comfortable in her new skin to ever believe she had been truly happy as a snob. The woman was wide-eyed and clung to the wounded man's arm.

Becca imagined she came from a well-to-do family and never had to do anything for herself, let alone try to survive in a post-apocalyptic world.

The man was tall and willowy. His long greasy brown hair hung in clumped strands past his shoulders. He had a patchy beard as if he'd tried to trim it at one time, perhaps with a knife, and gave up. He was in obvious pain with each step he took.

"What about the pregnant one?" Becca asked. "Is she unable to come out?"

The man started to speak, but the teen talked over him. "Nah. She's just too afraid. I think she thinks she's gonna get raped or something. Too late for that." The girl had found gum someplace and cracked it constantly. It was annoying and made Becca want to pry her mouth open and rip the gum and perhaps her tongue from her mouth.

The man frowned at her then said, "So? Now what?"

"Come, my son," Father Bernardo said. "Inside where I might take a look at that wound. Let's try to get you patched up. Becca, dear child. Dig out some food and get the grill going, would you, please? I'm sure they must be hungry. You know where I keep it. Have your friend help you."

Father Bernardo guided the man up the stairs and inside the rectory. The wounded man winced audibly with each step. The debutante walked next to him, more in the way than any assistance.

The teen tried to portray defiant confidence, but Becca could see the fear and insecurity in her eyes. "There's a picnic table out back. Go grab a seat and we'll get some food on."

The girl looked unsure whether to go or not. She swayed from foot to foot. The little girl paid none of them any attention, choosing to walk along the landscaping beams along the side of the church. She had brown curly hair and the light brown skin of a mixed race heritage. Her eyes were blue and her broad, innocent smile infectious.

Becca went inside to the chest freezer and surveyed the contents. The freezer was still well stocked even after their wonderful meal the other day. She found ten burgers and pulled out three. She doubted any of them had a burger since the pandemic struck, so having half of one was still a reward. She also took out a pack of frozen hamburger buns. Outside she found Jin had already lit the grill. She handed him the food, told him to get started, then went back inside for plates and condiments. When she returned, Jin had the frozen patties over the fire and the buns on the top rack to thaw.

Becca set ketchup and mustard on the table along with napkins and paper plates. She waited a few minutes for the burgers to thaw, then took them off the fire and used her knife to cut them in half. The centers were still frozen, but with a little pressure, they parted. She set them back on the grill.

The teen leaned forward, her mouth open and sniffed. "Oh my God. Are those real hamburgers? I mean, not those plant-based things that everyone says tastes just like a real burger but don't even come close?"

"Yep," Jin said. "Real." He mooed.

The teen looked from him to Becca. "Is he for real?"

"Real real," Becca said. "And I'd show him some respect. He could slice you into pieces with no effort, just like I did the burgers."

Jin smiled at the girl and raised his eyebrows a few times.

"Whatever." The girl said.

Chapter Twenty-Eight

While the burgers cooked, Becca walked toward the truck. She kept an eye on the windows for movement, but under the reflected sunlight, was unable to see inside. She reached the driver's door, opened it, and stepped up. She was greeted by a gun inches from her face. "If you know what's good for you, you'll back your ass up and get out of here."

Becca bristled. In a snarl, she said, "And if you know what's good for you, you'll lower that gun before I jam it down your throat and blow that baby out your snatch."

The woman flinched under the harsh tone and hard eyes. "You the one who killed my man?"

"No, but I was there." She softened her tone a bit. "Sorry for your loss."

The woman snorted. "Don't be. Wasn't much of a man. Truth be told, the only reason I was with him was cause he fathered this child and that only happened cause the bastard raped me."

Becca was talking to a medium-height black woman with a pretty but strained face. Her belly was huge, and she looked ready to pop. She also looked formidable. Becca wondered how it was possible for either of the two dead men to have been able to rape her.

The woman winced, and the gun wavered. Becca almost snatched the weapon away from her but decided to wait her out. She clutched at her massive, half exposed belly and stepped back until her legs hit a folding patio chair, and she dropped heavily into it. She lowered the gun as she went into a breathing routine. Once the pain subsided, she said, "Whew! That was a long one." She dragged an arm over her sweat-soaked forehead. "Guess it won't be long now." She blew out a breath. "Can't wait, though I'm a little nervous about having this child without a doctor. No, that ain't true. I'm a lot nervous. Scared even. Not so much for myself, but if something bad happens, what's to become of my Pandora? Who's gonna take care of her? And if my baby survives, who will keep her alive?"

Large tears rolled from her eyes. Becca wondered if she'd ever brought up her concerns with the others in her group. She felt sorry for the woman. "What if I told you I know where there's a doctor?"

The woman's eyes widened, and she wiped away her tears. "For real? This ain't no scam?"

Becca shook her head. We come from a rather large community where there's not only a doctor and nurses but a hospital, too."

"Get out. Around here? We been all around this area and save for them creeps at the old prison we ain't seen nothing like that."

"It's about two hours east of here. If you want to go, you let me know. Think about it. No pressure, but it will be a whole lot safer giving birth there than in this truck." Becca backed up a step. "Foods ready by now. You need help getting out?"

"Yeah. Maybe. Can you meet me around back?"

Becca stepped out and shut the door. The truck swayed as the woman walked toward the back. The door rolled up. "If you look down, there's a metal ramp that pulls out. It's the best way for me to get out since I kinda waddle when I walk."

Becca saw the ramp. The truck was just like the ones people rented to move when they wanted to save money and do it themselves. She lifted the ramp and pulled backward. The ramp was heavy but not to the point she couldn't move it. However, when she bent to set it down, she lost her grip and it banged on the blacktop.

"That should be good. You ain't gotta set it in those holes. I think I can step down that far."

Becca moved closer and extended a hand for the woman to hold for balance. She thumped down on the ramp, vibrating it. For a moment, Becca feared the woman was going to topple over the edge, but she righted herself and walked down to the parking lot. They moved toward the church. The woman did waddle and moved slow, but Becca matched pace. They came to the picnic table and the woman had to work and maneuver to bring her bulk down. She called to her girl. "Pandora. Pandora quit playing in that dirt and come over here."

From inside the rectory, a scream startled them. Becca smiled. Shamika ran to her mother.

"Must be digging out the bullet," Becca said. "Maybe I should help."

As Jin set the burgers in front of them, Becca entered the rectory and followed the groans and whimpers. She found Father Bernardo standing over the dining room table of the heavily wooded and ornate room with a magnifying glass and tweezers. He seemed flustered.

The woman who accompanied them inside was sprawled in a chair, her head hanging to the side. She had clearly passed out from the sight of blood and the barbaric surgery. Becca thought she'd never seen a human that pale before.

"Oh, dear child, can you help me? When I insert the tweezers, I can feel the bullet but can't see it through all the blood."

"Have you ever taken a bullet out of someone, Father?"

"Well, no, I guess that's a skill and an experience I lack."

"Then allow me." She stepped next to the priest and gently hip-checked him out of the way.

"Wait. What?" the injured man sputtered.

"Oh, don't worry. I've seen butts before." She was trying to distract him from what she was about to do. She took out her knife. Then pressed her eye to the magnifying glass.

"That's not what I meant."

"Good. Cause as far as butts go, this one seems to be lacking. Father, take a wad of that tissue and blot the wound." She widened the gap of the tweezers. They weren't made for bullet width.

"What do you mean, lacking?"

With the hole momentarily clear, she spotted the bullet. She knew she wasn't getting it out unless she widened the hole, which is why she wanted him distracted. "Yeah, it's kind of flat. There's so little meat back here I'm surprised the bullet didn't pass right through."

"It is not—ahh!" he screamed and bucked as she made a slice in the meat all the way to the bullet. He kept screaming while he tried to talk, making the word unintelligible.

She shoved him hard back down to the table and worked the tweezers into the wound. His scream rose to a piercing level. "Father, hold his legs."

Bernardo moved to the end of the table and fought to catch the flailing legs. Once he had them under control, Becca leaned an elbow on the man's back and wiggled the tweezers deeper until she hit something solid. She prayed it wasn't a bone. After several failed attempts, she managed to snag the bullet and pull. It moved but slipped. Two more tries brought the bullet to the surface where it pulled free with a sucking sound. The man stopped moving. Had she killed him? She bent to look at his face. His eyes were open and rolled up. *I did kill him.* She placed a hand on his chest and felt the rise and fall. With a relieved breath, she realized he had fainted. Good. That was for the best. She had to work fast before he woke.

Fifteen minutes later, after spreading antibiotic cream around the opening and using white thread and needle, she stitched the man closed and stepped back with a satisfying, "Yeah."

Father Bernardo made the sign of the cross. "You didn't kill him, did you?"

"No, Father. I promise. He'll wake in a bit and be in a lot of pain, but he should recover as long as infection doesn't take hold."

"Do you have medication to combat infection?"

"Not sure. I'll have to hunt through the medicines we found and see if any will work."

"Well, child, you did blessed good work here today. Well done."

They exited the rectory and were greeted with, "Did you kill him?" in almost unison from the two women. The teen rolled her eyes.

"He's resting," Becca said. "We'll give him some time. Remember, one of those burgers is for him. He's going to need the protein."

A disgusted and disappointed look crossed the teen's face.

Father Bernardo said, "You didn't cook enough for everyone."

"Father, we didn't want to impose and eat up your food. You're going to need that to get through the winter months."

"Nonsense." He turned and went inside, coming back moments later with five more burgers, a pot with water, and a bag of frozen corn. "Here now, my good man. Cook these up for yourself and Becca. We'll split up the rest to whoever's still hungry."

Jin pointed. "You?"

"Yes. If there's enough when everyone is finished."

Jin said, "Enough."

Becca smiled. He might not be religious, but he too had respect for the priest. He'd see to it Father Bernardo got some of his own food.

While they waited for the food, Father Bernardo went inside and revived the debutante. She did not look well. He had to support her every step until he sat her on the picnic table bench. She laid her head on her arms and moaned. Becca was finding a lot to smile about this day.

Jin slid a whole burger to Bernardo and raised a hand to quell his objection. "You eat." It came out as an order, and Bernardo complied. He gave one to Becca, kept one for himself and divided the other two in half, setting one in front of the moaning woman, one in front of the teen and two in front of the mother and her child.

The pregnant woman said, "I'm not sure she can eat another. Best you give this one to someone else."

Becca liked her for doing that. She could have hoarded it but chose to be courteous and share. Becca pushed the plate back. "Let her eat what she can. The rest we'll give to the wounded guy when he wakes.

They talked while they ate, and Becca questioned the pregnant woman, whose name was Shamika.

"Pandora and me came from Cleveland. We was trying to get to Chicago, where my people is. My car got stolen when we was less than an hour from home. Men just stepped into the street, made me stop, then dragged me from the car. I was scared 'cause I thought they was gonna take off with my baby in back, but one of them unbuckled her car seat and set her next to me where they threw me to the ground.

"The man inside, Glen, came by and helped me. We walked for a bit until he found this truck. Along the way, we picked up a few people. At one time we had twelve of us living in that truck. Some died from various reasons, and others just left until you see who remains. Anyway, we just kept driving west, not sure where we was going, but just trying to stay alive."

"You're the first decent people we've met in a long time," the debutante, Debbie, said. "Most everyone else wanted our food or our truck, or—" her voice trailed off.

Becca could imagine what the *or* was. She was an attractive woman and men would have desired her. "Well, we're glad you're here and that you found us. I'm sorry it started off with such violence." She glanced at the teen. "What about you?"

She shrunk in on herself and shrugged. Becca tried to remember her own teen years and how she had been so unsure of herself, but she had never lacked self-confidence as this girl apparently did. Oh, sure, she was full of attitude too, but in a more self-assured way. As she fought to contain the dislike for this girl, she thought, God, how my parents must have hated me. She tried again. "What's your name?"

The teen hesitated, looked at Becca, then away. "Star."

"Star! That's a good name. Is there a story behind it?"

"Ah, yuh! Cause I'm going to be one—a star. Least I was before all this stupid pandemic stuff happened."

The annoying, singsong tone of her voice combined with the attitude grated on Becca.

Shamika said, "Yeah, it's a shame all these people died just to mess up your dreams."

Becca laughed.

The teen rolled her eyes.

Becca said, "What's your talent?"

Star gave her a blank expression.

"You know, the one that was going to make you a star."

"Oh!" the girl, her mood brightening. "I'm a singer."

"A singer! That's great."

Across the table, Shamika's eyes widened and she gave a discreet shake of her head as she mouthed, *No.*

Becca fought the smile. "That's wonderful. Maybe you'll sing for us one day."

Shamika spoke quickly as if to change the subject before Star began to sing. "What about this community hospital you been talking about? Can we go there?"

Before she could answer, the sound of a loud engine echoed down the street.

Becca looked at Father Bernardo, who shrugged. "Hurry, everyone inside. Now."

Jin was already moving toward the police car. He jumped in and drove it onto the grass behind the building out of sight from the street. From the increased volume of the engine, they didn't have time to move the truck. Jin sprinted behind the garage. Becca ushered everyone inside. Father Bernardo helped Pandora up the stairs while the teen took Shamika's hand. Debbie appeared ready to faint again.

Becca waited on the top step and peered around the building. Seconds later, two identical, souped-up black pickups with extended cabs, tandem rear wheels, and lightbars drove side by side down the street. As they passed, she let out a relieved breath only to suck it in and hold it seconds later at the sound of screeching of tires. The trucks reversed and stopped in the street below the driveway. Four men were inside each cab.

"Please, drive away," Becca said to herself. But it was not to be. A hollow and sinking feeling filled her stomach as one by one, the trucks turned up the driveway.

Chapter Twenty-Nine

Bobby's eyes fluttered open. For a moment he was confused about where he was. A dark figure stood off to one side, his back to him. He peered through a parted white curtain hung from the ceiling. He watched the figure for a while, letting memories come back to him. Finally, he said, "Lincoln?"

The large black man turned, then displayed a wide smile. "You're awake. That's great. Let me go get Doc." He slid through the seam in the curtains and disappeared. He could hear the murmuring voices, then the curtains parted again, and Doc entered, followed by Lincoln and Lynn.

"Okay, before everyone starts talking, allow me to do what I need to first."

Lincoln and Lynn exchanged glances but stayed out of her way and silent.

"Glad you're awake. Other than shot, how do you feel?"

"Sore."

"Where?"

"Down here." He pointed toward his lower abdomen.

"Okay. Anywhere else?"

"I have a slight headache."

"Okay. And?"

I guess that's it."

"No nausea?" She stuck a thermometer in his mouth. He shook his head. When she withdrew it, she said, "Slightly elevated temp. We'll have to monitor that." She lifted his gown, undid the bandage and examined her handiwork. "This looks good. A little seepage, but it's dry. The stitches look good." She left to get some fresh bandages.

"Rule still applies. I'm still talking to him." She returned and while she rebandaged the wound, said, "Here's the situation. You had a gunshot wound to the lower left abdomen. It did penetrate a kidney. I have repaired the kidney and closed the wound. I am not worried about the wound healing, but I am worried about the kidney. You cannot afford an infection there. I have started you on meds to combat that and hopefully, we have a good start in the fight against infection. We should know more by tomorrow."

"What happens if there is an infection?"

"We'll keep you on the meds and monitor your progress. If the infection continues, I may have to open you back up and go in to evaluate the problem."

"How long will I have to stay?"

"Haven't you been listening? It depends on infection. Your stay has no set time. If no infection develops, you'll be out of here fast. Maybe three days. If there is an infection that we can't corral, it may stretch on for a couple of weeks."

"Weeks? No."

"Hey. I'm not in the mood to argue. I'm the doctor. What I say goes. You want to get out of here faster, don't get an infection." She turned to leave. "He's all yours."

"Wait. Doc."

She stopped and looked at him, clearly annoyed though he was unsure of what he did to make her that way. "Did you see the stuff we brought back? We found a lot of medical stuff."

She softened and rubbed her eyes. "Yes, and some of it is useful."

"What about that oxygen concentrator thing. Is that what you needed?"

She sighed. "No. We need a ventilator."

"What's the difference?"

She took a step closer. "A ventilator actually forces air into the lungs of a person who cannot breathe on their own. The machine you brought is helpful in that it creates air, but it's for people capable of breathing. They just need help doing it. The most important thing we're lacking is the IV bags with solution. We are getting extremely low. There is some potentially good news though. Myron is awake."

Bobby tried to sit up at the news. It was a huge mistake. The sharp pain in his side caused him to cry out and slump back.

"Easy boy. You'll ruin my work and I'll have to start over." She pushed him down and lifted the bandage. She studied the stitches under a stern glare. Satisfied everything was still all right, she gave him an annoyed look. "Anyway, he's still not strong enough to do anything on his own but is showing signs of improvement. Hopefully, soon we can take him off monitors and IVs, which means there's more for your father. Anyway. Rest. You felt what happens if you get too excited."

"Okay, Doc. Sorry."

"Don't be sorry. Just stop getting shot."

She exited, leaving him wondering what he did to offend her.

From a distance, Doc called, "I'm stepping out for some air. Don't stay too long."

The door banged open and she was gone.

"What did I do?" Bobby asked.

"She's overworked and upset about a few things," Lincoln said. "You don't need to worry about it. Believe me, it's not you as much as it is us."

"Why? What's going on?"

"You don't need to worry about it. You just rest and recover, but a little later, we are going to move you."

Lynn said, "There are some things going on that we need to be sure the patients are protected. We're handling it."

"I take it Doc doesn't approve of how you're handling it?"

"That's affirmative," Lincoln said.

"And, since you're not being forthcoming with details, it must involve my dad. Has there been a move to take him off life support?"

They looked at each other, and Lincoln shrugged. "Might as well. He might be of some help."

Lynn said, "Supposedly, Edwards and Merchant are on their way here to kill your father."

Bobby nodded and waited for more and when it didn't come, he prodded, "So, you're taking steps to stop them. With our new safety measures, they shouldn't be able to get on campus."

They exchanged glances again, this time more nervous.

Lincoln said, "We're not going to stop them. We want them to come."

Bobby looked from one to the other as the connections were made. "Ah! No wonder Doc's upset. Reasons?"

Lincoln shifted uncomfortably. "Several. If we let them in and capture them, we don't have to be on constant guard for them. If we don't get them now and somewhere down the road we let down our guard, it might open an opportunity for them to accomplish their goal later."

Lynn picked up. "Or they may ambush our people off campus."

"They already kidnapped Ruth."

"What?" He stopped himself from sitting up too fast, remembering the pain the last attempt caused. "Have you—"

"Yes," Lincoln said. "We rescued her. We have someone watching the house where she was being held. As of now, Edwards and Merchant still believe they have her as leverage. She's being kept out of sight."

"So, in essence, you're using my dad as bait."

Lincoln averted his gaze and rubbed at his whiskered face.

Lynn said, "Yes." Her voice was cold and hard. "Do you have an objection?"

Bobby thought about that for several moments. "No. It's what Dad would do. I have one change to your plan. I'm staying." Before they could air their objections, Bobby said, "If this place is empty of patients, it will look suspicious. If the goal is to lure them in where they can be taken without threat to others, then it has to look normal and normal means patients." He raised a hand. "Hold up. Before you shoot the idea down. How else were you going to get to these guys before they got to my dad? This way, you have someone on the inside who can help. An extra gun if needed."

"An extra person to worry about if there is a shootout," Lynn said. "Not to mention one who is already wounded."

Lincoln said, "I'm going to be in one of the beds. As soon as they enter, Milo and a team will surround the building. They'll be trapped."

"With only you to protect my dad. Even trapped, they'll still have him as a hostage or to kill. No. Sorry. With my dad unable to speak for himself, as his son, I do not give you permission to use him in this way."

"You mean not unless you're part of it," Lincoln said.

Lynn turned away. "This is crazy. It's bad enough we're risking your father's life, but to involve you too? No. We need to rethink this idea and just take them as they enter. We still have enough on them with the attempts on yours and Jarrod's life and the kidnapping of Ruth. We can still have a trial."

"A trial? That's what this is about. Accountability?"

"Bobby," Lincoln said, "you have to understand. We're at a delicate time in our development. We have to be seen as being open and fair. There is a major split within our ranks that can only be healed if they believe everyone is treated fairly. A fair trial with the entire community involved is the best way to accomplish bridging that gap."

"I do understand that, but you're risking my dad's life to make that happen." He glanced at them. "I can understand why you might not care," he said to Lynn. To Lincoln, he said, "but you're supposed to be his friend."

Hey!" Lincoln said.

Lynn gasped. Her jaw clenched. Fire lit her eyes, then tears quelled it and her face melted with emotion. She turned and fled the hospital.

"That was uncalled for—on both accounts."

Bobby felt guilty but used it to fire his anger rather than seek absolution. "If you plan on going through with this plan, I am staying to protect my dad. You may not think so, but this is a life worth dying for. That's all any of us wants in this crazy world—to be able to have a life to die for. That's what I thought we were building here. Someplace where everyone looks out for everyone else. But look what happens the moment you try to reestablish the old-world order. Things break down as they always did before and apparently always will to the end of time.

"My dad would stand up for, fight for, or give his life for anyone in this community, and has done so on many occasions, regardless whether that person liked him or not. Now, the first time we have a problem under the new order, they want to throw my dad to the dogs. He deserves better. He deserves everyone's respect."

Bobby hadn't realized he was crying until the tear dropped from his chin.

Lincoln frowned. "Okay, Bobby. You're right. About all of it. This community owes your father for its inception. However, many believe he was responsible for bringing the danger and the battles to our home. Recent events have left some hard feelings that we are working to soften. It takes time and sometimes doing things you might not like or approve but know this, I consider your dad to be a good friend. He is someone I look up to and respect. But if putting his life in jeopardy helps to resolve some of those festering issues, you better believe he'd be the first one to say, *let's do this.*

He turned and walked away, then stopped and faced him, "But boy, you better believe he'd also be the first one to tell you how disrespectful you were to Lynn, a woman, despite their current situation he still loves." He pointed at Bobby. "You owe her an apology."

He left, leaving Bobby feeling angry but small.

Chapter Thirty

Darlene walked across the street with her father doing his best to keep up. "Dad. I'm going. We left people out there and they need to be found. Becca deserves to know that her brother has been shot and-and, that it was all my fault."

"Darlene," her father pleaded. "You cannot do this alone. You are not in your right mind. You are filled with grief and guilt and a need to be forgiven or perhaps even to be punished. Yes, Rebecca needs to be told, but it shouldn't be by you. You are too emotionally distraught at the moment. Your arm is still in a sling, and you have pain medications in your blood. Now is not the time to be taking a long drive. Let someone else go in your place."

She whirled on him. "No, Dad. It has to be me. It is the right thing to do."

"Then at least take others with you. The danger you and Bobby faced may still be out there. You should not face it by yourself. That is foolishness and emphasizes my point about not being in your right mind."

He glanced to the right and spotted Lincoln leaving the hospital. "Sir, please talk some sense into my daughter before she gets herself killed."

"What's the problem?"

"She wants to go tell Rebecca that it was her who shot Bobby."

Lincoln glanced at father and daughter. Both were determined to have their way, and both were too emotionally involved to listen to reason. The young woman had just been released from the hospital a short time before and still wore a sling. As if reading his thoughts,

Darlene slid the sling over her head and moved her arm. She tried to hide the wince.

He ran through the options, none of which included her going alone. If he told her no, she was very much like Becca and would find a way to go anyway. Perhaps even sneaking off during the night when they already had one stressful event planned. If he said yes, her father would never forgive him, especially if something happened to her. He was screwed either way.

On the other hand, she knew exactly where Becca and Jin were. He noted she held the key to the van. It had already been unloaded, so he couldn't use that as a stalling technique. He could lie about the van still being worked on, but one of Milo's crew had changed out the damaged radiator and the van was running well. Besides, Darlene would just find another vehicle.

He wiggled his fingers for her to give up the key. Instantly, her face glowed with rage. Her temper was almost as bad as Becca's. "Unh-uh! Don't give me attitude. Give me the key."

She slapped it into his palm and pivoted. "Fine, I'll walk, but I am going."

"You can go."

"What?" Elijah sputtered.

"What?" Darlene said, facing him.

"You can go, but you have to take two others with you, and you have to return today, with or without Becca. Those are my terms. Take them or leave them."

"I'll take them." Her face was suddenly flush with excitement. She reached for the key, but Lincoln pulled them back.

"Nope. Not until I see your two traveling partners and have a chance to speak to them."

She nodded, spun, and ran toward the camp to recruit her team. As she did, he noticed she slipped her arm back through the sling.

Elijah was beet red. Lincoln feared the man might have a stroke. "Elijah, listen."

"How dare you override me, her father. You have no right."

"Listen, she was going to go anyway. You know that's true."

The man ceased his rant. His shoulders slumped as the truth of Lincoln's statement rammed home.

"This way, I'm forcing her to take others with her and she has a time requirement. She also is the only one who knows the exact location of where Becca and Jin are. That makes it easier."

Elijah regrouped and pointed a threatening finger at Lincoln. "If something happens to her, you will answer for it." He turned and hobbled away.

"Man," Lincoln muttered, "this job just doesn't pay enough."

Darlene came jogging up with two young men in their twenties who Lincoln knew by sight but struggled recalling their names. "Okay. Here's my team." She held out her hand for the key.

Lincoln ignored her and spoke to the men. "Here's the deal. You go to where Becca and Jin are. You pick them up and come back."

"They'll have things to load," Darlene said. "A lot of things."

Lincoln paused at the interruption, ready to explode at her. "If there's something to load, do that, then come right back. If there's trouble, things aren't as important as lives. Leave everything and come back. You protect each other and don't take any side trips, or you'll be doing whatever the worse duty is here for a month. You understand?"

The two men looked at each other then nodded. One said, "Yes, sir."

"That's What I like to hear," Lincoln said. He glared at the other man until he said, "Ah, yes-yes, sir."

"Okay. You have your orders. Do not let her out of your sight." He looked at Darlene. "Stay out of trouble."

"Oh, yes, sir." Hers came out sarcastically and was accompanied by a salute.

He frowned but gave her the key. She started to run, then stopped. In a more sincere voice, she said, "Tell my dad I'll be back and not to worry."

"He's a father. No words will ever stop him from worrying. Just don't give him anything to worry about, or you may never get off campus again."

She nodded and they climbed into the van and were gone.

As the van disappeared around the corner, Lincoln had second thoughts. There was already enough going on tonight. He lifted the radio and called for the lead guard at the western gate.

"Yes, sir."

"You see the white van approaching?"

"Yes, sir."

"It's okay to let it through, but when it comes back tonight. Hold it there until I clear it. Understood?"

"Ah, yes, sir."

He ended the call and scrapped the antenna across the stubble under his chin. He had a lot to do before tonight. It was time to get prepared.

Chapter Thirty-One

Becca glanced back to see what might have drawn their attention. Her eyes settled on the steam rising from the pot boiling the corn. Her heart fell. They were coming. Nothing she could do about it now but prepare to defend.

The first truck angled toward the parked truck Shamika and friends had arrived in. The second came at a slow pace along the side of the church, coming toward the rectory.

Becca pressed against the brick wall next to the door, steadied her breathing, and began plotting her moves. Once they came even with her position, she had to unleash a withering barrage that took out at least two of them. It was up to her to keep the pressure on and prevent them from getting off many good shots while Jin found a way to deal with the other truck.

She wished she had more firepower and glanced at the police car parked behind the rectory. Did she have time to reach it and pull out a rifle or even a spare magazine? She only had the one in her gun. It was full though she'd have to make every shot count.

In the distance, she spotted Jin darting across the property next door. She plotted his movements and figured he'd come up from the street side to take the other truck from behind.

She heard two doors open and assumed from the distance and direction of the sound it was the truck near Shamika's truck. The engine noise of the near truck drew closer. Becca fought to calm her racing heart and lifted her gun hand, ready for the first shot.

The grill of the truck came into view. It moved at a snail's pace, at least to her. Her nerves were on fire and she struggled to keep her body from shaking. She needed a steady hand to make her first shot count. She had no idea who they were or their intentions, but if she hesitated to find out, it might be too late.

The long black hood crawled by as if it would never end. As the base of the windshield appeared, she pulled the hammer back and added pressure to the trigger. The dash came into view, then the steering column. She didn't want to shoot too soon. She needed a line of sight at the back seat before she fired.

The truck stopped before the driver was in view. Come on! Her legs twitched with nervous energy, anxious to be in motion. The front passenger leaned out the window. "Anything?"

One of the men from the other truck said, "No one's here, but it's obvious someone has been recently."

The passenger said, "Looks like we interrupted a picnic. That's perfect cause I'm hungry."

"I hope they got enough for all of us."

The second man out of the truck said, "I hope it's a female cook. I'm more hungry for some company."

The men laughed.

Now, Becca had no qualms about pulling the trigger. The truck moved forward and the driver's face came into sight. It was a big, hairy head, with a wide sideways grin. His eyes were angled toward the picnic table and the grill. Becca stayed still, not wanting to be seen too soon. The frame between the front and rear door came next. *Just a few more feet,* she pleaded.

Whether she moved or the driver caught something in his periphery, he turned his head and the smile vanished as his jaw dropped. He was in the process of ducking when her bullet plowed through the side of his head.

She stepped forward and triggered one shot after another. The passenger was hit in the leg, hip, and chest before he could raise the AR he held across his lap. The driver's side passenger ducked below the front seat and stuck a handgun out the window. He fired blindly to keep her back. The passenger side rear door opened and the man sitting there slipped out using the truck for cover.

Shots chipped away at the brick near there as two of the men from the second truck ran toward the building with their ARs blasting. If she stayed on the porch, she was dead. Becca darted for the far side and vaulted the railing, landing awkwardly on the grass five feet below. She rolled on her side and came up running with a slight twinge of pain in her left ankle.

Becca sprinted for the far corner of the building, reaching it before shots followed there. They were still being fired but more to keep her from shooting than to hit. For the moment, they had no idea where she was, just that she was on the move.

She rounded the corner and scanned the area. A few possibilities to hide existed, however none for the long haul. She chose to duck behind the massive air conditioning unit, hoping to take one of her pursuers down. If they were smart, they'd split their forces, sending someone around the street side of the church and trap her. Perhaps it was smarter to keep running. The length of the rectory combined with the church made that a long distance to go unprotected.

As she settled in and lined up her shot, she wondered what Jin was doing. She hoped like a good Euchre partner, she could rely on him to take one. Of course, in Euchre, you only lost the hand, not your life, if your partner let you down. She knew Jin could be counted on to take his share.

Becca decided to duck and stay hidden rather than shoot as soon as a target came around the corner. The shot was long for her handgun and she had to make sure of hitting at least one pursuer. She crouched low and focused her ears on running steps, heavy breathing, or whispered voices. The wait wasn't long, but it wasn't any sound that gave her notice. It was the rising hairs on the back of her neck like some supernatural alarm system that told her it was time.

She popped up and acquired a target twenty-five feet away. Her opponent already had his AR up and sighted on the unit. He loosed a barrage as she fired. The difference was she had some cover, though not perfect and he had none.

His rounds tore up and through the unit. She fired as fast as she could pull the trigger, knowing she had to get on target before he did or she'd be cut in half. He grunted, staggered back, and stared at her with a stunned expression. He glanced down at his chest to see the red blossom spreading.

Becca took the opportunity to fire once more. The shooter dropped like he no longer had muscle tone in his legs. As soon as he went down, the next man was firing. Becca dove to the ground and pressed low to the brick wall of the rectory. She covered her head more because she had nothing else to use as cover than for any actual protection. The rounds walked toward her, pinging and ricocheting off the air conditioner.

He was moving and keeping her pinned until one of the rounds found her. For a fraction, the bullets stopped. She heard the click of a dropped magazine and realized she had seconds to fire before a new one was slammed home. She popped up, aimed and saw the AR leveled at her. A wicked smile creased the man's face as he knew he had her. He had faked her into believing he had changed the magazine. He had her. She knew it and he knew it.

"Works every time," he said and tightened his finger on the trigger.

Blood flew from his mouth. His head rocked, his knees bent, and he fell. Behind him stood Jin. He had come through for his partner. He waved for her to come. "Hurry." He turned and ran back in the direction she had come. Before she reached the corner, shots were fired from behind her. A man shouted a name, then he flung curses at her that were lost when she made the turn.

They ran toward the first truck. Becca saw two bodies at the second truck. Jin opened the passenger door and tore the AR from the still dying man's hand. After checking the magazine, he said, "Two," and pointed toward the street. "You," he pointed toward the back of the rectory. "Me go." He didn't wait for her to acknowledge or question. He sprinted toward the front of the church.

Becca ran around the front of the truck and opened the driver's door. The dead man had an AR on the floor sticking up between the two seats. She climbed up and leaned over the body. The smell hit her hard. The man's bowel had released upon his death. She snagged the barrel and pulled the AR out, then ran around the back of the truck as she heard angry words uttered about her.

"I swear, I'm gonna kill that bitch. I'm gonna make her suffer."

Was he talking to himself or was another man with him? She stalked around the tailgate and squatted, aiming along the side of the truck. The man only had two options. Going between the rectory and the truck, which was tight, or around the front, which was death. She waited patiently, but by the time she thought he might appear, he still hadn't and she began to get twitchy.

Becca wanted desperately to lift her head to peek and find where he was but having fallen for one trick already, she wasn't about to do so again. Plus, she knew Jin was close enough to save her.

The man wasn't muttering to himself anymore. Had she done something to alert him or had the hairs on his neck given him warning? She tried to relax her breathing to force a calm she no longer felt. She could not hold the squat much longer. Her legs were beginning to shake from the effort.

She had to find him. Though it made her vulnerable if her opponent came around the truck, Becca lowered slowly to a level that allowed her to see beneath the truck's high clearance. No feet. Where was he? Behind the tire? She lifted back to her squat, the tension making her breathing feel strained.

Shots came from the opposite side of the church. The sharp crack caused her to jump and almost fire a round. She took a chance and lowered to look under the truck. The man was not in sight. Where had he gone. Perhaps he ran around the garage to come out on the other side of the parking lot like Jin had done. She swung her gaze in that direction. She didn't see him, but if he did come out from there she was in the open. Where else could she hide?

Pushing back into a crouch, she duckwalked along the side of the truck keeping the AR up and ready to fire. She made it just behind the passenger door when movement made her duck and pull back. The shooter was right there—Where? Wasn't he at the front of the truck? That's where she caught the movement. He should be in sight by now. With the rifle aimed forward, she glanced up and to the left. There he was. He wasn't in front of the truck. He was up on the porch where she had been, waiting for her to show herself. She had caught his reflection in the big side mirror.

He had his AR sighted near the back of the truck. He had no idea she had moved. She crept toward the hood and rounded the oversize front bumper. Just before she stood to take her shot, her elbow hit the bumper, announcing her presence.

He turned and they both fired wildly. Becca ducked, but the shooter had no cover, so opted to rip open the storm door and push through the inner door of the rectory.

To Becca's great fear, the shooter was now inside with a host of possible victims and hostages.

Chapter Thirty-Two

Without hesitation, Becca bolted up the stairs, fearing for those inside. She had enough control not to push through the door. She stepped to the side and elbowed the storm door open. The inner door had been shut but not closed. With a toe, she nudged it open and raised the AR.

Screams came from further down the hall, just past the kitchen.

"Shut up all of you, or I swear I'll kill you. All I want is the bitch who killed my friend. Now, all of you stand up."

"Son," Father Bernardo said, "if you just calm down and lower your gun, I'm sure we can help you."

The man fired a shot evoking more screams. Becca feared the gunman shot Father Bernardo.

"You're not listening to me. Do as I say, or the next shot goes into someone's head."

Becca eased inside, taking her steps with slow precision and caution. An archway to the right led into the dining room, which connected with the living room. The hallway in front of her also led to the living room as well as the stairs leading to the bedrooms.

Shamika said, "Don't you point that thing at my daughter."

"Then move forward." His voice was more of a growl now, telling Becca he was close to killing someone.

She moved to the archway to the dining room and stopped at a position where she could see down the hall. The wounded man was no longer on the table. Only the remnants of his surgery remained, the bloody towels and instruments.

"That's right. Everyone stand still. You two on the ends curl back a bit, so you're in a semi-circle. Perfect. Now we wait for the bitch."

You do that, asshole, cause the bitch is coming for you.

Becca took a quick peek around the archway. The partial wall of the archway leading from the dining room to the living room obscured full vision. She could see the teen-age girl and Shamika but only the arm of the gunman and none of the others. The gunman was using them as human shields. That added to Becca's already high rage.

She slid along the dining room wall to the partial wall. She caught sight of her target in a mirror mounted to the wall above the fireplace to her right. He shot glances toward the dining room, but his main focus was on the archway leading to the hall. Somehow, she needed a distraction.

Father Bernardo said, "Son, please put the gun down. These good people mean you no harm. They aren't even armed. At least let Shamika and her daughter go. They are no threat to you."

The gunman rammed the point of the barrel against the priest's head, causing him to cry out. The others stifled cries of their own, not wanting to be the next one hurt.

The debutante next to Father Bernardo was white. In the reflection, Becca saw the woman's eyes roll back, and her legs gave way. She fell in a heap.

The gunman yelled, "Hey!" and swung his gun toward her. Becca had her distraction. She stepped out with her gun leveled. She didn't have to motion for Shamika to move. She leaned on her daughter and the teenage girl, driving them all to the floor. The gunman whirled toward Becca but was too late. She walked the rounds up his chest to his face. He was blown back from the impacts, landing on the sofa behind him, then slid to the floor.

Jin came into the room from the hallway with his gun up. She never heard him enter the house but wasn't surprised he was in a position to help.

Once the screaming stopped, Becca said, "It's all right. He's down. You're safe. Everyone get up and move out of this room."

Though she didn't need to, she kept her gun trained on the body as she reached a hand down to assist Shamika up. "Nice job," she told the pregnant woman.

Shamika glanced at the dead man. "Back at ya."

Jin dragged the body outside and placed it in the bed of the nearest truck. Then he collected all the bodies, stripped them of their gear and drove the truck north out of town. Becca would have offered to follow him to drive him back, but he was gone before she realized. Instead, she stayed to help ease the stress and tension back to a semi-normal level.

Once everyone had settled down, they moved the forgotten food inside to finish eating. Father Bernardo was ashen but gathered cleaning supplies and went into the living room to clean up the mess Becca made. She offered to help but he said, "Thank you," his voice quivered, "but I'd rather do it myself if you don't mind."

Becca backed out of the room, upset that she had brought pain to this good man. She had warned him the violence and brutality of this new world was coming, but that did little to quell her sorrow at being part of that indoctrination. Not in the mood to eat, Becca went outside for some air and to allow her own adrenaline rush to ebb.

She found the pile of weapons and gear Jin had left next to the stairs and moved them to the car leaving extra magazines for the ARs. She sat on the second step and began thumbing rounds from the near empty magazines to fill the nearly full ones. While she worked, her mind wandered to the recent gunfight. So much death and destruction. If only it hadn't come during their stay here. She prayed it didn't change Father Bernardo's outlook on life. This mad, out of control world needed more calming voices like his.

As her thoughts drifted, they eventually turned toward her brother. *Bobby should have been back by now.* She stopped loading. *How long had it been since he left?* A chill of premonition raced through her. Either Darlene was still having her way with Bobby, or they were in trouble. Knowing her brother, she was betting on the latter.

Jin sat on the top step. She glanced up, surprised he was back so soon. As if reading her mind, he said, "We go."

She nodded. "Yep. Let's load what we can in the car and the pickup trucks, so we're ready to move. We can come back for the rest. If Bobby isn't back by the time we're done, we go."

Jin stood, stretched, and said, "Eat first, then load." He winked at Becca and went inside the rectory. Becca sat stunned for an instant then broke out in a loud laugh. She got up and went inside to join him.

Jin finished eating first and took one of the trucks back to the house they'd been staying in to begin loading. He was gone before Becca got outside. She glanced down at the unfinished loading job and decided to complete that task before following Jin.

Exhausted from their ordeal, most of the others had settled into naps after clearing the dishes and cleaning up the mess. She could hear someone moving around inside and was sure it was Father Bernardo. She feared their presence was too much for the old priest. He was pale and looked tired. She wished he would just take a nap like the others but knew that wasn't his way. He'd make sure everyone else was taken care of before he ever thought about himself.

Fifteen minutes later, she heard an engine. She moved up the stairs using the building to shield her from the street, then leaned out to see what was coming. Jin turned the laden pickup into the parking lot and parked between the camper truck and the rectory. He hopped out and walked toward her. Becca moved down the stairs to meet him.

The sound of an engine reached her, growing louder by the second, coming fast. The two moved fast and separated. Jin broke toward the large motor home truck used by their guests.

Becca stopped at the end of the pickup truck next to the rectory, knelt, and aimed her newly reloaded AR toward the street. The engine sound grew. Seconds later, the dirty, battered white van slowed as it passed the driveway. Becca recognized Darlene in the driver's seat, stood, and waved. The van braked, reversed, and drove up. It stopped a few feet away and Darlene leaped from the seat.

"I was just starting to wonder about you guys." Becca stopped when she saw the nervous look on Darlene's face and the sling that supported her bandaged arm. Instantly, the chill returned. "What?" She glanced at the two men exiting the van. "Darlene, where's Bobby?"

At the mention of Bobby's name, Darlene grew more anxious. She stumbled over her words enraging Becca. "Tell me, now."

"Bobby's been shot."

Before Becca could explode, Darlene rushed to finish. "He's all right. I got him back and Doc worked on him. He's in recovery and is fine. Honest." She became aware that tears were falling when one slid off her chin. She wiped at it.

Seeing the anguish Darlene was in, Becca stepped forward and embraced her. She knew Darlene had strong feelings for Bobby and her released emotions emphasized the extent. She held the other girl as she cried. Darlene muttered, "Becca, I'm so sorry."

"He's all right, right? You said he was going to be fine." Then something clicked, and she pushed the other woman back to arm's length. "Wait. What are you sorry for?"

Darlene's face scrunched up as if she was in physical pain. She couldn't look at Becca.

"Darlene, what happened?"

Darlene brushed away her tears. "We were chased by a bunch of men. I think they were from the prison. They trapped us in a house and we had to fight." Her head lowered, and Becca knew something bad was coming. "The battle was moving so fast. I was up front, and Bobby was outside. I was wounded but still functional. Suddenly, I heard sounds from the back of the house. Someone broke in. I was sure if it was Bobby, he would've said something, so I whirled and fired. It was Bobby. I shot Bobby."

Darlene sniffled, but with the confession, her tears stopped flowing. She lifted her head. Becca saw the red-rimmed eyes and wanted to reach out and comfort her but was unable to move. The one thing that kept repeating in her mind was, *she shot Bobby.* It repeated over and over like some tortuous loop. With each replaying, her anger grew. Knowing she had to move or risk attacking Darlene, Becca walked past her without a word.

"Becca," Darlene pleaded.

Becca moved toward Jin. "Use them," she motioned with her head toward the two men who came with Darlene, "to load the van. If the others want to come, have them load stuff too. Caravan back to the farmhouse. I'm going back now." She turned toward the pickup and said over her shoulder, "Try to convince the priest to come to."

She ignored Darlene's pleas as she sat in the truck. The keys were still in the ignition. She gave her a hateful glare as she started the engine. She fed gas, then shifted, squealing the tires in an angry exit.

Her anger had just begun to ebb as twenty minutes later, with the sun setting, she saw the armored truck. More importantly, it saw her.

Chapter Thirty-Three

Becca braked hard as the armored car picked up speed and barreled toward her. With drainage ditches on both sides of the two-lane road, she had little room for error to turn around and not much time. The heavy truck was a quarter-mile away and closing fast. She was forced to reverse to gain more room to complete the turn, then shoved the pedal down hard. The truck was slow to accelerate. She urged it on by rocking hard in the seat. "Come on, you pig, move."

A glance in the side mirror showed the armored car still closing. They were less than a hundred yards apart. The truck's speed edged up at a steady but excruciatingly slow rate. She was sure the truck could outrun the weighted armored car, but she had to get the speed up first and it was taking too long.

As the armored car cut deeper into her lead, the back window shattered, causing a flinch and a momentary drop in speed. A glance in the mirror showed a man leaning out the window, firing at her. She ducked low and pressed the accelerator down again. She didn't think a bullet could hit her through the bed wall and the seat as long as she stayed down. It would take a lucky shot to find a path through the tread of the tires to reach the thinner rubber between. Besides, she had double wheels on each side. Maybe that's why it was taking so long to get up speed, she thought. As long as she didn't turn and give them a broadside shot, she should be able to outdistance her pursuers. She urged the truck to gain more speed.

As the gap began to expand, Becca felt more confident about her escape. The shooter was leaning further out the window and had the gun angled down. He was trying to take out a tire. She kept the pedal pinned and glanced at her gauges. Everything looked good. Then she did a double-take at the fuel gauge. It appeared to be dropping steadily. Heart sinking, she knew what had happened. One lucky shot had punctured the tank. She had started with a half tank. Now it was barely above a quarter.

Her mind raced for a solution. They might not be able to keep up with her, but all they had to do was keep her in sight. Soon the truck would run out of gas. Did they know that? Maybe if she increased the lead enough before the tank went dry, they might give up and turn around.

Becca kept the pedal down and the truck ran hard. She kept glancing in the mirror for a sign that her pursuers were slowing and turning around, but it never happened. Her anger grew. She had to find someplace to fight from that forced them out of the armored truck. If they caught her inside the pickup, she was dead. They never had to move from their safe positions to riddle the truck with bullets. She had to make them chase her on foot where she could deal with them on even ground.

The shooting had ceased for the most part. That was one good thing. Of course, now that she knew she'd have to fight it out with them, she'd rather they kept shooting and use up their ammo. She'd been so angry with Darlene and in such a hurry to get to Bobby that she didn't think to bring extra rounds or magazines. She had her handgun, the AR with only one mag, and her knife. She wondered now how many were in the pursuit vehicle? She knew there were two in the front but were there any more in the back?

Her lead had grown to more than a hundred yards. Still, her pursuers showed no sign of quitting. A ping made her cringe. They were shooting again. She looked in the mirror. The shooter was sitting on the window with one leg through, hanging over the door. He was no longer using the AR. Now he had a scoped rifle and was working hard to take accurate shots.

The next shot punched through the windshield a few inches to the right of her head. She scooted lower again. She had sat more erect as her lead grew. A look at the fuel gauge showed less than an eighth of a tank and falling. She needed cover and soon.

In the distance she spotted a farmhouse. She made for that. If she got out and made it behind the house, it would be her turn to stalk them.

Another shot was followed by a whoosh. She looked back and saw the last round had sparked off the road and lit the dripping gas. It rushed toward the truck. There wasn't much gas left to cause a significant fireball, but with the tank that empty, it was the fumes she had to worry about igniting. They would, in turn set the gas ablaze and cause an explosion.

She looked at the farmhouse as it grew larger. It was set back about fifty yards off the road. She had to reach the rear of the building and get out of sight. That would force them to get out to pursue her.

The flames reached the truck. She didn't have long. She had to get out of the truck and run. Still, she kept the pedal down, straining to get every bit of distance possible. She didn't want to be in the open too long with the shooter in possession of a scoped rifle.

A loud whoosh of air like it had been sucked into a void was followed by a boom. The rear end of the truck was lifted off the blacktop. With the driving wheels no longer keeping the truck moving forward, momentum was all that carried Becca. Speed bled off fast, but she was no longer concerned about her lead. Now she feared being crushed as the bed of the truck went perpendicular to the road.

Becca lunged for the seat, wrapping her arms around whatever she could to prevent being tossed like a crash test dummy. As the rear end dropped over the cab, Becca closed her eyes and gripped with all her strength.

The truck landed hard, skidded, and spun in a metallic grinding and shrieking. The roof caved under the impact. The windows were still intact and shattered, sending glass shards in and out of the cab. Becca winced as sharp pricks of pain came from many spots on her body. A warm trickle rolled down her cheek. Her body bounced, driving the air from her lungs, but she held tight. She kept her head pressed hard to the seat to avoid whiplash. As the truck slid to a halt, Becca released her death grip and lunged at the door. She knew her time was short and the armored truck would be on her in seconds.

The door refused to budge. Without turning, she rolled to her back, lifted her legs and tried to kick her way out the other door. Both had buckled under the impact and were jammed. Without pause, she scooted through the narrowed opening that had once been the windshield. Once out, she remembered her AR and turned quickly to retrieve it. She spotted the gun and reached it, slicing her torso on glass at the base of her ribs. She cried out but did not stop as she reached for the AR.

Her hand gripped and pulled it as she heard her pursuer's brakes screech. The truck had stopped spinning with the cab away from her pursuers, who were right behind the overturned pickup. She backed out of the windshield, causing further cuts. Once on the ground, with the hood overhead for cover, she spotted the front wheels moving alongside the pickup. She scooted to the other side to keep the truck between her and the shooter. If they wanted to find her, they'd have to get out, which gave her a slight edge, depending on how many of them there were.

As the truck crept forward, she slowly got her breathing and fear under control, replacing it with cold hard anger. It was time for her to become the hunter now.

Chapter Thirty-Four

The armored truck inched forward. The shooter in the passenger seat had exchanged his rifle for a handgun and was leaning out the window to get a look inside the cab of the overturned pickup.

"I can't tell from here. I don't see her, but I can't see all the way inside. I'll get out and check."

Another voice said, "No. You stay there and cover the cab. I'll send the others out to surround the truck."

Becca heard a rapping, then a third voice said, "What are we doing?"

The second man Becca guessed was the driver, said, "Go out and see if that bitch is still alive."

"What should we do if we find her alive?"

"I don't care as long as she's dead when you're done."

Becca slid with stealth along the side of the pickup. The bed of the truck was off the ground. She slid part of the way underneath to see the men as they exited the rear of the truck. She needed to even the odds a bit.

The rear door swung up with a loud creak. It clanged hard against the body of the truck and a booted foot touched down. She held back firing in case more than one exited. She wanted to get two at once if possible.

The first man out said, "I'll go around this way, you go straight down."

There were at least two of them. She had to take them before they separated too far, making the shot too difficult. The first man moved around the tail of the truck as a second set of boots stepped to the ground. A few more steps, and the first man would see her legs sticking out from under the truck. She had to take him now and hope for the best.

She triggered a short burst into the man's legs. She heard the scream but didn't wait to see him fall. Instantly, she swung the AR toward the second man who was now running. She fired but was too slow. Her shots missed.

As the body of the first man crashed to the ground, she whirled back. Her victim rolled on the ground clutching both legs. His eyes bulged as he spotted her crawling toward him. He tried to roll away, but she followed and drove her knife into the back of his head as she came out from under the truck.

The passenger door of the armored truck opened and the shooter inside stood on the floor and looked over the pickup. He had his rifle pointed but not aimed. When he spotted her, he lifted the rifle, but Becca was already on target and hosed him down. He did a death dance then hung over the door.

Shots pinged off the chassis of the pickup forcing Becca to duck. The armored car moved forward. To her, that was a big mistake. Had the driver been out of the truck, he might have had a shot at her when she fired at the passenger. As she ducked, she dropped the AR, unsure of how many shots she had left and scooped up the dead man's. It was a pump-action shotgun. She had never fired a shotgun before, but a gun was a gun. Point and fire.

She ducked under the bed again and walked in a crouch toward the overturned cab. Her opponent was somewhere in front of the cab. He must have guessed where she was. The truck rocked hard a few times then the bed tipped downward. It hit the pavement with a solid crack cutting off her best escape route. She could still escape left or right, but when she heard the armored car's door shut she knew the driver had entered the fray. She was cut off. Either way Becca went, she was dead.

She didn't move. How long would they wait before making a move on her? If they were smart, they'd come from opposite sides at the same time. She might get one, but the other had her. Were they willing to bet their lives on who might die to flush her out?

Becca looked at the broken rear window and got an idea. She crawled through, trying hard not to move the truck. She lay on the roof above and between the seats, then rolled on her side and moved the shotgun to her shoulder. An arm appeared through the broken window of the driver's side. The man there was signaling to his partner coordinating their attack. She did not have a good line of sight, nor was the gun snugged against her shoulder, but she knew where he was and thought the door would not stop all the pellets. She aimed slightly above the door frame, hoped the previous owner of the shotgun had buck rather than birdshot loaded, and pulled the trigger.

Pain erupted down her arm and spread across her chest. Becca rolled, clutching her arm to her chest and gasping for air. She was sure she had been shot but saw no blood. It was the savage kick of the shotgun. Screams came from the outside of the truck. Small holes perforated the door. A shadow fell over the window on the passenger side. Though in pain, she had enough sense to move. She slid back out of the rear window as the surviving shooter slid the barrel of his AR inside the cab and unloaded.

Becca managed to scurry from the cab, cover her head, and press against the outside of the cab as bullets ricocheted everywhere. She winced as a bullet creased her calf and drew her legs in tighter. She had to get ready to fight. Becca forced her hands down then realized she no longer held the shotgun. She had released it after it kicked her so severely. She slid her still numb hand down and withdrew the handgun. As the firing ceased, she sprawled on the blacktop and peeked out from under the cab.

The man was changing out magazines. It was her chance. She moved her gun arm along the roadway, trying to get her still throbbing arm to respond. It did but with agonizing slowness. The man spotted her and stomped down on her arm, pinning the gun to the ground. The wicked smile told her all she needed to know about what came next.

He slapped the magazine into place, cycled the round, and his smile widened as he took his time lowering the barrel toward her head.

Becca was unable to move her arm, but her hand and fingers still worked. Though the overconfident man had her arm pinned, he had never kicked the gun away. She angled the gun at the man's other leg and fought hard to get enough leverage to break the trigger. A second before she was staring down the barrel of his AR, she got enough pressure to fire. The bullet hit his shin, breaking the bone. The leg bent at an awkward angle and collapsed under him. He shrieked in pain as he fell. Part of his anguished mind understood if he didn't shoot, he was dead. He fired a continuous burst all the way to the ground.

As his weight lifted from her arm, Becca pivoted and fired, even as rounds stitched up her left arm toward her head. Her only target was between his legs and she kept firing. With each impact, his body danced and bucked as his screams went from shrieks to shrill. Becca wasn't sure when he stopped moving but didn't stop until the gun was empty. When the trigger would move no more, she lowered the gun, set her head on her uninjured arm, and allowed the darkness to take her.

Chapter Thirty-Five

"So much for Lincoln's security," Edwards whispered. "That was easy." In the darkness, no one was aware of their presence or their breach.

"Yeah. Too easy," Merchant said. "Maybe we're walking into a trap."

"Relax. No way. They wouldn't wait to spring a trap if they knew we were coming. They'd already be chasing us. Besides, even if they do catch us we still got the girl to use as leverage. They'll let us go if she's returned."

"Leverage don't help us if they shoot us. It only works if they capture us."

They were moving crouched through the open ground that had once been a cornfield behind the barn.

"I think the boy got caught and squealed," Merchant said.

"Hey, you want to do this or not? I'm telling you we got in so easily cause they got a bunch of kids keeping watch. You know they ain't got the attention span of a gnat." He pointed. "Look. We're almost there. Yes or no? You know you want to kill that son of a bitch as much as I do, but I'm going with or without you. Now's the point of no return."

Merchant scanned the darkness around them. "Okay. Okay. Let's get this done and get out of here."

They moved to the rear of the hospital. The door was still the old sliding barn style. Plans to replace it with something that sealed better were in the works but still on the long list of construction plans for the community. It was held closed by a hasp and padlock, and the seam between the door and frame had been duct taped to cut down on drafts.

Edwards took the small metal snips from his back pocket and worked on snipping the lock. They were made more for cutting items the thickness of wire fencing. The cutting blades weren't wide enough to get a good grip on the lock. It took enormous pressure using both hands to make a dent in the metal. After several attempts with little progress, Merchant, who had already sliced through the tape, lost patience and pulled out a small pry bar.

Edwards grabbed his arm to stop him. "It'll make too much noise," he whispered, his voice full of warning.

Merchant shook him off. "You're not getting anywhere on the lock. If we wait for you to finish, someone will see us." He inserted the bar between the hasp and door and pulled. The screws gave grudgingly but with little noise until they tore free of the wood. Both men crouched and paused, listening for signs they were heard.

A minute later, Merchant grabbed the door and slid it back far enough to slip inside. They stopped to get their bearings. The outer office was dimly lit by a desk lamp, but otherwise the entire building was dark save for the ambient glow of the various machines keeping their target alive.

Edwards moved. This time Merchant grabbed his arm. "Isn't there usually someone on duty?" he whispered.

Edwards shrugged and the two men moved toward the curtained section of the hospital where they knew overnight patients were kept. Edwards parted the first curtain and peered through. Of the six curtained recovery rooms, only two had there's drawn. Edwards held up two fingers, indicating two patients. He wasn't sure which one Mark was in, so motioned for Merchant to take the right and he went left.

He crouched and moved the curtain to see in. A lone figure on a hospital bed was in the room. He slid the long hunting knife he wore on his belt from its sheath and entered. He focused on listening for sounds that he was both undetected and in the right place. No one came to help. He crept forward, knife raised. One slow step at a time brought him closer to the kill. He stood three feet from his prey when he realized it was not Mark.

Disappointed that Merchant was going to get the kill, he backed from the room to join him, but before he slipped through the curtain he heard the sound of a struggle, then a gunshot ripped through the silence, and a body hit the floor. Exhilarated by the thought they had accomplished their mission but worried about the attention the shot would bring, he readied to sprint for the rear door when the figure on the bed in his room sat up and pointed a gun at him.

The lights went on, blinding him for a moment. He reached for his gun, but something hard pressed into the back of his head. "I wish you would pull that gun, you bastard."

He froze. They'd been tricked. How did they know? It had to be that kid. Why hadn't he been shot already? That was a mistake. He might not be able to clear his gun, but he still held the knife. He was only going to get one chance and it had to be now

He whirled, whipping his arm to slash across Lincoln's gun arm. If he got the man to drop his weapon, he might have a chance to get away. Anticipating the move, Lincoln stepped forward and blocked the arm, then drove the gun into Edward's face. A painful white flash of light exploded in his head. He yelped, stepped back to clutch his face, and Lincoln ripped the knife from his hand.

Blood flowed freely between his fingers and down his face. He pulled them away and stared at his bloody hands in shock. The sight caused anger and the anger turned to rage. With a roar, he charged at Lincoln. Somewhere in the back of his mind he noticed the wide smile on the man's face and he realized he had done just what Lincoln wanted.

A straight hard punch plowed into his face. His legs went rubbery before giving way, and he dropped to his butt, stunned. He shook his head. Lincoln was saying something. He missed it.

"Can you hear me?"

Edwards was still trying to clear his mind.

"With the authority vested in me by the community council, I'm arresting you for attempted murder, kidnapping, treason against the community, and a bunch of other shit I'll come up with later."

Bobby hopped off the bed, grimaced, then came forward and took the handcuffs Lincoln held out for him. He snapped the cuffs on Edwards tight, then pointed at Bobby, "You get back in that bed."

Bobby didn't argue. He smiled and slid back onto the bed. Lincoln hoisted and led Edwards out of the room. In the lobby area he saw Merchant cuffed and unconscious on the floor, bleeding from a head wound. An expressionless Milo stood over him.

The doors opened and three more armed men entered.

"Wh-what are you going to do with us?" Edwards asked with genuine fear in his voice.

"You are going to be the first person to be put on trial under the new laws of the community."

"Trial?"

"Yep. You'll be given a fair trial and hopefully, once convicted of your many crimes, I'll get to be executioner."

"There's no way we'll get a fair trial."

"Hey, fair or not, you get to live long enough to have one instead of us just shooting you now."

"We still have a lot of friends here. They won't let you execute me."

"After what you've done, I doubt anyone will admit knowing you."

"We still have leverage. We have the girl. We'll trade her for our freedom."

Disgusted, Lincoln said, "Get him out of here, boys."

Milo and three other men dragged the prisoners outside. Ruth burst from the farmhouse, leaped down the stairs, and sprinted toward them. Lynn followed shortly after. "Ruth, don't," but the young girl had a head of steam and a laser focus. She darted around Lincoln, who tried to capture her and ran straight for Edwards.

Lincoln swore and shouted, "Milo, stop her."

The big man stood watching and made no move. Neither did his men. Ruth stopped in front of Edwards, who gaped at her sudden appearance.

"Hey, asshole. This is for kidnapping me." She planted a kick between his legs that drove all the air from his lungs in a high-pitched keen.

Milo stepped forward and put his hands gently on her shoulders. "I got her Lincoln. Don't worry."

Lincoln shook his head and squatted in front of Edwards, whose face had gone from bright red to a ghostly white. "How's that leverage now?"

The men hoisted both Merchant and Edwards and carried them to the new building that was constructed, yet unoccupied near the rear of the property. They would be kept there under guard until the trial.

Chapter Thirty-Six

Lynn jogged to Lincoln and Bobby as Ruth walked past, heading toward the house.

"I don't want to be a tattletale," Lincoln said, "But your daughter swore."

Lynn shook her head. "That's what you're tattling about?"

"Well, yeah. The girl swears today and who knows what she might do tomorrow. You best get that girl under control before something bad happens. Hell, she might end up being another Becca."

Lynn narrowed her eyes and scowled. "I'll wash her mouth out with soap."

"There ya go. That'll learn her."

"Everything go okay?"

"Yep," Lincoln said. "Not a problem."

"I saw Merchant was being carried. Is he hurt?"

"Nah. Got hit on the head somehow. Can't hurt nothing up there."

"Should I get Doc?"

"I think Doc's mad enough at us as it is. If she has to get woken up to deal with a problem we caused after voicing her opposition to our plan, I think she might lose it."

"Yeah. Good point. I'll see to him. Besides, I have a few things to say to both of them about kidnapping Ruth."

"Ah, you're not going to hurt them, are you?"

She gave him a sweet *would I do that?* look and said, "Not any more than necessary."

"Just make sure they're capable of standing trial."

"Oh, they'll get their trial. I make no promises about standing for it." She moved toward the building now being used as a jail.

Lincoln looked back and noticed Bobby had followed them out. His smile had grown. "What are you grinning about, boy? Get your ass back in that bed."

Bobby blanched at the force of the words but went inside.

Lincoln looked skyward, thankful everything had gone without anyone getting seriously injured. "Whew!" He walked toward his house. He needed some sleep.

A loud bang stirred a memory disturbing his slumber. For some reason, he was unable to open his eyes. Was he still asleep? Had the loud noise been part of a dream? He struggled between a state of sleep and a dreamlike fuzziness that nagged at his level of consciousness. He fought to return to the peace of sleep, but the memory stirred again, this time making a connection with something that was very real and extremely painful. What was it? He tried to force the memory forward, but it refused to come. He hoped he remembered the feeling once he woke. Perhaps Lincoln or Jarrod would know what he couldn't remember.

That thought connected to another memory. Something about Jarrod and the pain he had just experienced. Had Jarrod hurt him in some way? No. He'd never believe that unless it was an accident.

Accident became the next keyword to make a connection. He tried to piece them together. Bang. Pain. Jarrod. Nothing came. The thoughts swirled and became jumbled with many others until they were lost to him. The effort left him tired. He drifted near sleep, but his subconscious mind did not allow for a smooth transition back. He bounced back and forth ever closer to rest, yet still, the nagging persisted.

He latched onto distant and distorted images of his children. Bobby. Rebecca. Was one of them in trouble? Didn't he remember hearing that from someone? Yes. No. He began to relax and allow sleep to take him.

Shot!

The word leaped to his mind and stood alone, highlighted in bold letters. His body jerked. Pain slammed him. He gasped. Connections were made. Shot. The loud bang had been a gunshot. Had that happened or had it been a memory of something else?

He broke free of sleep's pull and tried to rise. It was like swimming underwater and searching for the surface. He could not feel his body. What was wrong? Someone was in danger and he had to help. If only he could wake up.

Early the next morning, as he was leaving his house, Lincoln was confronted by a small group of Edwards' followers. One of the men, Jim Blake, got right in his face. "What's this we hear that you have Edwards and Merchant locked up?" He didn't give Lincoln a chance to reply. "What gives you the right to detain anyone?" He ranted on without waiting for a response, this time with a threatening finger in his face. "We think it's time for change in leadership. You think you're God almighty and because you're the council leader, you can do what you want when you want. Well, we're here to tell you that ends now."

Finally, he ran out of air and Lincoln could take no more. He snapped his teeth down on the extended finger and bit hard. The man cried out and tried to pull the finger free. The other three men and two women stood shocked. Lincoln released the finger and growled at the man. Blake recoiled, holding the finger. Then Lincoln advanced and the man cowered back.

"Let me handle these in order. First, yes, they are being held for some pretty serious charges. You'll find out all about it at their trial." He stepped forward again and the collective group gave ground. He felt his anger roiling and his fists opening and closing.

"Next, I have the right because it was granted to me by popular vote, and I have exercised that right pending trial." Another step, more retreating. "You want to change leadership? That is your right as voters. Next election, you should run for council yourself. That way everyone can see what an ass you are. No, I'm not God, but as council leader, I'm the next best thing here on Earth. If you don't like it or can't wait for the next election, you know where the door is. I'm sure someone might miss your belligerence and stupidity." He paused in both his rebuttal and his advance before saying, "And, oh yeah, if you ever put a finger in my face again, you will walk away minus one.

"Now, if you want to know more, there will be a preliminary hearing in front of the entire community after the evening meal. Answers will be given then. If you have any more questions, you can ask them then."

One of the women said, "We want to see them. We want to know they are unharmed and have not been mistreated."

Lincoln thought about that. "Yeah, that's a good idea. They will need someone to act as their attorney. I'm not letting you all in, so decide who will go and I'll let two of you in."

The group stood back and after a few moments of deliberation, chose Blake and the woman who spoke up, Gloria Updike, as the defendant's counsel.

Lincoln led them to the building being used as a jail. A guard had been posted at each of the three doors. "Tony," Lincoln said to the guard in charge. "Gloria and Blake are acting council for the defendants. Let them in to speak with their clients. Lock the door once they are inside." To Gloria, he said, "Knock when you want out." To Tony, "If they attempt to break them out, use whatever force necessary to prevent that from happening."

Gloria gasped.

"Then keep them locked up and we'll have a second trial for them."

"That's uncalled for," Gloria said. "We're members of this community too. We have rights."

"I agree," said Lincoln. "That's why you're being allowed in to see the prisoners. I merely pointed out what Tony and his guards should do if an escape is attempted. Take all the time you need to prepare their defense but know this, the evidence against them is overwhelming."

Blake turned to him. "You may think you're in charge and can have your way, but mark my words, your fall is coming soon."

Lincoln said, "If you want to take me down, I'll be standing in the opening by the house right after the preliminary trial. Feel free to take me down then." He offered the man a smile, then turned and walked away. His anger was still high and he couldn't wait for the trial to be over. But right then, the thing he wanted most was mouthwash. He had no idea where Blake's finger had been.

Chapter Thirty-Seven

"Get us out of this," Edwards said to Blake. "I don't care what you have to do. Get us out." Spittle flew from his mouth. He wiped it with the back of his arm.

Gloria said, "Is what they're saying true? That you plotted to kill the council?"

"What?" Edwards said. "That's bullshit. That," he paused, thinking better of using the word that came to mind, "man has got it in for us because we dared speak up against his friend. He's the one who needs to go."

Blake switched his gaze from Edwards to Merchant. "Lincoln don't strike me as the type to make this stuff up. He's not the only one saying things. They say you kidnapped Lynn's daughter."

"More lies," Edwards said, slamming his hand against the wall. I'm telling you, they're setting us up. Don't let them do it. If you allow this farce of a trial to go on, we're both dead. You need to come in with guns blazing and break us out."

"Let me do some thinking," Blake said.

"Thinking?" Edwards exploded. "What's to think about. We're being set up and led to our executions. There ain't no time for thinking. It's time for action."

Blake took an angry step toward Edwards. "And I need to think how best to do that without getting us all killed."

"All right. All right." Edwards lifted his hands in surrender and backed up a step. "Don't mean to be angry with you. Just we're under a lot of stress here with our lives on the line. You do your thinking. Just find a way to get us out of here. Please."

Gloria said, "You're sure there's nothing they have against you that's true and can be proved?"

"Hell no! They probably brainwashed that little girl to tell lies against us. Ain't that right," he asked Merchant.

The other man merely nodded his agreement.

She eyed both men with clear suspicion. "Okay. We'll figure something out."

Blake said, "We'll be back."

Gloria knocked on the door. Edwards took a step forward as the door swung open, hoping for a chance to escape, but all three guards were positioned there to prevent any such attempt. Blake and Gloria exited and the door was shut and locked.

As they walked away, Gloria asked, "What do you think?"

"Ha! I think they're guilty as hell."

"I agree, but what are we going to do about it?"

"Not sure yet. Can't say I like the idea of friends being put on trial, but if we break them out, we're gonna have to run which means leaving here."

"Yeah, I do like it here. It's a lot better than being on our own and always moving and scrounging for food." She stopped and faced Blake. "Does that make me a terrible person?"

"No. In truth, I respect what they're trying to build here. I've always been pretty much a loner, but I have to say, it's nice to know someone's got your back when times get tough. I can survive out there, on my own, but I'm not sure I want to."

"So, what do we do?"

"Like I told them, I'm gonna think on it a bit."

"Will you let me know?"

"Depending on what I decide, you sure you want to know?"

She shivered despite the warmth of the day. "I guess."

He smiled at her knowing it was better not to tell her.

Lincoln watched Edwards' and Merchant's legal team stop and have a deep discussion. He wondered what their plan was about the trial. He hoped they weren't stupid enough to try to break the two men out. That would only lead to more violence and death. He made a mental note to assign additional security to the guard detail.

He hated that they had to have a trial but also knew it was important to what they were trying to build. There must be rules and with them, consequences. He was glad he didn't have to preside over the trial by himself. The entire council, minus Lynn and Caleb, would hear the case and pronounce judgment. Since it was Lynn's daughter who was kidnapped, she and her son were excluded.

It wasn't so much the trial that had him concerned. That had to happen and the two men were guilty. His worry was how certain factions within the community might react to a guilty verdict. Any violence was another strike against the good people of the community. They'd seen their fair share of conflict and death and desperately needed a break from the violence. He didn't want to alienate anyone and knew he had to do a better job of remaining impartial.

Gloria and Blake ended their talk and started walking. He thought it a good opportunity to mend a fence or two. He moved toward them. As he closed he could see them both bristle and stand more erect. That was exactly the kind of reaction he wanted to suppress.

"I just wanted to apologize for my behavior and my actions. Tensions are a bit high, but that's no excuse for causing strife amongst community members. Is there anything I can do to help you with your defense or any information I can give you?"

They glanced at each other, surprise evident on their faces.

"Like you really want to help," Blake said with attitude.

Lincoln kept his temper in check. "Look, I may not like those men, but I do believe in being fair. Despite my feelings, they deserve a fair and unbiased trial. I won't stand in the way of that. You may think otherwise, but that's not the way I am."

"What happens if they're found guilty," Gloria asked.

"That's a good question. Since we've never had a trial before, I'm not sure. That would be for the council to decide, but if you have recommendations to put forth, I'm sure they'll be taken into consideration."

"Don't try to BS us," Blake said. He stepped forward aggressively. "They're already guilty in your mind and you plan on executing them."

Lincoln was no longer able to hold back his anger. He stepped forward, narrowing the space between the two men to a foot. "If you're asking if I believe they're guilty, I'd say no. I *know* they're guilty. I was there. I was one of the intended victims. We have multiple witnesses and victims, and we caught them inside the hospital after breaking in the backdoor with the intent of killing Mark, a comatose patient unable to defend himself. Will I push to execute them? No, but I won't balk from that punishment if the council votes on it."

Lincoln turned his head and found some calm. "Look, Blake," he said in a less confrontational tone, "I know they're your friends. I get you want to protect them. But these are some bad men and have done some extremely bad things. These are not the sort of people we want within our community."

Gloria said, "Then banish them. Don't execute them."

Lincoln looked at her. "I don't have a problem with that, as long as they don't come back. If that satisfies you, then make the recommendation for banishment to the council. In fact, if they plead guilty to the charges, we might be able to get it done without a trial where emotions are running high and there's no way of knowing what might happen."

Blake said, "Maybe you'd like not having a trial. Maybe your case isn't as strong as you think it is."

Lincoln smiled. "Guess that will be up to you and your clients to decide. Either way, let me know." He turned and walked away.

Chapter Thirty-Eight

Lincoln looked at his watch. It was nearly time to begin the trial. The community had turned out and brought a buzz of extra tension to the proceedings. Lincoln had spent the better part of the afternoon in session with his fellow council members deciding on how the trial would go. As much as possible, they wanted to adhere to the standard rules of a trial. The difference was that there was a council of judges rather than one. The biggest sticking point was whether they needed a jury. No decision had been made up to twenty minutes ago when they took a break.

It was late afternoon. Lincoln wanted the trial to be done during daylight. If there was trouble, he wanted to see it coming. He had armed guards on every side, and no one was allowed to carry a weapon into the trial.

With the weather still pleasant enough, the trial was being held outside where the community would be less packed together than inside the new building. Besides, since it was being used as a cell, the council thought outside made the trial easier. As many chairs as they could find had been set up in rows in front of the three large firepits. The stage had been constructed on top of the picnic tables and folding tables and chairs lined up along its width. Milo and Elijah were already up there talking.

A massive pickup truck drove up and parked next to the house. Jarrod, Maggie, and a host of others exited and moved toward the crowd. Jarrod joined Lincoln.

"How's things here?"

Lincoln shrugged. "So far, they're under control."

"Expecting trouble?"

Lincoln sighed. "Yeah, I guess I kinda am."

"Anything new with Mark?"

"Not that I've heard."

"You think he's ever gonna come out of it?"

"I don't know, but regardless, we have a council decision that he either wakes or gets unplugged."

"Man, I hope it don't come to that. He deserves better."

"He's certainly fought to live a life worth dying for."

Jarrod said, "Huh! I gotta think on that one for a bit."

Lincoln smiled and patted the big farmer on the shoulder. "I guess it's time we got this trial rolling."

Lincoln hadn't gone two steps when his radio crackled. "Lincoln."

"Sir," the guard said, "we've got a convoy coming our way."

"Which gate are you?"

"Western."

"Any of the vehicles look familiar?"

"Yeah, there's a white van leading the way."

The white van could be the one Darlene left in. He looked at his watch. Good. She was back. She was late, and he had to avoid Elijah last night and avoid his angry glares during their sessions today, but the return should ease some of that tension. Then he had a thought. "How many vehicles?"

"Four."

Four? They must have picked up another, but if that was the case, maybe they found a lot of useful items. He hoped some of those helped Mark stay plugged in longer. Thinking he had to organize teams to unload, he asked, "What are the vehicles."

"Well, the white van, a police car, a pickup and, ah, a larger moving truck."

That gave Lincoln pause. "How far out are they?"

"Two blocks."

That was close. "Okay. Hold them there. I'm coming."

"Problem?" Jarrod asked.

"Not sure. Can you give me a lift?"

"Sure." Jarrod moved toward his truck.

Lincoln motioned to Milo to come, then waved at the two guards closest to him. As they approached, he said, "Get in the back of Jarrod's truck."

Milo sauntered over, not happy that he had been summoned. "What's going on?" he asked with annoyance in his tone. "We need to get this trial started. People are getting antsy."

"There's a convoy of vehicles approaching the western gate. For the moment, that takes precedence. I'm going out there in case there's trouble. Handle things here until I get back." He took a step, stopped, and said, "Please." He jogged to the truck, climbed in the passenger's seat, and Jarrod backed down the drive.

In less than a minute, they arrived at the western gate. The convoy was already there and the guard was speaking to someone inside the van. The other two guards assigned to the gate stood behind it with their weapons ready but barrels aimed downward as they'd been taught.

Lincoln slid down from the oversize truck and sent each of the two guards he brought to split wide to the sides for extra coverage, and then he strode toward the gate.

The gate had been constructed by Milo and his crew. It consisted of a four-by-four post set between a larger post which was cemented in the ground. A drop-down leg was on the opposite side to keep the heavy beam supported. Cement barriers had been placed on each end of the gate, and sections of a ten-foot-high fence had been started on each side but was a long way from completion.

Lincoln ducked under the gate and moved toward the van. Darlene was in the front seat and one of the two escorts sat next to her. She spotted him through the windshield and raised both arms in exasperation. "Lincoln, what gives? Why have we been stopped?"

Lincoln moved next to the guard captain. "Lose the attitude. You're late. We had no idea you were coming and certainly not with so many vehicles. With what's going on today, I wasn't taking any chances that you might be a group of Edwards' people come to break him out."

"That's crazy. You saw me drive away. You told me to be back, well yesterday, but we had so much stuff to load it was late when we finished and didn't want to drive in the dark. Didn't Becca tell you we were coming?"

Jin walked up next to the van. Lincoln nodded at the man.

"I haven't seen Becca. I assumed she was with you. After all, you went to get her."

"That didn't go so well. She came back before us, leaving us to load everything up." Her body jerked like she'd been slapped. "Wait. Becca's not here? She left yesterday around sunset. She should be here by now."

That drew Lincoln up straighter and Jin tense.

"Becca no here?" Jin asked.

"I haven't seen her since she left days ago."

Jin whirled and hurried back to his vehicle. The police car made a U-turn and sped back the way they came.

"Can you tell me anything about her path?"

"It's all pretty straightforward. You get on Route Two and take it all the way back. There's just a short part at the beginning where you take another road."

Who's in the other vehicles?"

"People we met along the way and a priest."

"A priest. God, I hope that's not an omen. You vouching for them?"

"I don't know them. Jin and Becca met them, but they accepted them, so I guess that means we should too."

Lincoln thought that over then said to the guard captain, "Check the vehicles and if nothing looks off, let them through." To Darlene, he said, "Park on the street in front of the farmhouse. Parking is tight right now with the whole community here. I'll have someone meet you there to escort the new people." He turned and ran back to Jarrod's truck. As the farmer reversed, he said, "Tell me. You having fun yet?"

Lincoln snarled.

Chapter Thirty-Nine

Lincoln jogged to the council table. All the other members were already there. They turned to face him and Milo stood. "What was the big emergency?" he asked, annoyed.

Lynn joined them, standing next to Lincoln.

"It's Darlene and Jin with a group of strangers, which evidently includes a priest."

"A priest!" said Elijah.

Maggie said, "Talk about timing."

"Also, Becca left them to come here yesterday afternoon, but she never arrived." That announcement silenced them. "Anyone seen her?" He looked at each person. No one had.

Lynn said, "Any idea where she might be?"

"No, but considering the trouble Darlene and Bobby got into on their way here, I have a bad feeling the same group might have sidetracked Becca. I'm going to send teams out to search for her before it gets dark."

Just then, the caravan pulled up on the street.

Caryn said, "With all this going on should we postpone the trial?"

"No," Milo, Doc, and Elijah said together.

Elijah said, "It's not fair to Edwards and Merchant to put off whatever is going to happen. They deserve their day in court."

"Besides," said Doc, "We brought everyone here. We need to proceed."

Lincoln looked at the others for their opinions.

"I'll do whatever everyone else decides," Caryn said.

Maggie said, "I don't want to wait, but I don't want to delay searching for Becca either."

"I can still send out teams," Lincoln said. He turned to Lynn. "Since we're going to continue with the trial, can you see to the new arrivals? Perhaps steer them away from here, so they don't serve as a distraction?"

"Yeah, sure."

Lincoln climbed on the stage and lifted his hands for quiet. The buzz in the crowd had grown a bit hostile and a few comments were hurled his way. "'bout time." "Let's get this thing started already."

Lincoln waited them out, and finally they quieted. "I am sorry for the delay. Several things have come up that have nothing to do with the trial. We have several new arrivals." An instant murmur began. "And one of our people has gone missing. I'd like a few volunteers to form search parties." A few hands went up. Caleb came to the back of the stage and called to Lincoln. "I'll go since I can't serve on the council."

Lincoln nodded. "Those who are willing to go, meet with Caleb to organize your search areas." He turned to Caleb. "Ask Darlene about the route. Jin is already out there searching. He's in a cop car." He gave the searchers a few minutes to move out of the crowd, then said, "Okay with that done, we'll begin. The council has deliberated for many hours on how best to proceed. I want to set down those rules before we get started. I will explain everything. Then if needed, we can take a few questions."

While Lincoln took control of the trial, Lynn moved to meet the new people. She met Darlene and asked, "Can you introduce me to our guests?"

"No." Her manner was brusque. She moved past Lynn, then stopped and hung her head. "I'm sorry, Lynn. I don't know them. Ask Father Bernardo." She walked fast toward the hospital.

Father Bernardo stepped forward and offered his hand. Lynn accepted it. "I'm Father Bernardo. Thank you, dear lady, for allowing us to visit your fine community."

"You're very welcome, Father. Who are your companions?"

"Ah, yes. This is Shamika and her daughter, Pandora."

Lynn nodded at the pregnant woman. When are you due?

"I have no idea."

"Oh, well, maybe our doctor can help determine a due date. Nice to have you both here." She looked down at the girl who was staring at the large gathering. "Pandora is a pretty name."

Shamika said, "Yeah, I thought so too until her father told me he gave her that name because she was the surprise that came out of my box."

Lynn was dumbfounded and didn't know what to say.

Shamika laughed. "Yeah, that's most people's reaction."

Father Bernardo shook from his shock first. "This is Debbie." He motioned to tall, slender, late twenties to early thirties, woman. She gave a quick smile and looked away. "That's Star back there." He pointed to a skinny teen in ragged clothes. "And this gentleman is Glen. Glen was wounded and may need medical help if you can spare any."

"Oh," Lynn said. "Is that how you came to meet our people?"

"Yeah, you can say that," Glen said. "That scary woman and the Asian guy shot me."

Again, Lynn was stymied.

"Wow!" Shamika said, 'She wasn't lying. You got a big ass community here."

"Yes, it's constantly growing," Lynn said.

"May I ask what this gathering is about?" asked Father Bernardo.

"Ah, well, we have a monthly meeting to keep everyone informed as to what's going on. This is a very important one, and we need to keep our distance."

Twenty yards in front of them, two men with their hands bound were led toward the gathering with four armed men around them.

"Ah, this isn't a firing squad, is it?" asked a nervous Father Bernardo.

"No," Lynn said. "It's a trial. Let's go check out the hospital, shall we?" She ushered them away from the crowd as voices began to climb upon seeing the two defendants.

"A trial," Shamika said. "That's scary. What did they do?"

Lynn tried to determine the best way to answer that without sounding like the community was communist ruled. She decided on a portion of the truth. "It's our first trial in five months of being a community. Those two men are accused of kidnapping and attempted murder. That's all I'm willing to say for the moment. I don't want you to get the wrong idea about us. We are a very caring and strong community, and we work very hard to be a safe and happy place to live. Everyone pitches in and helps. It's the only way it can work."

"So, it's like some glorified commune," Debbie said.

"No, not at all. We recognize the importance of hard work for our survival, but we also do a lot of fun things too. Such as, we have a Halloween party coming up in a few days. If you're still here, you are welcome to attend."

"Wait!" said the teen. "You expect everyone to work?"

Lynn opened the door to the hospital and let them enter.

"The barn is the hospital?" asked Shamika.

She waited until they were all inside before addressing the questions.

"Yes, Star, if you decide to stay, you will be expected to do your fair share."

"What if we don't?"

"Well, we've never had anyone who refused, but my guess is you will be asked to leave."

"Seriously? You'd just throw me out knowing I might die out there?"

Lynn sighed. She was so glad her daughter Ruth had not been a typical teenager. "That's your choice."

"So, what?" Debbie said. "You'll put her on trial or something?"

"Like I said, we've never had that problem, so I'm not sure how it would be handled, but I do know if everyone else is working and they see that you're not, it'll be in your own best interest to move on."

Glen said, "But you don't kill no one for not working, right?"

Lynn smiled. "No. We only kill when forced to. Listen. I'm not sure what you're used to, but here we try to abide by the rules we've been used to before the pandemic. It may not be for you and that's fine. You are free to leave at any time. No one is going to stop you. If you decide to stay, that's fine too. Just know you will be expected to contribute your fair share of the labor."

While Lynn was talking, Shamika looked around the hospital. "So, this looks like a barn on the outside, but inside it's like a real hospital."

"Yes, we're very proud of what we've accomplished here. We've had two births over the past few months."

"Aw, I don't mean to be rude, but did they live?"

"Yes. Both mothers and babies were fine and still are. One is three months old, the other two. Our doctor and staff were for the most part medical professionals before the pandemic."

"Pandora. Girl, where you at?" Shamika said.

"Oh," said Lynn. "We have patients back there." Lynn moved toward the curtained partition as the girl stepped out.

"Mommy. Mommy, there's a man back there."

"That's one of our patients," Lynn said.

"He was moaning and saying something."

Lynn stood erect, trying to process what the little girl said. "Please, wait here." Without waiting to see if they did, Lynn hurried through the curtain and toward Mark's cubicle. Bobby was out at the trial and Myron had been moved to his bed over the garage. As she approached, she heard his voice. She stepped through the curtain with hopeful tears beading in her eyes.

Mark was still out but was moaning and saying something in a low voice. "Mark?" Please open your eyes. "Mark, can you hear me?"

He moaned again and said something. She leaned closer. She thought she heard the word "trouble."

"In trouble. Help." He moaned.

Was he coming out of the coma? She whirled and raced from the cubicle. She burst into the main room, causing quick screams from Star and Debbie. "Please. Wait here and don't touch anything."

She went through the outer door and ran for the meeting.

Chapter Forty

Jin reached the point where he had to turn to return to the church, but he knew Becca was not in that direction. She was nowhere along the route and he had seen no signs of an attack. Only one thing would have prevented her from reaching her wounded brother. An opposing force greater than her.

He continued straight. He had a little more than an hour of daylight to complete the search. He was realistic enough to know that if he didn't find a trace of her by then, he might not find her at all. He had two choices. Continue searching or drive back to the prison in Stryker they had passed days before. If she was anywhere else, she was lost.

With his eyes moving in a constant scan of the area and roads on each side of his route, he tried to imagine the scene that made her alter course. Something, no, someone, most likely a group of someones had confronted her. It had to be a group, or he'd have seen a lone body on the road someplace. That confrontation had to be in a vehicle, or again, bodies would be strewn about the road and she'd be home. No, something else happened that resulted in her changing course. It had to be a vehicle chase.

Where would she have gone? Since she wasn't anywhere on the route to the farmhouse, it had to be the direction he was moving. Becca was smart and tough. He had a lot of respect for her and her abilities. He knew many strong, hard, and tough women, his wife included. In fact, until he met Becca, his wife was the toughest woman he ever knew. With grudging acceptance, he was willing to put Becca on an even keel with her though he'd never admit that to his wife.

Because Becca was smart and ferocious when confronted, she would not go down easy. Signs of a fight had to be somewhere along this path. If she was killed, her body would be along here. If taken, evidence of destruction would be left behind. As he came to each cross street, Jin paused to study its length in both directions ruling most out and leaving one with a maybe.

A short distance later, sunlight reflected off something on the side of the road. He parked and got out. He found a brass casing. He examined it and found a stamped circle with an x in the center. It was a NATO 5.56 cartridge. An AR, perhaps. Who was he dealing with? Military? It was a strange cartridge to find in a rural setting in Ohio. One thing was for certain. He was on the right track.

He pocketed the cartridge, got in the car, and continued his search.

Lincoln said, "Okay, with that settled and understood, we're going to proceed. Do either council have anything to say?"

Blake stood. "How about a mistrial?"

Adrienne, the prosecuting attorney, stood immediately. "On what possible grounds?" She had been an attorney before the world went crazy. The council had relied on her trial knowledge in setting up how the proceeding would go.

"On the grounds that my clients won't get a fair trial."

Adrienne put hands to hips and faced Blake. "And where do you think this trial can be moved? Do you see other communities willing to take it? Do you even see other communities? No," she pronounced in an authoritative tone. "That's not happening."

"How is this a fair trial?" Blake continued. "Everyone here is against them."

"Well, then maybe they shouldn't have committed so many crimes against so many people."

"All right. Hold on," Lincoln said. To make things official, he consulted with the other five council members. They all agreed. "Motion denied. This is the court we have. This is where the trial is held."

Blake looked as if he wanted to say more, but Gloria put a hand on his arm and he sat. She stood in his place. "What about my client's rights to an impartial jury?"

Elijah said, "Since we are hearing the case as a council, we will serve as jury."

"So, you're both judge and jury. Isn't that a conflict?"

"We don't think it will be. We have discussed this and came to the conclusion it might be more difficult to seat a jury than to handle it ourselves."

"This is too important to leave it in your hands. These men's lives may depend on having an impartial jury to weigh and decide the evidence. If anything, because of your positions on the council, I would think you'd rather distance yourself from the final judgment and allow peers to decide their fate."

Lincoln said, "You make a good point. What if we put it to a vote within the community?"

This brought a scowl from Elijah and some concerned looks from the others.

Maggie said, "We discussed this. Picking a jury will drag this out longer than we want. We need to finish this today."

"I agree, but not at the expense of alienating those we are here to serve. If we're seen as railroading them, the community may never trust us again."

Caryn and Milo nodded their agreement.

Lincoln stood. "All those in favor of having a jury decide the justice of this trial raise your hands." About a third of the hands went up. He breathed an inward sigh of relief. "All those content with having the council be judge and jury, raise your hands." Though not every hand went up it was clear the community had confidence in the council to handle the matter fairly and impartially. "The motion is carried. We will serve as the jury. Counselor, it can't get any fairer than that. A vote was taken."

Gloria wasn't happy but realized she had nothing more to argue.

"If there're no other motions," Lincoln said, "Adrienne, are you ready to begin?"

"Yes, your honor, oh, ah, do I call you that?"

Lincoln shrugged and looked at the others.

Elijah said, "Since we're hearing this case as a council, perhaps address us as such."

"Then, yes, council. I am ready to proceed."

"Call your first witness," Lincoln said.

"The community calls David Bedrosian."

Lynn scanned the crowd until she found Doc. She was sitting four people in, so Lynn leaned over the first person in the row. "Doc," she said in a low voice. When Doc saw her, she frowned.

"Sorry, Doc, but it's important." She motioned her with her hand and walked away from the gathering. She waited impatiently for her to arrive.

"What is so important—"

"Mark is talking."

Instantly Doc's manner changed. "Is he awake?"

"No, but I think he might be close." Lynn could not contain her excitement.

Doc moved past her and hurried toward the hospital. Inside she paused for a second. "Why are all these people here?"

Lynn entered behind her. "I was giving them a tour and had no place else to take them."

"Everyone, please stay to the side and don't touch anything." She snagged gloves from a box on a stand and snapped them on as she pushed through the curtain. Lynn followed without taking gloves. Doc was already checking vitals when Lynn pulled up next to her. Mark looked much the same as he always did. He was not moaning or speaking, just resting. The only evidence that something was different was the bead of perspiration along his forehead.

"Something caused him distress," Doc said. "But I can't be sure what. I wish I could run a CT scan to see if there's any activity, but all I can do is wait and see if anything else is going on."

"I promise you he was muttering and moaning," Lynn said, her tone defensive.

"I'm not doubting you, but whatever you saw might have been exaggerated by your desire to want him to wake rather than any actual sign he is."

Lynn was about to respond, but Doc cut her off. "No, it's all right. The beads of sweat tell me there's an internal struggle going on. However, that may also be an infection of some sort. We'll watch him for now and if this activity increases, I'll run some tests." She put a hand on Lynn's shoulder. "I don't have a lot of experience with this sort of thing, Lynn. Be patient and pray for the best."

Jin stopped the car. Two vehicles sat down the road a half a mile away. Neither of them had moved since he spotted them. He also didn't see any bodies moving. The pickup truck was the one Becca drove off in. It had been flipped on its roof. He believed the other vehicle to be an armored car.

He edged closer and could make out bodies strewn about the road. He increased speed. When he was close enough to make out Becca's body, he punched the pedal down and raced forward. He hit the brakes hard and exited with his gun in hand. He first had to clear the area before checking on Becca, but a quick glance showed her unmoving and bleeding. Though he feared for the worst, he made a complete circuit of the scene, checking for any signs of life. The four men were dead. He hurried to Becca's side and checked for a pulse. Though weak, it was there. Her injuries appeared minor, but the cumulative effect of several gunshot wounds to her left arm had drained her, and a jagged cut below her rib cage looked nasty and deep.

He quickly bound the wounds as tight as he could. Her other injuries were scrapes and bruises and unimportant. He scooped her up in his arms and walked to the car. It was still full of items collected from the town. He pitched the few things from the front seat to the back and slid Becca in. He buckled the seat belt and her body slumped. Afraid moving her had been too much, he checked to ensure she was still breathing, then got in and raced with all the speed the car had back to the farmhouse.

Along his route he passed two other vehicles coming toward him. His first thought was they were part of the group that took out Becca. It didn't matter. They were not stopping him. He blew past, angling onto the shoulder of the road to get clearance. As he went by, gun up and ready, he spotted Caleb in the driver's seat of the first car. They weren't enemies. He pushed the car harder.

Chapter Forty-One

Lincoln glanced at his watch and wondered if they should take a break. They had heard from both David and Thomas Bedrosian. The testimony had stirred the crowd into high emotions. It was difficult to cease the steady murmur.

Neither Blake nor Gloria could do much to contradict the testimony. Blake tried to leave the thought the two had made the testimony up. As friends of Mark, he suggested their purpose was to have Edwards and Merchant thrown out of the community because they voiced their opinion for having Mark unplugged.

Adrienne quickly buried whatever damage was done by asking both father and son if anyone else could corroborate their stories. With all others dead except for Edwards and Merchant, the only witnesses were those involved in taking the assassins down.

Adrienne skipped Jarrod, and the guards involved in shooting Lincoln's would-be killers and went for something more solid. She stood and said, "I'd like to call Ruth to the stand."

The crowd murmur grew. As she took the stand, which was a kitchen chair brought from the farmhouse and set on top of a picnic table, the crackle of a radio drew everyone's attention to Milo. He lifted a hand to fend off any objections or comments and said, "Milo."

An excited voice came from the other end, but the only one who could hear it over the loud voices of the crowd was Milo. "Say again." The speaker repeated and Milo stood. "Where's Doc?"

Someone said, "Lynn came and got her and they hurried to the hospital."

"One of you go tell her she's got an incoming patient." He leaned over the table and said less loudly to the council. "Jin found Becca. She doesn't look well."

To the crowd he said, "We'll need a few of the nurses to go get prepped and two others to get transport ready for an unconscious patient."

Movement from several areas showed the response.

Lincoln stood and said, "We'll take a short recess. Guards, you watch them." He pointed toward the prisoners.

Minutes later, a police cruiser raced up the drive, slowed only to avoid the milling people, and braked hard in front of the hospital. A gurney was already waiting and gowned medical staff did a quick examination of Becca while still in the car before moving her. She was inside in less than a minute.

Lincoln moved next to Jin. "What happened?"

"Not know. Find Becca, on ground with four," he held up four fingers to emphasize the number, "other bodies around her. All dead. They run off road. Flip truck. Becca shot many time. Very weak. Still breathe. I bring her fast."

"Good. You did good, Jin."

Elijah came up next to him. "We need to get everyone back, or we'll never finish this."

Lincoln nodded. "Yeah. You're right. Let's do this." He shouted, "Everyone, we are continuing the trial. Please return—"

A commotion broke out near the defendant's seats. Loud voices turned to shouts followed by a lone scream.

Lincoln ran. When he got there he found Edwards with his arms wrapped around Gloria's neck. He had a gun pointed at her head. One of the guards was lying on the ground with blood flowing from his nose.

Merchant had been wrestled to the ground by the other guard and several community members.

Blake moved forward. "Edwards, I swear, if you hurt her, I'll kill you myself."

"I ain't letting them railroad me. I'm not going down for this."

Someone asked, "You saying you didn't do those things?"

"It don't matter if I did them or not. What matters is we need a change of leadership. These people got to go. Mark and Lincoln and all of them. We was just trying to make people see it was time for someone new to be in charge."

"You mean like you?" someone else shouted.

"Well, no, but what would be so wrong with that?"

"You mean other than what you're doing now? You're just admitting your guilt. No one here is going to support you no matter what we might think about Mark. This is wrong. Let her go."

"No, I need her. Let Merchant go and we'll leave. We ain't gonna let you execute us."

Blake stepped closer. "Let her go, Edwards."

"Don't you take a step closer, or I'll—"

Jin appeared through the crowd and pressed a gun to the side of Edwards' head. "Wh-what are you doing? I'll kill her. I will."

"Don't care," Jin said. "I kill, too."

"Blake, tell him to get away from me."

"Jin. Please," Blake pleaded.

"He drop gun or die. His choice."

"Even if I shoot her."

"Choose. Live or die." He cocked the hammer for emphasis. Edwards flinched, and the crowd gasped. "Last chance. Three, two—"

"Okay. Okay. Don't shoot. He raised his hands and Jin snatched the gun away. Blake pulled Gloria away, then busted Edwards in the mouth with a long arcing fist. Edwards folded.

Lincoln said, "Put them both back in the new building. We'll discuss what to do with them and continue this later."

Edwards was lifted and carted with Merchant back to their cell.

Milo shouted above everyone. "Go on home for today. The sun is setting. The council will meet and decide what to do. We'll continue the same time tomorrow."

The new arrivals were ushered out of the hospital. Father Bernardo made his way to Lincoln. "My, is it always this exciting here?"

"No, Father, not normally. It's a very quiet and close-knit community. You just happened to catch us at a bad time."

"Well, if you are in need of my services, let me know."

"Will do. Sorry for not greeting you when you arrived. My name is Lincoln."

"Father Bernardo."

They shook hands.

"You are welcome to stay as long as you want, Father, but forgive me, I have things to attend to."

"I quite understand."

Lincoln met at the council tables with the other four members. Blake, with his arm around Gloria, came up to them. "Under the circumstances, we're resigning as council for the defendants. We hope you understand but don't care if you object."

"I don't even care if they're guilty," Gloria said, "though I'm certain they are. They deserve what they get. I just want them gone. We don't need that kind of bad blood here. These are good people. They don't need to be subjected to that kind of evil."

Blake led her away.

"So, now what," Maggie asked.

"Good question," said Milo.

To make this a fair trial, we need a new defense council, but I doubt we'll find anyone willing to do the job."

"Can't blame them," Caryn said. "I think Edwards made clear his guilt by his actions."

"So, how do we handle this?" asked Maggie.

"What if we just make a decision right now," said Elijah.

"You want to execute them without a trial?" Milo asked.

"No. We don't have to execute them. What if we just banish them from all contact with the community."

Lincoln said, "I've been thinking the same thing. It spares the community having to go through this again and solves the problem."

"What if we let them go and they come back and cause trouble from the outside?" Caryn asked.

Milo said, "We make sure they understand their sentence has been commuted. If they return, they will be instantly executed. That puts the choice of life and death in their hands and releases us of the burden."

"That works for me," Lincoln said. "Shall we vote?"

It was unanimous.

"Let's keep this to ourselves and announce our decision tomorrow in front of the community," said Lincoln. "We don't want anyone to think we're doing something wrong."

"What if they object?" asked Maggie.

Elijah said, "Then we start over and ask for their recommendations."

"What if they recommend execution?" Maggie asked.

No one had an answer for that question.

"Let's go with what we decided and if they disagree, we'll reconvene and try again," said Milo. "But Lincoln's right. To avoid problems, it's best not to leak our decision."

With that decided, the council split and went their separate ways.

Jin found Lincoln. "I do okay?"

"Yes, my friend, you did fine."

"Bad men. Should just take away and kill."

"I hear you. It would be simpler, but we have to do it this way. We can't have the community think we're no better than them."

"You may be better. Not me."

"Jin, please. Don't do anything to cause more problems."

Jin smiled. "I good guy. I behave."

Jin walked away, leaving Lincoln wondering if that was meant to ease his mind or make him more worried.

Chapter Forty-Two

Bobby sat in the small cubicle with his father while his sister was in surgery. He had been assured that Becca's wounds were minor. It had only been the cumulative effect of the combined injuries that had weakened her. While he sat he thought. Then, he voiced those thoughts, because he had been doing it ever since his father had been in a coma.

"I don't know, Dad. Maybe they're all right about us. It's not just you. It's a family thing. After all, you're in a coma and Becca and I have been shot and needed surgery. Maybe we are danger magnets. I mean, we've all been shot multiple times. Eventually, our luck is going to run out. Maybe it is time for us to move on."

He sat back and stretched his long legs out. So much was swirling through his mind he had to organize his thoughts. He focused on his most recent injury at the hands of Darlene. He knew it was an accident, but he couldn't get over the fact she had shot him. Though she had professed her sincere apology numerous times, he had trouble listening to her. He could see the hurt in her eyes at his lack of response. He liked her but was no longer sure he could trust her in a tight situation, which occurred too often not to be a concern on several levels. On the other hand, he was well aware that he had to shoulder some of the blame. He didn't announce himself.

When she returned from getting Becca, she had walked toward him, stopped, and changed direction. He hadn't seen her since. That did sadden him. He wanted to tell her it was all right, but he had to believe that to say it, and right now he didn't. Maybe he never would. To tell her without sincerity behind the words was too easy to see through.

Perhaps time is what was needed. Time away from seeing each other and time between the event and reconciliation. He just didn't know how he felt about, well, any of it.

"I think I need a vacation, Dad. Any ideas? Other than fishing, that is." He smiled at his own joke and hoped his dad was smiling somewhere inside that shell, too.

The curtain parted and Doc entered. He stood. She looked tired and he motioned toward the chair. She smiled and sat. "I'm done. Your sister is fine. She had five minor wounds, three of which were nothing more than grazes, but two went through her arm. She won't be able to use it for a while though. Barring infection, she should get full range of motion though perhaps not full strength. The bullets went through muscle."

She stretched and rubbed her neck. "She also has a mild concussion, a large gash on top of her head and a severe gash in her abdomen. Wait until she wakes and sees the shave job I did on her hair. Other than that, she has bumps, scrapes and bruises, but all have been treated. I put her two cubicles over. I expect her to wake shortly. You can see her then."

She nodded at his father. "Have you noticed any change?"

"Change? Like what?"

"I'm not sure. Lynn said he was mumbling to himself."

"Really! That's good, isn't it?"

"Yeah, if he did. No one but Lynn heard him, so I hate to say it but with time running out on the council's mandate, it might have been wishful thinking. Just thought you should know."

She stood.

"Doc, thanks. Not just for this and my sister but for all you do for everyone."

She smiled. "You're a good man, Bobby." She left him alone with renewed hope.

Lincoln stood near the firepits as the tables were cleared for the evening meal. It was later than usual for them to be eating but that couldn't be helped. He wanted to go home, sit down and have a semi-chilled beer from the stock he kept hidden in his garage. However, people kept coming up to him with problems or questions so he gave up on that wonderful idea and waited for the next person to arrive. It was Milo with Jin in tow.

"Jin tells me the pickup, car, van, and big truck are full of food and gear. Guess they found an untouched area and struck it rich. We're going to need a lot of help unloading, but I'm not sure where to put it all. I hate to say it because it's piling onto my already monstrous workload, but we need to build a storage building to house our inventory. It will make it easier to check supplies and know what we have. Right now, it's piled everywhere we can find space."

"For now, why don't you use a small portion of the garage until we can figure something out. Some of this will be alleviated once the house is finished."

"Is that a dig to get my ass moving on that project?"

"Milo, come on, man. You are busting your butt on several projects at once. I got no complaints and certainly no demands. It will all get done in its own sweet time. I'm just saying that once the house is finished, we'll be better able to decide if more storage is needed, that's all."

He nodded, accepting Lincoln's statement. "I'm going to organize some teams to begin unloading."

"Great. I'll lend a hand in a minute."

The two men moved on and a small group took their place. He gave up thinking about that beer.

Five minutes later, Father Bernardo and his group came up. "Mr. Lincoln—"

"Just Lincoln, Father."

"All right, Lincoln. I have a few requests. Glen here was shot and Shamika, as you can see, is quite pregnant. They were wondering about seeing your doctor."

"Just go into the hospital and ask. She's been busy, so may not do it today, but I'm sure she'll set something up for tomorrow."

"I wasn't sure if we were allowed inside. We were kind of ushered out in a hurry."

"I believe that's because she was going into surgery and didn't want anyone else in the way. Just go ask. She's a wonderful person. Ah, here's Ruth. Ruth, would you take these good people in to see Doc and maybe schedule an appointment."

"Sure, right this way. I was heading there anyway."

As they walked away, Father Bernardo said, "I've been approached by several of your people in regards to doing a mass. I don't have a problem doing a mass. In fact, I'd relish having someone to share it with but wanted to clear it with you first."

"I think that'd be a great idea."

"I'll have to go back to the church and get my things. Perhaps we can set it up for tomorrow."

"Father, let's plan on it. However, we do have some un-finished business to take care of first. If not tomorrow, then the next day for sure."

"Very well." He stepped back and a teenage girl moved forward with a long-legged woman. At first he took them for mother and daughter.

"Hey," the teenager said with attitude. "You the man in charge?"

"I'm council leader."

"I was wondering. We were told if we don't do what you say, you'll kick us out of here. That true?"

"I guess that depends on what this is in reference to." He looked at the mother for help. She seemed to be on her daughter's side.

"We were told that if we didn't work, you'd kick us out like you're some Gestapo dude." Her attitude was grinding.

From the word *"Hey,"* Lincoln was sure he wasn't going to like this girl. Now he wanted to smack her. He gathered his thoughts and his self-control. "Did you ever have a job?" He already knew the answer so didn't wait for her reply. "Well, if you would have, your boss was not likely to pay you if you didn't do the work. That's the same way here. You want to eat, do the work. It's simple. And the nice thing is if you don't like our rules, you are free to leave. Now, if you'll excuse me, I suddenly have an urge for some cheese."

He walked away and heard the older woman say, "I think he just insulted you."

Chapter Forty-Three

The next morning, Bobby helped his sore but determined sister to her feet. Doc poked her head through the curtain, rolled her eyes and said, "Whatever."

"Is she mad at me?" Becca asked. "I mean, it's not like I asked to be shot." She put her good arm around his shoulder and they walked just to be moving.

"I think everyone's tensions are running high."

"Because of the trial or us?"

"I think they're related. And don't forget, Dad only has another week before they pull the plug. Regardless of what she thinks or our current conditions, we can't afford to laid up too long."

"As if we'd ever let that happen."

"I'm not sure we'll have a choice in the matter."

"Of course we have a choice. We kill anyone who tries."

"Then what, Becca? We gonna kill everyone? Even if we manage to stop them from unplugging him, what will our future be here? We've made friends. We've worked, fought, and bled with these people. I can't just kill them. We're in a no-win situation."

"Well then, what's your solution?" she snapped. I will not let them kill our dad. If you won't stand by him, I'll do it alone."

"Relax. I'm not going to let them do that, but I think there's a better way." He pushed open the door and they went outside. The late October sun was bright, but the air carried a chill. They shielded their eyes from the glare and turned away from its path.

"So, what's your big idea?"

"Just hear me out. I think we should take Dad and leave."

Becca stopped moving and faced him. He expected her to yell and to argue. Instead, she said, "But if we move him, isn't that the same as pulling the plug?"

"It may be, but if it is, it will be on our terms, not theirs. I think Dad would be okay with this plan."

"Where would we go?"

"I was thinking Blakely. We already know there're supplies and some food. We won't starve and we'll be on our own to do our thing without anyone making comments and wondering what trouble we'll get into next."

"I'm not saying it's a bad idea. I'm just concerned about Dad."

"If they get their way and pull the plug and he dies, there will be huge long-term resentment. We'll end up leaving anyway and go on bad terms. This way, he's with us. If he dies, we'll all be together and his death will be on us alone. Face it, Becca. If he doesn't wake and the IV solutions Doc gives him run out, he will die anyway. He wouldn't want us to use up the last of the supplies to keep him alive if someone else might have benefitted. You know that's true."

Her eyes filled, and she lowered her head.

"The odds of us finding more of the IV bags that are still useable are slim. We need to face the facts and do this for Dad. Besides, Dad is a survivor. Maybe the jolt of not having his nourishment fed through an IV wakes him up. At any rate, I'll bet Doc lets us keep the bag he's hooked up to, which gives us a little more time with him."

"Oh, Bobby. I'm not ready to let him go."

He pulled her into an embrace and let her cry against his chest. "I know, Sis. Me either. But whether it's today or in three days or even a week, if he doesn't wake up, he dies, no matter what we do. This way, we get him back to that house and stay with him until," he was suddenly unable to continue.

They stood silent for several minutes.

"Okay, Bobby. Let's do it. We still have a day or two. Let me heal up a bit, and then we'll go."

There was an old wooden and wrought iron bench against the front wall of the garage. They eased down there and sat in silence for a while.

Becca said, "I see your girlfriend over there. You gonna be able to leave her?"

"She's not my girlfriend."

"You gonna let a little thing like her shooting you get in the way of true love?"

"Stop."

"Do you believe her?"

"That it was an accident?" He didn't answer right away. "I believe her. I accept her story and her apology. It was an accident. In fact, it was my fault. It happened. It's over. I'm moving on."

"But..."

He frowned. "I'm just not sure I can trust her again."

"When she told me I was angry. I wanted to hurt her. The fact that she had the courage and the decency to come tell me herself went a long way to my not harming her. I walked away. Now, after understanding what happened, I'm not as angry, but in the back of my mind, I keep hearing a voice say, *she shot your brother.* It's hard to forget. I don't know what I would have done had she killed you."

Bobby sighed. "I understand. Leaving is for the best."

"Are we going to tell people we're leaving?"

"I was debating that myself. I think yes. There are good people here. People who have stood by Dad and us that we should respect enough to say goodbye. I know Lincoln would be upset, Lynn too."

"Screw her. She gave up on dad."

"Doesn't mean she stopped loving him."

"Fine, but the fewer, the better. In fact, let's wait as long as we can before we tell anyone. I don't want some long, drawn-out goodbye. Let's pack while they're doing the trial and sneak our bags out."

"We need to get permission to take one of the vehicles. We'll need something big enough for Dad."

"We'll take the van."

"We'll ask for the van."

"Whatever. We're taking the van,"

"Becca, remember, we don't want to burn bridges. Some day we may want to come back. It'd be nice if we were allowed to."

"Okay. I promise to try it your way."

"Yeah? Until?"

She didn't answer which, Bobby thought was an answer.

Chapter Forty-Four

Later that afternoon, the community came together to decide the fate of Edwards and Merchant once again. When they were led to their seats, they found themselves sitting alone. Though Lincoln had asked the community for volunteers to represent the two defendants, no one else was willing to serve as defense counsel. It was as if the entire community, including one time Edwards's supporters, had already convicted the two men. That was reason enough not to continue with the trial. If the verdict was guilty, which it surely would be, there might be a clamor for an execution. Lincoln wanted to avoid that at all costs. As much as he disliked the two men, he didn't want their executions to be on his watch.

After calling the crowd to order, Lincoln stood. "Since there is no defense counsel and to save our community from further distress over the fate of these two men, the council has decided not to continue with the trial."

This was met with the uproar he expected. After a shout for quiet from Milo and Elijah, Lincoln continued. "Instead, we have passed judgment. Our unanimous decision is that Edwards and Merchant will be banished from our community for life. They will have no further contact with any member of this community. To do so will result in our secondary judgment of death by execution."

Though not quiet, the crowd was still listening.

"Edwards and Merchant, do you understand our decision?"

Neither man spoke.

"I'm going to need a verbal response."

"Fuck you," Edwards said.

"Then I take that as refusal, which automatically puts judgment number two into effect." Guards take them to the street. I will need six shooters to serve as a firing squad.

Both Merchant and Edwards exploded to their feet.

"What? No. You can't do this?" Merchant said.

"No. No," said Edwards. "We'll take the deal. We'll take the deal."

But the crowd had surged around them and Lincoln feared he could not get them back. He shouted and whistled, as did Milo. Still, they did not stop. Edwards and Merchant were dragged toward the street.

Lincoln jumped down from the table and pushed to get to the front of the crowd. A gunshot caused everyone to duck and freeze. Milo stood on the tables with his gun slowly descending toward the crowd.

"You gonna shoot us all, Milo?" one man asked.

"To get justice and order restored, I will."

"Hold on," Lincoln said. "They have not had their final say yet. All I did was explain what would happen. It hasn't been pronounced yet. Now, before you do something you'll be sorry for, we need to hear their final answer. "Do you Edwards and Merchant accept banishment for life as your just punishment for the crimes you have committed?"

"Yeah. Yeah. Please, just don't kill me," Edwards babbled.

"Yes," said Merchant, though fire lit his eyes.

"Then so be it. Return them to their cell. You will be released in one hour. And let me warn all of you that since they have accepted this judgment, no harm shall come to them. They are free to go, never to return. However, if anyone from this community sees them again, they will be captured and returned here for fulfillment of the execution. Now, take them."

The two men were hauled away with their feet barely touching the ground.

Lincoln's heart pounded like he'd just run through the toughest defense he ever faced. He joined the council.

"Well, that almost blew up in your face," Maggie said.

"Yeah, thanks, Maggie."

"Hey, just saying."

"We going to send them out there with nothing?" Caryn asked.

"Why should we give them anything?" asked Milo.

Elijah said, "It's the Christian thing to do."

"They weren't being Christian when they plotted to kill our people."

Lincoln said, "Let's not be them. Caryn, can you please put enough food and water into packs for two days?"

"Sure."

"We gonna give them weapons, too?" asked an annoyed Milo.

"Knives. One each. Would you pull them from the weapons cache, please?"

Milo narrowed his gaze, letting Lincoln know he didn't like the request. He turned and stormed away.

Caryn went to fill the bags.

Maggie said, "That went well."

"You hear the news?" Bobby asked as he stepped into Becca's cubicle. She lifted her head from the pillow.

"What?" She knew he was talking about the trial but purposely avoided going out to listen. She heard the loud roar from the crowd and thought they disagreed with something. The gunshot had been a surprise, but when no others followed, she assumed it had been fired to gain control over the angry mob.

"They got lifetime banishment."

Becca lowered her head, now angry. "So, they plot to kill Dad and all they get is banishment? How's that for justice?"

"At least it's over. We can plan on leaving tomorrow if you want."

Becca only half heard him. Her mind was running through ideas.

"Becca, are you listening?"

Annoyed, she said, "Yeah. What?"

I was asking if you think it's better to wait out the last few days they gave us to give Dad a few more days to come out of his coma?

That was a good question. One she hadn't considered. She ran the idea through her mind, taking into consideration that regardless of when her father left, she might have to leave sooner. "I don't know, Bobby. It gives him a few extra days. Ah, when are they releasing the assholes?"

Bobby didn't respond right away. Becca glanced at him. He was eyeing her with suspicion.

"What? Why you eyeballing me?"

"You're not planning to do something, are you?"

"Me?" she tried to sound surprised and innocent. Her brother knew her too well for that to work.

"Becca!"

"What? What can I possibly do? Look at me. I'm in no condition to do anything. I just didn't want to be outside when they let them go. If I saw them, I might try to do something. This way, I can stay out of sight and avoid the temptation."

He kept his gaze on her for another uncomfortable minute. "I'll be back later, Sis."

"Ah, yeah. Sure."

By the time he was out the door, she already knew what she was going to do. These men weren't going to get away with attempted murder. Not on her father. They were going to pay for their insult. Lincoln and his council had their chance. It was her turn to mete out justice.

She eased out of bed, found her possessions, and dressed. Her gun wasn't there, but her knife was. The long, well-honed survival knife her father had given her was the only weapon she needed. She strapped it on and went to the front door. She left the sling hanging around her arm but slipped her arm out. Anyone who saw her but wasn't sure it was her would remember the sling. With everyone milling around the cooking area waiting for the men to be banished, *Ugh!* the word was sour in her mouth, she slipped out, moved to the back of the garage, and used the parked vehicles to cover her as she made her way to the street.

She spotted Jin sitting on the house porch he and his wife and daughter shared with Lincoln and Jenny. She called to him but stayed behind the last car in line. He looked up and spotted her. As if understanding her need before she told him, he glanced around to see if anyone was watching, then he moved with casual nonchalance toward her. He stopped on the opposite side of the car and leaned his back against the front quarter panel. He didn't speak.

"Jin. I need your help."

He gave a slow nod to indicate he was listening.

"I need a ride with no questions asked."

Crowd noise rose as Edwards and Merchant were escorted from the new building. The sight of them was like adding another log to the already raging fire within her. When she glanced back at Jin, he was gone. A surge of panic choked her. Where was he? She needed him. He was the only one who would understand her need.

She was about to turn back when a car drove up in front of her with Jin at the wheel. She glanced back, rounded her shoulders, lowered her head, and moved to the car. Jin flung the rear door open before she got there so Becca could slide in. The car moved down the street.

"You no want people see, get on floor in back. Cover with blanket."

Pain lanced her arm, but she grunted and lowered to the floor, gritting her teeth. She found the raggedy blanket and covered her body. The car came to a stop. Jin spoke to the guard. "Go hunting."

"Cool," the guard said. "Good luck."

The car accelerated then made a turn. Down the road, out of sight from the guards, Jin pulled over and let Becca get into the passenger seat. She was about to explain what she wanted when he drove. She had a feeling he already knew.

Chapter Forty-Five

"You're sending us out there without a gun?" Edwards whined. "How fair is that?"

"We won't survive out there," Merchant said, with a lot less drama.

Lincoln said, "You can choose to stay here if you want, but out there, at least you stand a chance. Here," he put two fingers to his head like a gun, pulled the trigger and went, "*Pooh!* Gone."

"You're a real bastard," Edwards said. "Just remember, you're fair game out there."

Lincoln moved until only inches separated them. "Was that a threat? We can pretend we're out there right now if you'd like. Just pretend we're the only ones here. No one else will get involved. Just you and me."

Edwards glowered but didn't reply, nor did he make a move toward Lincoln.

"You should go now. The council has graciously supplied you with two days of food and water and two knives. Be happy you're not dead and buried already." To the guards accompanying the two felons, he said, "Drive them ten miles out. Let them out, then drive forward and leave their gear down the road. If they give you a hard time, don't give them anything. If they try anything against you, kill them." With that, Lincoln turned and walked away.

A large crowd had gathered to watch the men driven away. Lincoln feared some of them might try to take matters into their own hands. He didn't want it to happen, and in fact, warned them against doing anything to the two men, but he wasn't going to stop them. He did his part. It was up to others now.

The two cars drove away through the western gate. The crowd dispersed and Lincoln went to get the beer he had wanted since much earlier.

Jin drove west on a road parallel to the one transporting the prisoners. They went in silence. Becca fingered the knife, sliding it in and out of her sheath. They spotted the two truck convoy through gaps in buildings and trees on a periodic basis. It was enough to know they were still moving.

About ten miles out, they lost sight of them. Jin sped up and made a left turn. He slowed as he came to the cross-road the guards had taken. He stopped short of the road, got out and ran. As he neared the intersection, he ducked and crawled forward, working his way into the low brush. He waited several minutes before returning.

"They come. On foot."

Becca drew in a long breath and released it. "You know why I'm here?"

Jin didn't look at her. He nodded once.

"You know what I'm going to do?"

He nodded.

"You know I have to do this alone?"

One nod.

"You okay with this?"

He looked at her, his face and eyes expressionless. "Do what need to. I wait."

"You're a good man, Jin."

She moved to get out of the car. He grabbed her arm.

"You good, but hurt." He offered her his gun.

Becca looked at the weapon, considered taking it but stopped her hand short of touching it. "No. I'll use this."

His eyes softened for a moment. "If my daughter, I tell use." He lifted the gun. "But, if my daughter. I be proud."

His eyes hardened again. "Use knife must be good with knife. Whoosh! Whoosh!" He made slashes with his hand. "Fast. No talk. Action. Come back not hurt."

She nodded and got out. She cut across the corner of the open lot toward a small copse of trees, keeping them between her and her approaching prey. As she walked, she twisted and stretched, wanting to be free of any prohibiting adhesions in her muscles. There would be pain, though not nearly as much for her as her opponents. She just had to ignore it and do what she came to.

Becca stopped in the trees and waited. She tried to remain focused on the task she had undertaken, but her thoughts went to her father and what Jin had said. "Would her father be proud of what she was about to do? The answer bothered her. NO. He would have talked her out of her plan, talked her down from her anger. He would not be proud, but once the deed was done, he wouldn't dwell on it. He'd just be happy she was all right.

"Well, Dad," she murmured to herself, "I'm not you, and this is how I deal with things I see as wrong. I'm sorry. Like it or not, this is for you."

Five minutes later, she heard them talking. It was a lot of bravado speaking about what they were going to do to Lincoln and her father. She waited another minute before stepping out. They didn't notice her until she was almost on the street ten yards in front of them. They stopped.

"What? Who are—" Edwards said.

Merchant interrupted him. "It's Mark's bitch daughter."

"Ah, yeah. What do you think you're going to do, Bitch?"

She held the knife behind her in a stabbing grip with the blade pointing up her arm and obscured from view. She moved closer.

"Why are you here?" Merchant asked.

"Who cares?" said Edwards. "Here's our chance to get a little payback and have some fun at the same time."

Becca smirked. "You tried to kill my dad. Did you think I'd let you get away with that?"

Edwards snorted. "What do you think you're going to do about it, little girl. You think you're a match for us. You think you're tough?"

"You won't think you're so tough when you're squirming beneath me," Edwards said. "Girl, when I take you down, I'm going to mount you and ride you until you die."

Becca laughed. "Right. Like five seconds could kill anyone." She kept moving closer. They weren't smart enough to be afraid. She reversed the grip so the blade was pointing down behind her thigh.

Edwards snarled and took a threatening step forward. "Oh, I'm going to enjoy hurting you, you stupid little, cu—"

Before he finished the insulting word, Becca's knife was in his throat. Her face inches from his as his eyes bulged. She roared a warrior's cry, spun the man between her and Merchant, and used her foot to push him off her blade. He fell gagging and grasping at his ruined throat.

Merchant stepped back, his cockiness long gone. He fumbled for his knife as she advanced on him. His face went through several changes ending in fear. The knife fell from his shaking hand and he turned to run.

Already moving, Becca took flight and slashed at his back, scoring a long slice. He screamed and arched backward, slowing his pace. Becca landed and fell against Merchant's legs, tripping him. He went down. Becca rolled and felt the pain as she took the brunt on her knees. She felt the stitches in her arm tear but was beyond feeling the fire. She rolled onto her back and over to her knees. When she finished, Merchant's face was a mask of sheer terror. She didn't hesitate. Becca drove the knife through his eye. She plunged it with such ferocity her fingers touched the rim of the socket. She twisted once to the left as he bucked and shrieked, then once to the right. By the time she withdrew the blade, Merchant was no longer screaming or moving.

She pushed her body to her feet and screamed her triumph to the sky. The pain she had walled up rushed in now with savage fury. She cried out and dropped to one knee. For several moments, she fought for control. When she had managed to harness the agony enough to move, she cleaned the blade on Merchant's shirt, then stood and stripped the bodies of their packs and knives. With that done, she rolled the bodies into the drainage ditch on the opposite side of the road.

By the time she reached the car, she was staggering. No amount of effort could keep the pain down. Jin opened the rear door and she collapsed onto the seat and fought back tears. He laid the blanket over her. Jin put a comforting hand on her head. "Did good, little warrior. Father be proud."

The trip back was long. The guards recognized the car and Jin and had the crossbar raised as he approached, preventing any questions about the sudden appearance of Becca. Once there, Jin got her from the car and guided her to the hospital. A worried Bobby was pacing inside.

"Sis, where have you . . . what happened to you."

Jin said, "She walk. Trip. Fall. I bring."

They got her back to bed. Having just finished with an examination of the pregnant woman, a nurse got Becca situated on the bed, gave her some pain meds, then numbed her up to redo the broken stitches on two of her wounds.

As the nurse worked, Becca caught and held Bobby's eyes. He glanced at Jin, then back to his sister. After a few seconds, he nodded. "Get well, Sis. We have a lot to do tomorrow. He turned and walked away.

Chapter Forty-Six

The next day, after Bobby spoke to Doc then went to Lincoln and Lynn to explain what they were doing, a small crowd gathered inside the hospital. Speaking for the council, Lincoln and Lynn agreed to allow not only the partial IV bag, but one full backup bag since he hadn't reached the two weeks period allotted.

"I set the drip to its lowest level," Doc said. "It will extend the flow and his life a little longer. The monitor and portable ventilator are charged and have roughly six to eight hours of life before they need to be recharged. I'm not sure how you're going to do that, but it's the best I can do. I don't want this to sound bad, but at some point, I will want the equipment back. I still don't agree with what you're doing, but I understand and wish you well."

"It's what's best for us and the community," Bobby said. "I promise we'll get the equipment back to you."

"I'm sorry you feel the need to leave. This is your home. A home your father helped build. I think he would be disappointed to know you left."

"Actually, my father has been thinking about leaving for quite a while," Bobby said. He tried not to look at Lynn, not wanting her to feel this move was about her, but a glance he was unable to hold back showed her reaction. His words brought pain. That was not his intent. "He was acutely aware of a growing unease with his presence here and didn't want to be the cause of others leaving."

"I told him I thought that was an overreaction on his part and that those he upset were few and not of the mind that he should leave. With Edwards and Merchant gone, I doubt anyone left holds any grudge against your father."

"That may be true, but I think the time away will do everyone some good."

Lincoln sighed and looked to Lynn and Jarrod for help persuading them to stay. Both appeared willing to accept the sibling's decision. "You sure there's nothing I can say to change your mind?" Lincoln asked. "You two are a big part of things around here. We're going to hate to see you go."

Bobby said, "I think these people need a break from all of us, not just my dad. We'll be all right. Besides, we're only two hours away.

"And we won't be alone," Becca said. After telling Father Bernardo they were moving to Blakely, he wanted to return home with them. Debbie and Star decided they liked it better there as well. After Glen's appointment, he opted to go back too. Only Shamika and Pandora were staying. Shamika felt better about having a doctor nearby.

That morning they loaded the truck and cleared the back of the van. A mattress was set on the floor for Mark. They were ready. All that was needed was to transport Mark.

Lynn was unable to speak. Tears flowed in a constant stream.

Jarrod leaned over Mark with tear-filled eyes. "You take care now, my friend. I will miss you." He patted Mark's shoulder and backed away.

Mark was wheeled out of his room and the gurney was lined up with the van. It was then that Lynn lost control. She rushed to Mark and wrapped her arms around him. She sobbed. Through her gasps, she said, "You need to know that I always did and always will love you. I'm so sorry." She kissed his lips, brushed back his long hair, and Lincoln guided her back.

Jin, Caleb, and Jarrod lifted Mark and slid him inside while Becca and Bobby eased him in from the inside. When he was positioned, Becca sat next to him and Bobby got out the side door. A box of medical supplies for different needs had been placed on the floor. The front floor held boxes of food and water to help them get settled.

Lincoln made sure they had enough ammo and a five-gallon container of gas. He also handed them one of the radios. "If you ever need us, do not hesitate to call."

"Will do." Bobby closed the rear doors. He shook Jin and Caleb's hands. When he extended his toward Lincoln, the big man swatted it aside and drew him into a bone-crushing hug. "I love your dad like a brother. I will pray for him."

Lincoln choked up then and Bobby did as well. Jarrod followed with his own version of the Lincoln hug leaving Bobby breathless. Lynn hugged him much gentler but with more water. "I love you and Becca. I know she resents me, but I do love your dad." She kissed his cheek.

With nothing more to say, he gave a final smile and moved around the van to the driver's door.

"Bobby!"

He looked up to see Darlene sprinting across the grounds.

"Oh, Bobby, no. You're leaving." She started to cry. Her entire body shook. "Do you hate me that much?"

"Darlene. We're leaving for my father. It has nothing to do with you."

"Can you ever forgive me?"

He placed a hand on her cheek, and she cupped it with both hands leaning into it. "We're all right, Darlene. There is nothing to forgive."

She flung herself into his arms. "Please don't go. Don't leave me."

He held her for a moment, then eased her away. "This is something I have to do, Darlene. We'll see each other again."

"But, where are you going?"

Her voice had carried and they were drawing a crowd. That was what he wanted to avoid. "I have to go. We can't keep my dad out here too long. I'll be in touch."

He climbed into the seat and started the engine.

"Bobby!" she cried.

As the van started to move, Becca opened the sliding door. "Hey, we're not far. You can always visit. You know where."

Darlene cupped her mouth and nodded. "Thank you."

They drove away slowly as others became aware of what was happening and came to say their goodbyes.

They led the large truck down the drive through the throngs of gathering people and through the western guard gate.

"Can you believe we're doing this?" Becca asked. There was no excitement in her voice.

"It was long overdue."

"Bobby? Are we doing the right thing? For Dad, I mean?"

He glanced over his shoulder and saw his sister's quivering lip. "Becca, we're doing the only thing for Dad. He was going to die anyway. This way, it will be with us. We can spend whatever time is remaining with him. It's the way he would have wanted it."

"You're right. I know you are. It's just hard leaving, knowing this is the end. We had hard times there, really hard times, but in between those times, things were truly good. It was home."

"Yes, it was. We made some good friends. We'll see them again. I promise."

They drove on in silence. As agreed upon before they left, because of the speed they were forced to travel not to jostle their father, the bigger truck passed them. They'd be set up and ready to help move Mark into the house when they arrived.

They were on their own, but that's how they liked it and, especially in this case, wanted it. They had each other's backs always. They settled in for the drive, each lost in their own thoughts and memories. Then Booby caught movement in the side mirror. He leaned toward the window for a better view. It was a car. "Ah, sis. We've got company."

"What?"

"It's a car, and it's moving fast." He picked up his handgun.

He could hear her move in the back of the van and knew she had armed herself. He increased speed gradually.

"Any chance they're from the community?"

"Unknown but better to be prepared."

"Man, neither of us is in any condition for a prolonged fight."

"Can you handle my rifle?"

"Handle, sure. Shoot with your accuracy, no."

"That's okay. As long as you can hit the windshield, that should slow them down a bit. First things first though. Use the scope to see if you recognize anyone."

"Ah, how do you focus this thing? Nevermind. Are they flashing their lights at us? Should we stop and see who it is?"

"Not until we know for sure if they're friend or foe."

"They switched lanes."

"Can you see who it is?"

"No, the van is bouncing too much, and they're flying."

"Can you get a shot?"

"They'll be alongside us in a few seconds." She shifted to the side door, unlatched it but held it closed. Then she whipped the door open and pointed a gun at the car. "Oh, shit! It's Jin."

"Jin?" Bobby grew concerned. Whatever brought Jin out here at such a high speed had to be important. He slowed, as did Jin's car. He saw the man in the passenger seat but could not see the driver. However, Jin's daughter was in the rear seat with several backpacks.

Jin motioned for him to roll down his window. Bobby did and leaned out.

"You go. We go too."

Bobby now saw Jin's wife was driving.

"You always in trouble. Need help. We go be with friends. Keep you safe."

Bobby smiled. "That's great, Jin."

"See you down road." He motioned with his hand like an old wagon train master telling his followers to move out. Then their speed increased, and soon they were out of sight.

"How cool is that?"

Becca said, "Very." She closed the sliding door and settled in again.

Then they heard. "No." Bobby was so startled he slammed on the brakes and had to let up on them fast or risk pitching their father into the seats.

"Bobby. Becca. Trouble."

"Dad. Daddy, can you hear me?" Becca said. She leaned over him and stared into his eyes. She shook him.

"Trouble," he said again. His voice was so soft and raspy it was barely recognizable as his.

"Daddy. Please wake up."

Bobby parked and climbed in the back, taking up a position on the opposite side. "Becca, stop shaking him." She was so desperate for him to wake her emotions were running havoc with her mind.

"Daddy, pleaseeeee!"

"Bobby. Becca. Trouble."

The monitor came to life, the beeps more rapid. The heart rate was rising. The portable ventilator didn't seem to be keeping up with the rise and fall of his chest. *Did that mean he was breathing on his own? Was he in trouble? Had they killed him before he would have died?*

Somehow, they had to either get him calmed down or—wake him. "Becca, wait." Bobby had an idea. "He thinks we're in trouble. Play on that. Force him to wake up to save us."

Becca caught on. "Daddy. Help. We're in trouble. We need you."

"Dad. Help us. You have to save us," Bobby said.

Their father's face scrunched up as if in agony.

"Bobby, he's in pain. How do we stop it?"

"Push him a little harder." Sweat beads popped on his forehead. Some form of internal battle was being waged that they could not comprehend. All they could do was watch, spur him on, and pray they didn't kill him.

"Dad. Help."

Please, Daddy, come rescue us."

The urgency in their voices grew with each word they spoke.

Was it too much? Not enough. Should they be patient, get him to the new house and try again after he rested? They just didn't know. Their desire for him to wake won out for the moment, and they persisted in their efforts to force him from his coma.

Bobby and Becca needed him. He could hear them, but for some reason, they were not in sight. They were close. Their presence was all around him. He had to break free of whatever was holding him back.

"Bobby. Becca. Coming."

"Yes, Dad. Come for us."

It was Bobby. He sounded desperate.

"Daddy, please. We love you. We need you."

The urgency in Becca's voice was painful. He had to reach her. He fought. Pain pounded in his head and fire spread across his chest. Too much. He wasn't strong enough. *No! No!* The nothingness surrounded him again.

Chapter Forty-Seven

"Wh-what just happened?" Becca was on the verge of panic. She leaned over her father's body, pressed a hand over his heart and her ear at his nose. She ignored the monitor wanting to feel his life force for herself.

Bobby sat back and watched the monitor as hope drained. The beeps were descending rapidly. He prayed they slowed and became stable again and didn't keep going down. He had seen the agony contort his dad's features. He was in severe pain. His blood pressure had skyrocketed. Was it enough to cause internal damage? What happened when blood pressure rose too high? Heart failure? Brain damage? He didn't know enough about medical symptoms to be sure but knew it wasn't good. Had they just ensured their father never regained consciousness?

The heart rate continued to decline. What had it been before? Sixty? It was at seventy- two now and dropping. The sensor monitoring blood pressure flatlined, giving him a stab of pain, shock and panic.

"Becca!"

The sheer terror in his voice brought her upright fast. Before she could speak, he was on his knees searching. He found the blood pressure clip and snapped it back into place on a finger. The machine beeped. He looked at it, waiting for the numbers to come, but nothing happened.

"Come on!" He held the little monitor wanting to shake it into functioning. His panic and fear of loss had his head thumping to the point of explosion. Then he noticed the reset button and pushed it. Instantly the machine began to calibrate again. The fact that it was rising gave him hope that his father was still alive in there someplace. He glanced at the heart rate. It had settled at a steady sixty-two. His body sunk and he realized his own heart rate had climbed, too.

"What happened?"

"I think when you leaned over him you knocked the clip off."

"But that wasn't going to kill him."

"No," Bobby breathed out, trying to relax. "It just scared me because his heart rate kept sinking and suddenly there was no blood pressure.

"Oh." She laughed. It wasn't a real laugh but more a nervous bark. She repeated it again, then fell into Bobby's arms, sobbing. "Is this what it's going to be like as long as he's still with us? Us constantly in panic mode trying to stretch out his life as long as we can?"

"Yes. I'm sure it is. All we can do is the best we can. It's in God's hands after that."

"Well, God had better help him, or he's in trouble with me. He needs to either wake him or ease him from this world. This isn't fair for him or us."

"What are you saying, Becca? Are you ready for this to be over?"

She lifted her head, not bothering to wipe her tear-streaked face. "I, uh, I don't know. Isn't that what we're already doing?"

"We have the power to end it now if that's what you want?"

She glanced from her brother to her father and back. "Is that what you want?"

He thought about it for a moment, then shook his head. "No. I want to continue with the plan. If God chooses to take him, he'll do it in his own time. Let's go to the house, get him settled, and then sit around talking about memories."

Becca nodded as fresh tears welled. "I'd like that."

Bobby smiled and climbed back into the driver's seat.

Mark could feel the rolling and bumping and knew he was moving. He had heard the voices of his son and daughter and no longer felt they were in danger. He felt calm, his body relaxed. The fiery pain that had scorched his chest had subsided, and the pounding in his head was almost gone. He felt at peace.

Memories. His children had talked about memories. He sifted through his vault of favorites. There were so many. The time Bobby discovered where the car keys were and actually got the engine started before he ran out to stop him. That time at the zoo when Becca climbed to the top of the fence at the elephant's compound because she wanted to ride one. That should have been his first clue as to the kind of woman she would grow up to be.

He was so proud of them both. They had come so far and been so strong despite all that had been placed in their path. He was secure in the knowledge that they would be all right without him.

His memories became broader as he recalled family outings with the whole family. He thought about Sandra and Ben. Though he couldn't see them, he knew they were close. Maybe now was the time to go to them. He felt he still had some time, but soon.

Then his thoughts turned inward. Had he done all he could to prepare Bobby and Becca? Did he have regrets? Yes, many. Perhaps too many to recount. Had he left anything undone or unsaid? Wow! Yes to that. An image of Lynn displayed vivid and detailed. Every line, scar, birthmark, and blemish that made up her beautiful spirit came into focus. Maybe his one true regret was not finding a way to reconcile with her. It was too late now. He hoped she found happiness.

Overall, it hadn't been a bad life, well, all things considered. How does one plan for the apocalypse? He did his best to help others and to ensure his children were, if not safe, then at least prepared to face whatever came. A sudden sadness touched him. He really wanted to say goodbye to his children. Maybe there was still time. That was up to God now.

Was it time?

No. But it was time to make amends with one other. *God, forgive my sins and my disbelief at times. I tried to do what was right, as I'm sure you know. If I haven't strayed too far and it is your wish, I'd love to be with my family again. I think I led a life worth dying for.*

End

ABOUT THE AUTHOR

Ray Wenck taught elementary school for 36 years. He was also the chef/owner of DeSimone's Italian restaurant for more than 25 years. After retiring he became a lead cook for Hollywood Casinos and then the kitchen manager for the Toledo Mud Hens AAA baseball team. Now he spends most of his time writing, doing book tours and meeting old and new fans and friends around the country.

Ray is the author of forty-nine novels including the Amazon Top 20 post-apocalyptic, Random Survival series, the paranormal thriller, Reclamation, the mystery/suspense Danny Roth series and the ever popular choose your own adventure, Pick-A-Path: Apocalypse. A list of his other novels can be viewed at raywenck.com.

His hobbies include reading, hiking, cooking, baseball and playing the harmonica with any band brave enough to allow him to sit in.

You can find his books all your favorite sites.

You can reach Ray or sign up for his newsletter at raywenck.com or authorraywenck on Facebook

For a free book, visit raywenck.com and sign up for the newsletter.

Other Titles

Random Survival Series
Random Survival
The Long Search for Home
The Endless Struggle
A Journey to Normal
Then There'll Be None
In Defense of Home
A Life Worth Dying For

Danny Roth Series
Teammates
Teamwork
Home Team
Stealing Home
Group Therapy
Double Play
Playing Through Errors
Pitch Count

The Dead Series
Tower of the Dead
Island of the Dead
Escaping the Dead

Pick-A-Path Series
Pick-A-Path: Apocalypse 1
Pick-A-Path: Apocalypse 2
Pick-A-Path: Apocalypse 3

Stand Alone Titles
Warriors of the Court
Live to Die Again
The Eliminator
Reclamation
Dimensions

Ghost of a Chance
Mischief Magic
Twins In Time
When the Cheering Stops

Short Stories

The Con   Short Stop-A Danny Roth short

Super Me   Super Me, Too

Co-authored with Jason J. Nugent

Escape: The Seam Travelers Book 1

Capture: The Seam Travelers Book 2

Conquest: The Seam Travelers Book 3

The Historian Series

The Historian: Life Before and After

The Historian: The Wilds

The Historian: Invasion

Jeremy Kline

The Invisible Village

The Lost Tribe

Bridgett Conroy Series

A Second Chance at Death

Traveling Trouble

Ray Wenck

Ray Wenck

Made in the USA
Columbia, SC
07 October 2023

24089396R10154